MARTHELLEN
and the MAJOR

Also by Stephen Bly
in Large Print:

Hidden Treasure
The General's Notorious Widow
The Outlaw's Twin Sister
The Senator's Other Daughter

Also by Stephen & Janet Bly
in Large Print:

Columbia Falls
Copper Hill
Fox Island
Judith and the Judge

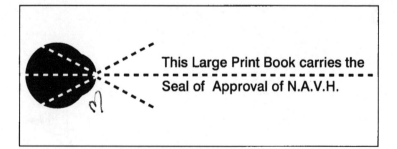

MARTHELLEN
and the MAJOR

The Carson City Chronicles: Book Two

Stephen & Janet Bly

Thorndike Press • Waterville, Maine

Published in 2004 by arrangement with Stephen Bly.

Thorndike Press® Large Print Christian Fiction.

The tree indicium is a trademark of Thorndike Press.

The text of this Large Print edition is unabridged.
Other aspects of the book may vary from the original edition.

Set in 16 pt. Plantin by Ramona Watson.

Printed in the United States on permanent paper.

Library of Congress Cataloging-in-Publication Data

Bly, Stephen A., 1944–
    Marthellen and the major / Stephen & Janet Bly.
        p. cm. — (Carson City chronicles ; bk. 2)
    ISBN 0-7862-5826-8 (lg. print : hc : alk. paper)
    1. Judges — Fiction.   2. Housekeepers — Fiction.
3. Real estate developers — Fiction.   4. Carson City
(Nev.) — Fiction.   5. Large type books.   I. Bly, Janet.
II. Title.
PS3552.L93M38 2004
813´.54—dc22   2003055461

For
W. Scott Walston

As the Founder/CEO of NAVH, the only national health agency solely devoted to those who, although not totally blind, have an eye disease which could lead to serious visual impairment, I am pleased to recognize Thorndike Press* as one of the leading publishers in the large print field.

Founded in 1954 in San Francisco to prepare large print textbooks for partially seeing children, NAVH became the pioneer and standard setting agency in the preparation of large type.

Today, those publishers who meet our standards carry the prestigious "Seal of Approval" indicating high quality large print. We are delighted that Thorndike Press is one of the publishers whose titles meet these standards. We are also pleased to recognize the significant contribution Thorndike Press is making in this important and growing field.

Lorraine H. Marchi, L.H.D.
Founder/CEO
NAVH

* Thorndike Press encompasses the following imprints: Thorndike, Wheeler, Walker and Large Print Press.

Behold, he shall come up as clouds,
and his chariots shall be as a whirlwind:
his horses are swifter than eagles.
Woe unto us! for we are spoiled.

JEREMIAH 4:13, KJV

CHAPTER ONE

Carson City, Nevada . . . 1880

"Judith, dear, where is that darling judge of yours? I need him desperately."

The long peacock feather emanating from the band of Daisie Belle Emory's wide, teal-colored felt hat rose two feet above her head, flagging her presence in the crowded, noisy lobby of the opera house.

Judith Kingston intertwined her ungloved hands and fought the urge to fiddle with her wedding ring. "He's escorting Marthellen home," she said. Even in the roar and laughter that bounced off the twelve-foot ceiling and crystal chandeliers of the antechamber, her voice sounded too loud and defensive.

"Was Marthellen ill?" Daisie Belle pulled on black silk gloves and stretched them up to her elbows. She slipped her arm into Judith's and led them toward the west wall in front of a thirty-foot mural of four grizzled prospectors and a mule on top of Mt. Davidson.

"No, not really." Judith glanced toward the front door, but her five-foot, four-inch height prevented her from seeing through the crowd. "It's a rather involved story."

"How delightful." Daisie Belle swirled in front of Judith, their eyes only inches apart. "You'll have to tell me right now."

Are those eyelashes real, Daisie Belle? Judith glanced at the abalone cameo pinned to Daisie Belle's high black lace collar.

"Doctor Jacobs' brother was scheduled to come to town today and he agreed to be Marthellen's escort for tonight's benefit."

Daisie Belle patted Judith's hand. "And he jilted her? Poor dear. I trust the judge will reprimand him for such spineless behavior."

"Well, it is understandable. Yesterday's snowstorm in the Sierras shut down the passes. Even the trains couldn't get through. He was to come over from Placerville. Doctor Jacobs was out on calls all night and just got word."

Daisie Belle scanned the crowd as she clutched Judith's hand and said, "You mean she got all dressed up to come to the opera, with no escort? She should have stayed. We could have sat together. I rarely

10

have an escort since my husband died." She tossed her head to look across the lobby, volumes of dark curls flowing across her shoulder as she turned her head.

I don't understand that, Daisie Belle. You might never have an official escort, but you are never without your flock of male admirers. Aloud, Judith said, "She felt too awkward after telling so many people she had an engagement this evening."

Daisie Belle flashed a toothy smile and talked without moving her lips. "How are my teeth?"

"What?"

"I just ate a Jordan almond and I think a piece got stuck in my teeth. Can you see anything?"

Judith inspected the perfectly straight white teeth. "I can't see anything at all."

Daisie Belle let out a deep sigh. "That is a relief. Sometimes I have nightmares about appearing in public with food stuck in my teeth. You must promise me that if it ever happens you will quickly and discreetly inform me."

"Only if you promise the same to me."

"Yes, we do have to look after one another. Someone told me recently, 'Daisie Belle, you carry the weight of Nevada culture on your shoulders.' And I told them that was nonsense. I said, 'Judith Kingston and I share that load.' "

Daisie Belle stood on the tips of her black French lace and patent leather boots, searching the crowd. "So the judge escorted Marthellen home?"

"The judge is quite insistent that no woman should have to walk in the dark alone," Judith said.

"What a gentleman," Daisie Belle cooed as she plucked a loose thread from the puffed sleeve of Judith's green tricot suit. "Next time I'm going out at night in the dangerous streets of Carson, I'll remember that."

Judith spun her wedding ring around. *Mrs. Emory, you try that and you'll have a lot more trouble than you can imagine.*

"I was merely teasing, dear Judith. My, you're a jealous one."

"I didn't say anything."

"Your fiery brown eyes said it all. However, I do need to see the judge for just a moment tonight."

"He should return soon." Judith's voice sounded flat. She winced under the widow Emory's discerning gaze.

"Oh, look! There's Mr. Penrose," Daisie Belle said. "I need to talk to him, too. I'm trying to get him to donate twelve plump geese for the church to distribute to needy families at Christmas."

"Geese?" Judith questioned. "Wouldn't they prefer turkey?"

"Why on earth would anyone want to eat a dry, tough old bird like that when they could have the moist, sweet meat of a goose?" When Daisie Belle sashayed across the lobby, the multitude parted like the Red Sea.

Judith moved to the center of the crowd, trying to avoid glass cups filled with rhubarb punch and hot coffee. She paused where she could watch the front door.

Levi Boyer walked up to Judith with Marcy Cipiro on his arm. He wore a white shirt tightly buttoned at his thick neck, with puffy gathered sleeves and leather suspenders. No tie. Marcy wore a dark blue dress trimmed in white lace gimp.

"Marcy, that's beautiful," Judith said.

"She made it herself, but I helped her choose the cloth," Levi boasted.

Marcy released Levi's arm and twirled. The skirt had three small flounces around the bottom, each with a piping of blue velvet. "My mother's the seamstress," she said. "I wouldn't even want her to look at this. She always tells me how I could do it better."

"You won't hear any criticism from me," Judith said. "If it weren't for Marthellen, there would be very little sewing in my house. However, I do like to quilt."

"Is the judge around?" Levi asked.

"He should be back soon." *Lord, I don't want to talk about Marthellen's misery, especially in front of this happy couple.*

Levi slipped his arm around Marcy's tiny waist. "Good, 'cause I need to ask him somethin' important."

"A legal matter?" Judith asked.

"Sort of. I was wondering what he was gonna do with them boys at Consolidated Milling out at Empire."

"Have they walked off the job?"

"Not yet, but there's gonna be trouble. Consolidated has lowered their wages two times since summer. The workers are all sayin' they're gonna quit. And the company says that if they quit, they'll hire a new crew, 'cause there's plenty around that's needin' work."

Judith studied Levi's strong jaw and chiseled chin. "I do believe they're right about that," she said.

Levi shifted his weight from one foot to the other. "Here's the thing. The boys at Consolidated are poppin' off that if anyone tries to get their jobs, they're in for a fight."

14

"They're threatening violence?"

"Violence to the workers, their wives, their kids, their homes, and their dogs."

"But that's like extortion," Marcy said and let go of Levi's arm.

"Yes, it is," Judith said. "But so is lowering a man's salary twice and threatening to fire him if he complains."

Levi strained his neck to peer above the crowd. "There's a rumor the judge has some kind of rulin' on the matter. But I don't know if it will help the owners or the workers."

Judith gave him a level look. "I don't know what he's decided, but I can tell you it's been hard on him. There doesn't seem to be an easy answer. What would you advise, Mr. Boyer?"

"I suggest stickin' to another profession. I had thoughts about quittin' the livery and takin' one of those mill jobs. But this convinced me to just sit tight. Sometimes makin' more money ain't worth the aggravation."

"I certainly agree with you there," Judith said.

" 'Course, after me and Marcy get married, she'll be quittin' her job at the children's asylum, and I'll need to bring in better pay."

Marcy's eyes widened. "I won't be quitting right away or anything."

Levi patted her gloved hand. "Darlin', what do you mean? We're gonna have our own kids. Remember what you said?"

Marcy pulled back. "I said I absolutely love children and want to have several of our own, but I didn't say immediately."

"Why of course you did, darlin'." Levi's eyes narrowed and creased at the corners. "You told me you wanted children during the first years of our marriage."

"First years, not first days." Marcy tried to release his grip on her arm, but he clutched it tight. "Levi, I don't want to quit the children at the orphanage the day we're married."

"That's not the way I figured it."

"I'm sure you can adjust," Marcy said.

"Me, adjust? Marriage ain't a time for the husband to adjust. It's the wife that has to do the adjustin', ain't it, Judith?"

"Oh, my, I believe you'll have to talk this issue through without me. Marriage was a grand adjustment for both the judge and me. In fact, we're still adjusting."

"Really?" Marcy said. "But you and the judge have been married . . ."

"Forever? Well, it does seem that way."

A blonde, curly-haired woman with

peach-toned skin and a full figure hurried up to them. "Have you heard from Roberta? Is she coming home this week? Did you tell you her secret? Is she getting married?"

"Peachy, I don't know a thing since I talked to you last week," Judith said. *My daughter is not getting married! She would never make such a critical decision without discussing it with her father and me. Why does Peachy Denair have such a difficult time believing that? Lord, why do I have such a difficult time believing that?*

The girl's face flushed rosy pink. "Since she's my very best friend in the whole world, I would think she'd tell me if she's not interested in Turner Bowman anymore."

"Turner's one of them that's protestin' havin' wages cut out at Empire," Levi declared.

"He's a shift foreman, you know," Peachy announced, her blue eyes squinting in a slight glare. "I never thought he'd end up working at the mill. When he was young, all he ever wanted to be was a railroad engineer."

"You've known him for that long?" Marcy asked.

Peachy's round cheeks could barely contain her full-lipped smile. "Roberta and I

17

have known Turner Bowman since the third grade."

"Yes, and you two have wrangled over him since the second day he moved to town," Judith chided.

Peachy's expression turned pouty. "Once we got to the eighth grade, it wasn't much of a contest. Roberta looks too much like her mother to make a fair contest."

"Her mother never, ever looked that good," Judith replied. "Besides, Roberta hasn't seen much of Turner in the past two years."

"Neither have I," Peachy said with a sigh. "He spends every moment working, or talking politics. You have to let me know the minute Roberta comes home. If I knew what train she was on, I'd ride up to Reno to meet her. Then we could ride back on the V & T together. I guess that sounds rather foolish, doesn't it?"

Judith brushed her curly, dark brown bangs away from her eyes. *I've thought of doing the same thing myself, but I would never admit it to anyone.* "Peachy, I'm sure you'll be one of the first to know when she arrives."

"One of the first? Don't you go telling Turner before you tell me. You've got to promise me that."

18

"I promise, but I can't make promises for my daughter."

A stout man with a wide-brimmed hat in his hand sidled up next to Judith. "Have you seen my deputy, Tray?"

Judith peered into the small, piercing brown eyes of Sheriff Hill. "Did you look backstage?"

"What would he be doing back there?"

"Visiting with the widow Willie Jane Farnsworth, I would imagine. She's singing tonight."

The sheriff tugged at his wrinkled brown tie that was already loose. "Nah, he told me that deal with Willie Jane was all through."

"When did he tell you that?"

"This mornin'."

"Well, I saw them at the post office right before lunch," Judith reported. "There might have been a change of mind."

"That don't prove nothin'."

"They were holding hands, Sheriff."

Marcy slipped her gloved hand into Levi's as the sheriff shook his head and said, "Keepin' up with them two is like playin' faro with your eyes closed. If you see Tray before I do, tell him to look me up right away."

"You got trouble in town, Sheriff?" Levi probed.

"Not yet. But a half-dozen hard-lookin' men have been filterin' in all afternoon. They rode to town in ones and twos, but they all ended up at Jack's Saloon and I hear they're all from Arizona. I wanted Tray to look 'em over."

Judith grinned. "Do you think they might be planning something nefarious?"

Before the sheriff could reply, Peachy said, "Do you think it's safe to be out on the street? What will I do? I walked all the way here from Aunt Estelle's."

"Ain't nothin' to worry about yet," the sheriff assured her. "The only thing out there that's dangerous is the cold. If that wind don't die down, you'll be frozen up before you reach the woodstove."

The sheriff peered around the lobby and surveyed the lower level of the opera house. "Maybe I'll just wait here for Tray to return. I don't want to barge backstage right before the program begins."

"I heard Willie Jane practice. She's very talented," Peachy said.

"Ain't bad for a . . ." The sheriff cleared his throat.

"For a widow lady?" Judith said.

"Eh, yep. That's what I was goin' to say. And speakin' of the cold, I saw Duffy Day shiverin' out on the steps. Said he wouldn't

20

come in, of course, but I couldn't seem to talk him into goin' on home. Said he's waitin' to talk to you, Judith."

"Then if you all will excuse me, I'll step out and speak to him."

"It's mighty frigid out there; you'd better grab your cloak," the sheriff said.

"I'll just be a moment," she replied.

As Judith wound her way through the crowd, she heard talk of growing concern over the depressed silver market and the trouble at Consolidated Milling. The brass handle on the oak and cut-glass front door felt cold, but it did little to prepare her for the blast of frigid air as she exited the building on Carson Street. She fought to get her breath.

The short, thin man in the shadows wore stovetop boots over the top of his worn wool trousers. His dirty, sheepskin-lined, canvas coat was fastened with a knot of hemp twine. A navy blue knit seaman's hat was pulled low over his ears and blended into his straggly beard. His deep-set brown eyes were shadowed in the flickering gas street lamp.

"Duffy, you must get out of this weather," Judith scolded.

"Yes, ma'am, it done turned cold real sudden like. But I needed to ask you a favor."

Judith hugged her arms to still her quaking shoulders. "Couldn't we step inside for just a minute, Duffy?"

"No, ma'am, I cain't do that. My mama taught me that if I didn't have an invite, I was not to go in."

"I'll pay your way."

"Oh, no, I couldn't do that. My mama said it ain't right for a woman to pay for a man's ticket. I jist need you to read a letter for me." He pulled a stiff piece of brown paper from his pocket and gripped it tight as it flapped in the wind.

"Duffy, you know how to read."

He shoved the paper toward her. "I was afraid I might have read it wrong. It ain't long. You tell me what you think it means."

Judith turned her back to the wind and gripped the paper with both hands. Her chin trembled so badly she had to bite down to keep it still. She tilted the letter toward the street lamp as a gust caught her black felt hat and tugged at her hair pins. "It says, 'I'll be home by Christmas, yours truly, Drake.' " She looked back at Duffy. "Your brother's coming back after all?"

Duffy's feet began to shuffle. "Yep, that's the way I read it, too."

"That's wonderful news, Duffy! You haven't seen him in years."

"I'm goin' to have a mighty fine Christmas," he said.

"You and your brother will have to come over to our house and have Christmas dinner with us."

"Can I eat out on the steps?"

"Not if it's this cold."

"I'll dress warm."

"And I wish I would have dressed warmer tonight, Duffy. I have to get inside before my lips turn to ice."

"I think I'll go home and stoke my fire."

"Good idea. Could you use a big, steaming cup of coffee?"

"Yes, ma'am, I reckon I could."

Even the lobby seemed below freezing as Judith scampered back inside.

"Judith," Peachy Denair called out, "the overture is starting."

"I'll be right there."

Daisie Belle Emory blocked Judith's path to the linen-covered table full of Marthellen's ginger snaps and Daisie Belle's pearlash cookies. "That nice Mr. Penrose agreed to donate twelve geese to the Christmas food baskets," she said. "Wasn't that sweet of him?"

"Excuse me, Daisie Belle, I'm in a hurry to get some coffee."

Daisie Belle raised her sweeping dark

eyebrows. "Oh, is the judge back? You never drink coffee."

"This is for Duffy Day outside."

"Why, he should come in. I can find him a nice seat up front with me. I would be happy to pay his ticket."

Judith turned the spigot on the coffeepot and filled the thick porcelain mug. *Daisie Belle, your sincere graciousness continues to amaze me.* "Oh, you know Duffy, he won't come into any building."

"Then, do hurry, dear. But while you're pouring, I have a request. You're so close to Mr. Cheney . . . could you ask him to donate twelve jars of pickled okra?"

"For the food baskets?"

"Don't you think they would be splendid with glazed goose?"

"I don't know if there are twelve jars of pickled okra in the entire state."

"Mr. Cheney would find an outlet for you. I happen to know that grocer Cheney has never, ever turned down a request of Judith Kingston's."

"I'll ask, Daisie Belle, but I'm not sure every family will enjoy pickled okra as much as you do."

"Enjoy it? I think it's slimy and disgusting. But we must uphold culture."

Judith glanced at the coat closet as she

24

scooted toward the front door. *The judge isn't back yet. It doesn't take that long to walk home. He probably went in to build up the fire for Marthellen.*

Another blast of cold air greeted her as she stepped outside and handed Duffy the coffee.

"Did you put sugar and cream in it?" he asked. "I'm sorry, but I cain't drink the stuff unless it has sugar and cream."

"Eh . . . no . . . I sort of got distracted and I . . ."

He held the cup toward her. "I cain't drink it unless it has sugar and cream."

"Perhaps, just this once you could —"

"They got sugar in there, don't they?"

"I'm sure they do."

"Thank ya, I'll jist wait right by the door."

As she entered the building, Judith could hear the swell of the Carson Orchestra playing a Trovatore waltz. The lobby was almost empty. As she stirred in two spoonfuls of sugar and a slurp of cream, she glanced toward the door. Through the glass she could see a tall man talking to Duffy Day.

The judge is back. No, that's not the judge. Something about the profile is different. A bit straighter. Not as thin.

The heels of her black dress boots tapped across the polished wood floor. Just as she reached the door, the tall man stepped inside, pulled off his round, neatly blocked black felt hat, and slipped off his black wool overcoat. He looked commanding in his tailor-made vest and suit with black silk tie. His straight white hair was carefully parted on one side; Judith couldn't help but admire the neatly trimmed sideburns that stretched down the side of his face. His nose was large but shaped to fit his face.

It is unusual to see a handsome middle-aged man that I don't know . . . and who doesn't have Daisie Belle attached to his arm.

"Miss, be careful when you hang up this coat. It's imported cashmere. Please don't brush it up against anything dirty or wet." His narrow-set blue eyes surveyed the empty room as he draped his coat over a startled Judith Kingston's arm. He obviously was used to being in charge.

He plucked the coffee mug out of her hand.

"Don't just stand there, hang up my coat," he said as he raised the mug to his mouth.

"Wait! That's not your coffee," Judith blurted out.

"It most certainly is not," he replied, giving it back to her. "I like mine black as aces. After you hang up my coat, you can fetch me some unadulterated coffee."

She nodded toward the end of the lobby. "The coffee urn is over there. You may fetch your own coffee."

"What impertinence."

"You think that is impertinent? If you don't immediately take your coat and hat, I will drop them to the floor, which is both dirty and wet."

He snatched the items from her hands. "I have never had staff greet me so rudely. Do you know who I am?"

"No. Nor do I care." Judith marched past him and pushed open the front door.

"Who is that fella?" Duffy asked her.

"I don't know, but I'm sure he'll tell me."

"He gave me two bits." Duffy took a sip of the steaming coffee. "Yep. He gave me two bits and told me to get off these steps or he would be forced to summon the constable."

Judith stamped her feet to keep warm and to register her disgust.

"I was wonderin'," Duffy said, "do I get to keep the two bits, or do I have to give it to the sheriff?"

"The man gave it to you. It's yours," Judith assured him.

A wide smile broke across Duffy's bearded face. "You still freezin'?"

"I think my blood has warmed up quite a bit, but I do have to get back to the program."

"Is Willie Jane singin'?"

"Not yet."

"She's a friend of mine, you know."

"Yes, she is."

"Thanks for the coffee, Judith."

"You're welcome, Duffy." Judith saw someone approaching the opera steps and recognized a familiar walk.

"Are we going to have mashed potatoes and gravy?" Duffy was saying.

"When?"

"On Christmas, when me and Drake come over."

"I'll be sure to tell Marthellen to make them."

"My word, Judith, you'll catch pneumonia out here without a cape," the judge chided as he wrapped his long arms around her.

"It was a little stuffy inside. I needed the air," she replied.

"Drake's comin' home for Christmas," Duffy said.

The judge glanced at Judith and she nodded. "Duffy got a letter from Drake."

"Well, Duffy, that's great. Why don't you celebrate by coming in to join us for the benefit?"

"I think I'll walk over to Cheney's and get two-bits' worth of bearclaws and then mosey on out to my place." The bony young man shuffled away, his back slightly humped over, head down, eyes intent on the ground.

The judge held the door open for Judith.

"Is Marthellen all right?" she asked.

"A little melancholy."

"She gets along well until she's in a crowd with everyone paired up. I know she gets lonely sometimes," Judith said, letting out a sigh. "She may be having one of her depressions. It's usually in December, isn't it?"

The judge pulled off his hat and brushed back his thinning, light-brown hair. "She talked of going to visit Charlotte and family at Christmas, but she doesn't want to leave us alone."

"Perhaps she should go," Judith said. *But oh my, I'll have to do the cooking.*

"I told her to invite Charlotte and family to come have Christmas with us. She said it was a delightful idea. I think it perked

29

her up. I didn't think you would mind."

"Of course not." *But where will we put everybody? I'll have to find the baby crib and . . .*

"If you think that's too much, I'll just tell Marthellen."

Judith waited as he pulled off his overcoat. *How on earth, dear Judge, do you tactfully do that?*

The orchestra had swung into the California Polka. "I'll get your coffee; you hang up your coat," Judith said.

By the time Judith joined the judge, the proud stranger emerged from the cloak room. "I see you have reconsidered your impertinence," he said as he reached for the coffee.

Judith marched past him and handed the cup to the judge.

The man spun around on the heels of his shiny boots. "Sir, I wish to register a complaint. I'm Major Fallon Lansford, originally of Philadelphia. Since the moment I've come into this opera house, the hostess has greeted me with unseemly indifference."

A smile crept across the judge's face. "Don't tell me she made you hang up your own coat and hat?"

Major Lansford glared at Judith.

"You know," the judge said, "she makes

me do the same thing . . . and I'm her husband, Judge Hollis A. Kingston." The judge held out his hand. "I don't believe we've met."

Major Lansford stared a moment, then bowed.

At least he has the grace to blush, Judith noted.

"I feel like a presumptuous, arrogant fool," the major said.

"You acted like a presumptuous, arrogant fool," Judith said as she also held out her hand.

"Now that the introductions are over," the judge said, "perhaps you'd like to join us for the program."

"You are most gracious. But I think I'll just retrieve my coat, slip out under the crack in the door, and fade into the night."

"Major Lansford, don't be so harsh on yourself," Judith said. "Life in Carson City, Nevada, takes some getting used to after living in the East."

"I trust I will adapt quickly. I do plan to stay awhile."

"Did you move your whole family out with you?" Judith asked.

The man hesitated, then glanced at the judge, who said, "That's my wife's way of

31

finding out if you're married and have children."

"I'm not married, Mrs. Kingston, due mainly to my previous military occupation, not by choice."

But I know nothing about whether you ever were married, and you avoided the inquiry about children, Judith thought.

"There you are," called a cheery voice. Daisie Belle Emory's silk skirt swished across the burnished floor of the lobby.

"When I saw your seats still empty, I got concerned." Daisie Belle scooted up beside the judge and slipped one arm into his and one into Judith's. "Your wife needs to make the announcement about the Christmas food baskets." She turned her eyes to Lansford and introductions were made.

"What a coincidence," Daisie Belle cooed. "My late husband was a major. Is your wife here with you tonight?"

"We've been through that," Judith said.

"Ah, I can tell by the judge's chagrin and Judith's response that you are not married. Is that true, Major?"

"You are an observant lady, Mrs. Emory," Lansford said with an attempt at a smile.

Daisie Belle abandoned her hold on Judith and the judge and slipped her arm into Lansford's. "We really need to go inside. I'm one of the judges in the amateur talent part of the program. I have no idea why they keep selecting me. I suppose they can't find any other volunteers who will give honest yet credible opinions. Now, what brings you to Nevada, Major?"

"A sanatorium."

Daisie Belle stopped at the doorway to the grand hall and dropped her hand from his arm. "Oh dear, are you ill?"

"Oh no, nothing like that." He offered his arm and she took it.

"Carson City doesn't have a sanatorium," Judith noted. "I'm afraid there isn't one in the entire state."

"I know," Lansford said. "I've come to build one."

The moment the judge opened the Nevada Street door of his house, he could smell the aroma of melted cheese over fresh-baked apple pie. Marthellen hurried forward to assist Judith with her coat.

"My word, Marthellen, you baked us a pie?" inquired the judge.

"I always feel better when I'm doing things for people. You know that, Judge. Besides, I needed to do penance for acting so irrationally."

Judith hugged Marthellen and said, "I have never been noted for my gracious handling of disappointment either."

Marthellen led them into the kitchen. The warm air fogged the judge's gold-frame glasses. He took them off and laid them on the small oak breakfast table. "I suppose you are going to tell me I'll have to wait until that pie cools?"

"Unless you plan on permanently scalding your tonsils. Let me fix us all a hot drink first."

"If you ladies will excuse me, I need to hunt in my desk for a map." The judge strolled toward the dining room.

"Perhaps Doctor Jacobs' brother will be here tomorrow," Judith offered as she looked in the cupboard for cups and saucers.

"And he might be one day too late. You know me, Judith. About once a year I go through this pitiful state. It's usually around Christmas. I get to thinking how life could have been . . . should have been." Marthellen banged a pot on the stove. "I sound ungrateful, don't I? But I don't have one pleasant memory before I met you and the judge."

"Nonsense. I'm sure there were many good times over the last four decades."

"There might have been, but I don't recall them. Mr. Farnsworth left us right after Charlotte was born. Bence was three years old. I lived hand-to-mouth for so long, I can't remember the previous years. Those were tough times. Up and down the line we moved, with me cookin' for the railroad men. All those shacks were just the same. Me and two kids in a single room, thin-walled, ten-by-twelve cabin. There were places like Tulasco, Deeth, Peko, Golconda, Argenta, White Plains . . ."

"I wish I could erase all that for you," Judith said.

"I thought it would be different when we moved into that three-room cabin at Ravenwood along the Reese River. All I had to do was cook for the mining superintendent and his family." Marthellen hung her head. "How can you let me prattle on with this melancholy tale? I do this to you every December. That's when it happened, you know."

"Go on, Marthellen, talk about it if you want to."

The woman's deep-set eyes were somber, her thin lips pursed. "What is there to say? He wanted more from me than just a meal and I wouldn't give it to him. He took it anyway. And I shot him."

Judith brushed the tears from her eyes but noticed that this December, Marthellen wasn't crying.

"I've lived that one scene over and over. How I wish I had never pulled that trigger. I knew it at the time. I just sobbed and cried over and over, 'What have you done, Marthellen, what have you done?'" She stopped speaking and sighed. "I'm doing better this time, aren't I?"

"I believe so."

"Isn't it strange how I can go all year and never even mention a thing, then comes the Christmas season and it all boils over again. Kind of like those donkey engines letting off steam. It's a safety valve. And every year you get scalded."

"You've never heard me complain."

"You and the judge are the best thing that ever happened to me. When the judge refused to send me to prison, you offered me probation by working in your home. That's when I knew there was a God in heaven."

"Marthellen, you know what a delight you have been to the judge and me all these years. You've been a good friend too."

The housekeeper sharply clapped her hands. "That's enough of that. I'm through my yearly melancholy. I'm glad Doctor Jacobs' brother wasn't here. This would not have been a good night to have a man around."

"There are other nights," Judith challenged. "Keep your options open."

"Not at my age."

"You're two years younger than I am."

"Maybe so, but I look ten years older."

"Well, let's celebrate old age by eating pie. I'll go pull the other old-timer out of his maps."

Marthellen took up a knife and started slicing the pie. "What is he looking up?"

"Humboldt Springs."

"Where is that?"

"That's what the judge wants to find out. Tonight we met an Eastern man named Fallon Lansford. He just came to town and claims he's going to open a health sanatorium at Humboldt Springs. He says it's only ten miles south of town."

"Is he a doctor?"

"No, he's a major."

"Did he wear his uniform?"

"Most of the evening he wore Daisie Belle Emory."

"I take it he's unattached?"

"That's the rumor," Judith said.

"What does he look like?"

"A little like the judge, only a bit grayer."

"You mean, he's our age?"

"I would guess so. Maybe it's a good thing you got over that need for a male friend. He's handsome if not exactly charming."

"I'm definitely in remission, but not entirely cured," Marthellen admitted. "Besides, I guarantee I will never be able to compete with Daisie Belle Emory. It's like looking at a sage after you've seen a rose."

"You didn't lose anything, Marthellen."

"What do you mean by that?"

"I didn't have a good first impression of him."

"That's the same thing you said about pickled okra." Marthellen pulled three china plates off the shelf and used an ivory-handled pie server to lift out one large and two small wedges of pie.

"You're right. Lansford reminds me of pickled okra."

"And what does Judge Hollis A. Kingston remind you of?"

"Hot apple pie . . ."

"With cheese?"

Judith laughed. "Oh yes, lots of cheese."

CHAPTER TWO

First District Judge Hollis A. Kingston brushed back his neatly trimmed graying mustache and goatee, then bowed his head over a steaming plate of liver and onions with brown gravy. As soon as a trio of amens greeted the conclusion of the blessing, he plucked up a silver fork, reinforced its cleanliness by wiping it on the white linen napkin in his lap, then plowed into the thick gravy.

"Sheriff, did you ever find out about those strangers hanging around Jack's Saloon?" he asked.

Sheriff Hill waved a hunk of pork chop skewered on the end of his knife. "They got spendin' money, I know that much. But they don't seem to be stirrin' up anything. They ain't causin' no trouble, and they ain't loiterin' around any of the banks. I reckon they're just passin' through."

"Why don't you just up and ask them what they're doing in town?" Doc Jacobs said as he performed an autopsy on the meatloaf.

" 'Cause law-abidin' folks has a right to privacy." The sheriff popped the pork chop in his mouth and kept on talking. "It ain't right to make 'em reveal things they don't aim to reveal."

"The sheriff's right, Doc," the judge said. "A law-abiding man should be able to keep to himself, if he chooses."

"Well, it doesn't hurt to know who is standing on the street corners," Doc said. He held up a bite of meat. "What is this stuff right in the middle of my meatloaf?"

"It sure is green," the sheriff said.

"It better be a green bean," Doc Jacobs muttered.

"Looks like okra," the judge remarked.

"Tastes like okra," Doc Jacobs shot back.

"I heard several of those fellas were killers from down near Wickenburg, Arizona," Mayor Cary reported.

The sheriff snorted. "Two of them were tried in Prescott for manslaughter, but acquitted by the jury."

"How did you find that out?" Jacobs asked.

"I wired the judge's friend Stuart Brannon, at his ranch in eastern Yavapai County, with a description of them."

Mayor Cary leaned forward. "I thought you said a man should have privacy."

"A trial is public record."

"What else did my legendary friend say?" the judge asked.

"That they were a hard lot, that it would be best to have them on your side in a gunfight." The sheriff waved his coffee cup at a waiter across the room.

"You see, they're up to no good," the mayor remarked. "Maybe they're goin' to rob the U.S. Mint."

"That's absurd," Sheriff Hill said. "That's the most secure building in the state. You can't rob the U.S. Mint. Even the superintendent couldn't sneak a coin out of there if he wanted to."

Doc Jacobs pointed to a round object on his plate. "What do you suppose this thing is?"

"It's a pickled crab apple dyed green," the judge announced.

"What for? A man comes in here for home cooking and he gets an art exhibit."

"You braggin' or complainin', Doc?" the sheriff said.

"Neither." The doctor pushed the crab apple off his plate. "The truth is, someday someone will try to rob the Mint. It's just too tempting."

"You saying you've been tempted, Doc?" the judge asked.

"I live in Carson City for my health and do doctoring just to keep me busy. Heaven knows I don't do it for pay."

"We aren't going to get some more of those 'poor doctor' stories, are we?" the mayor said with a groan.

"Not from me. I had a very good day yesterday. I received a bushel of apples, two scrawny pullets, four promises to pay by the end of the month, two bits in cash, and a baby named after me. They're going to call her Jake."

The sheriff hooted. "They named a girl after you?"

"And that was one of my good days."

"Judge, did you hear about that mill workers' meeting out at the river tonight?" Mayor Cary asked.

"Turner Bowman told me about it."

Doc Jacobs pushed his plate away and took a sip of coffee. "How come they're having it way out at the river?"

The judge shrugged. "It's outside the city limits. I reckon they figure there is less interference."

"You'd have to be mighty dedicated to the cause to stand out in the cold around a bonfire off company time," the mayor said.

"I believe that's the point," the judge replied.

"Well, it's about halfway to Empire down there. You think they are going to march down to the mill and protest?"

Doc Jacobs leaned back in his chair. "They haven't been fired yet."

"I don't think there will be any trouble," the judge said. "I'm going to the meeting myself."

The mayor glanced his way. "What for?"

"Turner invited me to observe. He knows there is pressure on me to make a ruling in the matter. And he wants some independent observer there to report on things, in case Consolidated wants to stir up rumors."

"I never would have pegged Turner for an agitator," the mayor said. "He's jeopardizing his position as assistant captain in the volunteer fire department."

"Turner's a bright young man. He asked if he could read law with me," the judge said.

Doc Jacobs sat up. "Turner wants to be a lawyer?"

"He certainly wants to know the legalities of the mining industry. I'm not sure he'll follow through all the way and take the bar exam, however."

The mayor picked his teeth with his fingernail, then used his napkin to wipe his bushy sideburns that grew to the bottom of his chin and up to an unruly mustache. "Then you're going to let him?"

"I don't have any reason for rejecting him."

"I heard they threatened to shoot anyone who tried to hire on and take their jobs," Mayor Cary huffed. "That doesn't sound like the type that would make a good lawyer."

The judge glanced around at the others. "I'm sure some have made threats. However, I've never heard Turner say such a thing. Have any of you?"

They shook their heads.

"Besides, I have a more serious dilemma to resolve."

"Roberta home already?" the sheriff asked.

"No. She telegraphed her mother that she'd be coming in on the eastbound on Saturday. I handle that situation come the weekend. The thing that troubles me now is Major Fallon Lansford."

"He's out at Humboldt Springs, I hear." The sheriff waved his hand to the north.

"Where's that, Judge?" the mayor asked.

"It's not out on the Humboldt River, that's for sure. The major claims it's southeast of the Carson River."

"Did you ever find it on your maps?" the sheriff asked.

"No, but they've changed the names of all those landmarks so often, who knows what is correct anymore?"

The sheriff rubbed the back of his hand across his flat nose. "Why won't he tell anyone exactly where it is?"

"He says it's got to remain secret until he secures a patent deed on the land," the judge said. "He's afraid some other developer will nab his mineral springs."

"I, for one, wish him success," Doc Jacobs said. "They've got a mineral springs in the Rocky Mountains along the front range, behind Colorado Springs, and it has been a great boon to the economy, not to mention the health aspect."

The mayor nodded. "Major Lansford claims it will create as much as thirty-six jobs for the area and thousands of dollars for area merchants. He's quite a visionary."

Sheriff Hill leaned across the table. "Ain't goin' to cut down on your clientele, is it, Doc?"

"I don't think so. Most of his customers will come from out of town."

"A big draw for rich Easterners if he builds a quality hotel like he said," the sheriff said.

The mayor looked around the table, waiting until he had caught everyone's eye, then said, "I, for one, like the sound of it. We've got to look beyond mining and milling. Sooner or later mines run out of gold and silver. We have to use this wealth to establish an ongoing level of prosperity."

"Whew-wee, you'd think this was an election year for Mr. City Magistrate," Doc Jacobs said.

"Don't start counting tourist dollars yet," the judge chimed in. "We've had other promoters come in with grandiose schemes that came to nothing."

"Yeah, remember that gentleman who wanted a four-story hotel with a gold-plated statue of Kit Carson on top? Can you imagine a four-story building in Carson City?" the mayor said.

"Is that the one who wanted a zoo in the saloon?" Sheriff Hill asked.

The judge grinned. "He called it a wild animal casino."

The mayor shook his head. "Things like that would make the great state of Nevada a laughingstock."

The sound of gunfire brought the sheriff to his feet. The second shot brought his .44 Colt out of its holster and the other three men out of their chairs.

"Where's that coming from?" the mayor said.

The sheriff stared out the window of the hotel dining room. "I hope it isn't the capitol. I'd better check it out."

"You need some help, Sheriff?" the judge asked.

"I hope not . . . but —"

"Come on, boys," Judge Kingston said, "it's time for the noon-hour posse."

His revolver now holstered, Sheriff Hill led the quartet out of Ormsby House and onto windswept Carson Street. Each man jammed down his hat and broke into a run.

Toady Scott sprinted across the street toward them.

"Where's the shootin'?" the sheriff hollered.

"In the alley behind Jack's Saloon," Toady called out. "One man dead, another wounded."

"It's those Arizona men," the mayor groaned. "I knew they were trouble."

A crowd of several dozen people huddled on the brick-lined alley behind Jack's Saloon. Most were men. Most wore heavy winter jackets and holsters strapped outside their coats.

A man sprawled face-down. Nearby, a

woman was crying. A tall, well-dressed man with a bloody white handkerchief wrapped around his left hand kneeled beside the fallen man.

"What happened here?" the sheriff demanded.

Major Fallon Lansford, clutching his bleeding hand, stepped forward. "I can't believe I shot him. It happened so fast."

Sheriff Hill glanced down at Doc Jacobs, who was examining the body. "Is he dead, Doc?"

"Two shots to the heart. He's dead, all right."

"You shot this man?" the judge asked Lansford.

The major plopped down on an empty nail keg, his head in his hands. "I shouldn't have done it."

The sheriff called out to the weeping woman being comforted by a couple of the Arizona men. "Fidora, what happened? Are you hurt?"

She shook her head and continued to sob.

"Did anyone see what happened?" the sheriff called out.

A barrel-chested man with two weeks' worth of beard and wearing a wool-lined canvas coat strolled over. "We was all inside of Jack's, Sheriff. We heard one shot and then another. So we came runnin'. That's all we know."

"Didn't anyone here see anything at all before it happened?" the sheriff shouted.

There was mumbling among the crowd, but no one stepped forward.

"Then you might as well go back to your faro tables and your swill," the sheriff said. "Doc, you make arrangements with Kitzmeyer's about this body." He called out to the retreating assembly, "Does anyone know who this man is?"

"He went by the name of Rudy Boca when he was in Silver Peak," one of the Arizona men said.

"He a friend of yours?" the judge asked.

"He was as worthless as a wet cowchip. He was a sneak thief, footpad, and lazy braggart. He probably deserved what he got," the man said.

The judge looked at him closely. "I might need to talk to you later. What's your name?"

"Ritter Crosley."

Sheriff Hill waved his arm toward the woman. "Judge, can you escort Fidora down to my office? I'll take the major. Mayor, you and a couple of these men help get this old boy to Kitzmeyer's. Doc, you grab your bag and come on down to look at the major's hand."

"I never should have shot him," Lansford said again. "I was trying to protect the lady."

A large crowd followed the procession down Carson Street. They were held back outside the sheriff's office by Deputy Tray Weston.

"How's Lansford's hand, Doc?" the sheriff asked.

"It's a fairly shallow cut. A little iodine should do the trick."

"You want to tell me and the judge what happened?" Sheriff Hill said to the major.

"It all happened rather sudden. I was on my way to the St. Charles Hotel for lunch."

"Through the alley?"

"I had gone one block too far and was cutting back when I heard the woman scream as she rushed down the stairs. As she ran by me, this man was pursuing her, brandishing a knife and shouting obscenities. I pulled my revolver out of my vest and ordered him to desist. He shouted something, then turned and lunged at me. I put up my left hand to defend myself. When I felt the blade slice, I thought he was going to kill me, so I pulled the trigger. I wish I hadn't done it. I hope he didn't have a wife and children. I couldn't bear it if I orphaned some children."

"If what you said is true, as far as jumpin' in and keepin' him from cuttin' Fidora," the sheriff said, "there ain't a man in this room who wouldn't have done the same. We're mighty protective of our women, no matter what part of town they're from. Isn't that right, Judge?"

"There will have to be a regular inquiry into the man's death," the judge declared, "but on the surface it does seem like justifiable self-defense."

"I've been out West less than a week and I've already killed a man. I never should have pulled the trigger," Lansford continued to moan.

"Pulling the trigger was a natural response," the judge said. "Pulling it the second time is a bit more difficult to explain."

Lansford jumped to his feet. "Twice? I shot the man twice?"

"He was shot twice, all right," the doctor said. "In the heart, close range, bullets not more than two inches apart."

"I had no idea."

"In the heat of conflict, we do a few things we don't remember," Doc Jacobs commented as he wrapped linen gauze around the major's hand.

"I haven't lost control like that since Gettysburg," the major murmured.

Sheriff Hill shoved his hat to the back of his head. "You were at Gettysburg?"

"I was wounded on the second day . . . but then, so was everyone else. We started out fighting for the grand cause of the Union. By the afternoon we were fighting for our platoon. By the next morning, we were fighting for personal survival. It's not a pleasant memory, nor is this."

The judge glanced over at Fidora, who sat hunched on a wooden bench. Her voluminous curly black hair paraded down her face, half covering her eyes. She wore a thin black wool shawl around her shoulders and rocked back and forth.

Judge Kingston marched over to an empty cell and tugged a gray wool blanket from the cot. He draped it gently around her shoulders.

Fidora looked up, smiled faintly, revealing the scar on her neck and two crooked front teeth. "Thank you, Judge. I ran out without my coat."

He sat down on the bench beside her. "How about you telling us your version?"

She looked quickly at the major, then away. "This is a lousy business to be in, Judge. Like I was telling your Judith last

52

week, as soon as I save up enough money, I'm pulling out. I figure if Willie Jane can walk away from it, so can I."

"Did you know the man that died?"

"Ain't never seen him before an hour ago. I was up at Callie Truxell's place. She had to go to the store, so I was sitting up there drinkin' coffee and waitin' when this man comes beatin' at the door. I thought he might be a friend of Callie's, but he thought I was her, so obviously he'd never met her. I told him she was gone and he should come back. He said he wanted to wait inside, but I told him no."

"And he didn't like your answer?"

"He said he didn't like waitin'. Said he'd just as soon be with me as with Callie."

"What did you tell him?"

"I told him it was my day off and I didn't have much use for a man that dirty who smelled like a dead cow."

"I don't suppose that went over too well?"

"He reached behind him and pulled that big knife. Bein' my day off, I hadn't thought of carrying my revolver, so I tried to slam the door. He kicked it open and came after me with the knife. I ducked his swing and tore down the stairs as fast as I could. I figured on running back to my crib and gettin' my gun and shootin' him if he didn't stop chasin' me."

"What happened in the alley?"

She paused. "It's pretty much the way this man said."

"Did you see the stabbing and the shooting?"

"I was runnin' away from it as fast as I could, Judge. I didn't see nothin'. For all I knew, that guy was shootin' at me."

"Well, I'm glad you aren't injured," the judge said.

"It ain't a very purdy business I'm in, is it?"

"You've appeared before the bench often enough to know how I feel about that, Fidora."

"But you and Judith treat me square anyway. Ain't one man out there on the boardwalk that would have gone and got me a blanket for my shoulders."

"Don't sell them too short, Fidora. You're a very independent and opinionated woman. Maybe some men feel a little threatened."

"You ain't threatened."

"No, but I'm worried. Someday, there'll be no one there to stop your pursuer and I'll have to read verses over you up at the cemetery."

She studied the judge's face. "You promise to read verses over me, even if I don't quit the business?"

"I promise. Now, how are you going to amend your behavior to see this doesn't happen again?"

"I'm going to tote my pistol even on my day off," she said. "Can I go now?"

The judge glanced at the sheriff, who nodded.

When Fidora stood, she was a good ten inches shorter than the judge. "Could you tell Judith I need to talk to her? It's mostly girl stuff."

"I'll tell her."

She tossed the blanket to the judge and left. As he watched her walk away, he thought, *A crib girl and a judge's wife discussing "girl stuff"? I have a feeling, dear wife, that you know much more "girl stuff" than I ever want to hear about.*

The judge abandoned any hope of returning to the Ormsby and finishing the now-cold liver and onions. He pulled down his hat, fastened the top button of his coat, and leaned into the stiff, frosty wind as he hiked back toward his office. He had just arrived at the corner of the state capitol grounds at Musser and Carson Streets when a woman under a buffalo robe hailed him from the back seat of Chug Conly's hack.

He tipped his hat to the woman with the stylish fox-fur hat. "Good day, Mrs. Emory."

"I heard Major Lansford was shot," Daisie Belle said.

"No, he was wounded with a knife. He shot his assailant."

"How dreadful! I do hope this brush with frontier violence doesn't dissuade the dear man from his ambitious project. Did you know he asked me to head up the Carson Community Auxiliary for the Humboldt Springs Sanatorium?"

"I didn't know that, but he made a good choice."

"I have something important I've been needing to ask you, Judge. Would you be willing to play the part of Good King Wenceslaus in the Christmas pageant? It is the male lead. There's just no one else in town who could play it like you."

The judge noticed that Chug Conly was fiddling with his wool muffler, trying to tie it more tightly around his neck. "I suppose I could do that."

"Oh, Judge! That is so generous of you. I'll be playing the princess."

"I don't remember a princess in the story."

"I've adapted it a bit, added a few lines here and there to give it more drama." She glanced west at the Sierras. Piles of white clouds skimmed across the tops. "I'm going up Musser. Can we give you a lift home?"

"No, thank you. I'm just headed across the street to my office."

Chug Conly sat up, holding the lead lines, and said, "Judge, tell Judith that eucalyptus leaf tea surely helped my wife's congestion."

"I'll tell her."

When the judge entered his office, Spafford Gabbs was busy writing at his desk. He shoved his garters higher up on his white cotton sleeves and adjusted his black tie. "I hear you had quite a busy noon hour, Judge Kingston."

"News gets around fast."

"Miss Fidora stopped by and gave me her deposition. Do you want to read it?"

"I heard the story. Just file it. The deceased went by the name Rudy Boca and came here from around Silver Peak. If the sheriff down in Esmeralda County needs any information, we'll have some to give him."

"Lawyer Grimshaw is in your office."

Garrison Grimshaw stood at the east wall, examining a large framed lithograph. A lit cigar hung from his bearded mouth. "My word, Judge, is this really Mr. Lincoln's autograph?"

"It's genuine. He gave that to me when he sent me to Nevada."

"You had a presidential appointment?"

"It was only a territory then." The judge sat down in the oak swivel chair behind his desk. "Have a chair, Counselor, and tell me what's on Consolidated Milling's mind."

Grimshaw pulled the cigar from his mouth and paced in front of the desk. He favored his right leg with a slight limp. "Judge, we need to know what you intend to do about that insurgent meeting tonight at the river."

"The right of free assembly is guaranteed in our constitution."

The man stopped pacing and puffed on his cigar. "But malicious rioting must be stopped."

"I haven't heard of any rioting."

"That's just the point. We must do everything we can to prevent it."

"Mr. Grimshaw, I'll tell you what I'll do. I'll attend that meeting tonight and observe what happens. I'm not the sheriff. I don't enforce the laws. But I interpret them. I'll see what's going on."

Smoke billowed around Grimshaw and wafted toward the ceiling. "Let me advise you to carry a weapon and drive some fast horses."

Judge Kingston leaned forward, his hands folded. "I believe you have an exaggerated idea of the situation. Most of your workers have grown up right here in Carson City. I've known them since they were rolling hoops up and down King Street. Some have learned their table manners sitting at my wife's supper table. I no more need to carry a gun to that meeting than I do to church."

Grimshaw's eyes narrowed. "Then I know which side of this conflict you're on."

The judge rose, towering over the attorney. "Mr. Grimshaw, I do not have a case before me. I do not take sides on any case. I am interested in justice and carrying out the law in a fair and impartial manner. And I do not appreciate your verdict about my fairness concerning a speculative matter."

"I suppose we'll find that out soon enough."

"Oh? Do you plan on bringing a suit?"

"We have contingency plans for emergencies."

"I trust they are legal and ethical."

"I assure you, they are legal."

The warm air inside Cheney's Grocery rolled over Judith as she tugged off her four-button kid gloves. Marthellen followed her in and picked up a wicker basket near the door. She leaned close to Judith and whispered, "Five . . . four . . . three . . ."

"Judith!" John Cheney's booming baritone voice came from the back of the store.

"He's a little slow today," Marthellen teased.

"I didn't see you come in," Cheney called out as he hustled down the aisle, fastening the top button on his shirt and sliding his tie tight.

"We just walked through the door, Mr. Cheney. Roberta's coming home this week, and I thought we should pick up a few of her favorite items."

He scurried to a shelf. "I have a wonderful tin of assorted English tea crackers. I remember how she loved those last Christmas. They come in a quite festive, reusable tin."

"I do need to keep within my budget," Judith said.

John Cheney glanced around the store, then scooted between Judith and Marthellen. "You know that when you try new items for me, you get them at wholesale." He hurried off toward the back of the store.

Marthellen chuckled and shook her head. "Judith Kingston, you are a continual inspiration to me. I've never known a woman who could get men to do so much for her without compromising her virtue."

"Mr. Cheney is a generous man."

"Only to you, Judith. He knows that if you have a decorated tin of English crackers in your kitchen, he'll sell a dozen more before Christmas."

"That's just a myth perpetuated by people like Daisie Belle Emory."

John Cheney returned with a large blue tin of English tea crackers. "Did I tell you what happened Monday, Judith? After you ordered those twelve jars of pickled okra, I sold fourteen more before quitting time. Can you imagine? I bet there's not a store in San Francisco that sells that much pickled okra."

"Maybe we could call Carson City the pickled okra capital of the world," Marthellen suggested with a gleam in her eye.

"Hi, Mom! Hi, Judith!" Willie Jane Farnsworth came toward them. "Mr.

61

Cheney, there's a freight truck in the alley."

"He can just wait. I'm looking after my favorite customer."

"I'll take care of Marthellen and Judith," Willie Jane offered.

"Yes, Mr. Cheney, please do take care of business," Judith urged. "I promise I won't leave until you've shown me all your new products."

"Splendid. Willie Jane, I entrust these two to your care."

Willie Jane gave both women a hug. "I didn't embarrass you by calling you Mom, did I?" she asked Marthellen.

"I would have been crushed if you didn't."

Willie Jane turned to Judith. "Isn't she something? I was married to Bence for only a few hours, but she treats me like real family." She glanced down at the wooden floor. "I spent all those years doing the stupidest, most horrible things. Then, on the darkest day in my dreary life, the Lord changed everything. I have had more blessings in the past four months than in my entire life up 'til then. And most of them are because of you and the judge."

"Blessings come from the Lord, Willie

Jane. He allows us to sit back and enjoy them," Judith said.

"I'm sorry I missed your song the other night," Marthellen confessed. "I suppose you heard about my melancholy streak."

"Willie Jane was exceptional," Judith said. "I'm going to ask our new minister, Reverend Fraser, to let her sing at church sometime."

Willie Jane dropped her head. "I couldn't do that. It wouldn't be right. Some of the ladies would object."

"Any woman who doesn't understand the forgiving and cleansing power of Jesus Christ needs to go back to Sunday school," Judith insisted.

"But what if the reverend doesn't think it appropriate?"

Marthellen grinned. "Are you serious, Willie Jane? There isn't a clergyman in Nevada who would dare refuse Judith Kingston's request."

"Don't you two start in," Judith said. "Mr. Cheney has already tried to butter me up. Which reminds me, we do need butter and eggs. Plain, ordinary ones."

"I'll fetch them." Willie Jane spun on her heel to head toward the rear of the crowded store.

"She's doing good, Judith," Marthellen commented.

"She's sincere about the Lord. I know that for sure."

"I was so afraid she'd never get off the laudanum."

"I understand that's a battle she'll have to fight for a long time."

"You know what's funny? She's my daughter-in-law, but most times she seems more like a daughter. It's like Bence's last present to me." Marthellen took a small handkerchief with embroidered violets from her coat pocket and dabbed her eyes. "Judith, will we ever outlive our middle-aged moodiness?"

"I suppose. But I'm not looking forward to the next step."

"What's that?"

Judith laughed. "Senility."

"Mrs. Kingston, have you heard from Roberta?" Peachy Denair walked toward them, the cape on her wool hood hiding her yellow hair.

"She's coming on Saturday, as I told you. That's all I know."

Peachy plucked up a tall, flat-sided, light green bottle. "Look at this olive oil. They bottled it in Italy without even straining out the twigs."

Judith took it from her hand and examined it, then placed it in Marthellen's basket.

Peachy frowned. "You're going to buy that? Maybe Mr. Cheney will give you a discount for taking the one with the twig."

All three ladies strolled down the aisle as Judith inspected several items.

"Did you hear about the rally at the river tonight?" Peachy said. "Turner called a workers' council. I was thinking about going. How about you two?"

"I'm afraid not," Judith said, "but the judge said he would probably ride out."

Peachy shoved her hood back. "I wonder if I could go with him?"

Judith looked at the girl. "I would imagine Sheriff Hill will accompany him."

"Peachy, why do you want to go?" Marthellen asked.

"You mean, besides the fact that Roberta's coming home soon and I only have a few days to snag Turner Bowman before she whisks him off?"

Marthellen grinned. "That makes perfect sense to me. But what does Mr. Turner Bowman say about that?"

"Oh, you know men. Women have to help them make up their minds."

"Now, here's a young woman who's wise beyond her years," Marthellen said. "I'll remember that advice."

Peachy pulled her hood forward and

covered her hair again. "Thank you, Marthellen. I have to run. I have an interview for a job at the governor's office." She swished out the front door into the December cold.

"The governor's office?" Marthellen said.

"She'd make a marvelous receptionist," Judith announced. "Governor Kinkead could get a lot of work done while Peachy was visiting in the foyer."

A breathless Willie Jane came up to them. "Sorry it took so long. Mr. Cheney had some special eggs he wanted you to try. There's a man in Genoa whose hen always lays double-yolk eggs."

"Well, that is different," Judith replied.

"And this butter is from our new separator. We ordered it from Holland. That's in Europe. Say, did you hear about Fidora?"

"I understand Major Lansford apprehended her assailant," Marthellen said.

Judith kept silent. *Apprehended? I hear he shot the man twice in the chest.*

"It was a very brave act. He seems like a real gentleman," Willie Jane declared.

"I've not even met the man," Marthellen said.

"You might get your chance real soon."

Willie Jane waved toward the front of the store. "Here he comes."

Holding his crisp black bowler in his right hand, Major Fallon Lansford marched toward the ladies. Judith thought she heard a slight gasp from Marthellen.

"Mrs. Kingston, how nice to see you again. I trust I will not make as big a fool of myself as I did at our last meeting."

When Judith held out her hand, the major transferred his hat to his bandaged left hand and winced, then shook her hand.

"I heard of your defense of Fidora, but I didn't hear of your injury," Judith declared.

Marthellen couldn't seem to keep her eyes off the major. "Oh my," she said, "did you get shot?"

"I was gashed with a knife, but I don't believe any tendons were severed, Mrs. . . . eh . . . ?"

Judith spoke up. "Major Lansford, this is my dearest friend and confidante, Mrs. Marthellen Farnsworth. She's like a sister to me." *Even more than like a sister, Major.*

The major took Marthellen's hand and slowly bowed. "I would have guessed you to be sisters."

Judith waited. *This would be a nice time,*

Marthellen, for you to mention that you are also my housekeeper and cook.

"No one has ever mistaken me for Judith Kingston's sister," Marthellen stammered.

"I definitely see a resemblance."

Judith peered into Fallon Lansford's eyes. They were friendly but not familiar. They were discerning but not pressing. They were also something else she couldn't quite figure. *My, he does know how to pour on the charm when he wants to.*

Willie Jane stuck out her hand. "I'm Marthellen's daughter-in-law."

"Very pleased to meet you. Does this store belong to your family?"

"Oh, no, I just work here."

"Willie Jane and I not only share last names, we share widowhood as well," Marthellen announced.

Judith bit her lip. *Nicely done, Mrs. Farnsworth. There's still a little steam in your kettle.*

"Fidora's a friend of mine," Willie Jane told him. "I want to thank you for savin' her from harm, perhaps savin' her life."

"I can hardly take the credit. It was a re-action more than anything," the major said.

"A heroic one, it sounds to me," Marthellen added.

"As I've said before, I deeply regret the

necessity of shooting the man. It is not the entry into Carson City society I had planned."

"Men of decision and action have always had a place on the frontier," Marthellen said. "Haven't they, Judith?"

"She's right about that. Our heroes, and our villains, make quick decisions and take determined actions." *Which are you, Major? A hero or a villain?*

"I'd better get back to work," Willie Jane said and gave a curtsy.

The Major nodded. "It was so nice to meet you, Mrs. Farnsworth."

"Just call me Willie Jane like everyone else. One Mrs. Farnsworth is enough."

Willie Jane weaved through the customers to the back of the store, her whole body swaying as she walked. A young girl about six years old hurried to keep up with her, feet skipping faster, hair bouncing. Judith noticed the major taking in the whole scene.

"I, too, much prefer that you call me Marthellen, Major," the housekeeper was saying. "Mr. Farnsworth met his demise in the Idaho mines nearly twenty years ago. I hardly remember what he looked like."

Judith marveled at the color in Marthellen's cheeks. *That's because he left you and the children years before that. It's amazing how quickly you're losing your melancholy.*

"He was involved in gold mining?" the major asked.

Marthellen nodded.

Judith curled her fingers in front of her. *And he also fell into a shallow stream and drowned in a drunken stupor, but there's no reason to go into that.*

The major turned to Judith. "The reason I came in is that I'm inviting a few community leaders to a dinner tomorrow night at the St. Charles Hotel. Just a dozen couples or so. I want to explain my plans for the sanatorium and I wanted the wives' opinions, too. I have learned over the years to greatly respect the convictions of thoughtful women."

Judith waited for him to continue. *I would guess those who agree with you are thoughtful and those who disagree are foolish. Lord, this is not fair. Please forgive me. I've got to stop this. I really must give the man a chance. My pride is getting the best of me.*

"I was on my way to the judge's office to invite you both and noticed you in the store," he said.

"You might want to go ahead and check with my husband," Judith advised. "I'm not sure of his obligations for tomorrow evening."

"Yes, I'll do that. And . . ." he stepped closer to Marthellen. "I would very much like to have you attend as my personal guest."

Marthellen glanced over at Judith, a startled look on her face.

Judith's eyes sent the message, *You don't need my permission to go to dinner with any man.*

"But before you answer, I have something to confess," the major said. "I would be delighted with your company. However, I must admit to an ulterior motive. If I don't bring someone to the dinner, I am quite sure Mrs. Emory would find a way to sit next to me."

"You don't enjoy Daisie Belle's company?" Marthellen asked.

The major spoke softly but firmly. "She is a charming woman in many ways, but she's a constant talker. I'm afraid I wouldn't have a chance to explain my project my way, especially if she thought we were a couple — partners in some way. It's very important that I present my case fully. I very much need community support for the sanatorium."

Judith studied him while he gave this candid speech. He seemed sincere, a man who knew what he wanted and how he should go about getting it.

"So you want me to attend just to divert Daisie Belle from the chair next to you?" Marthellen pressed.

"Not at all. I look forward to visiting with you. But I wanted to be honest that your highest mission will be to save me from the clutches of Mrs. Emory."

"I appreciate your honesty," Marthellen said. "I would be glad to help you in that regard."

"Until tomorrow night then, ladies."

Marthellen watched him leave the store, hat tall on his head, wounded arm tucked against his stomach. "Doesn't the major remind you of the judge?" she said.

Judith took the basket from Marthellen, then continued on down the aisle.

CHAPTER THREE

The star-filled December sky was a striking contrast to the warmth of the bonfire flames crackling near the Carson River. The angry faces of the men standing near the fire looked to the judge as if they were ready to explode — all except the one who stood on a large tree trunk, holding up his hands.

Shaggy, dark-brown hair curled out from under Turner Bowman's worn cap. Firelight flickered off his clean-shaven, square-jawed chin. His strong voice echoed through the leafless trees standing as shadowy sentinels along the riverbank. The crackle and pop of cottonwood provided a kind of percussive backdrop to his "sermon."

"I called this meeting because you and I know something has to be done. We are not being treated fairly. We've had our wages lowered twice, and no one at Consolidated Milling will guarantee they won't cut them again. They want us to quit so they can hire men for cheaper wages. That's not right. But all we've done so far is grumble around the street corners of Carson City. That hasn't accomplished much. There's been a lot of loose talk about what we could do. But whatever we decide, it has to achieve our goal."

Fremont, a big man with wild black hair and dirty canvas coat, hollered, "I say we just hang the whole lot of 'em."

Several in the crowd shouted approval.

The judge watched as Turner waved his hand to quiet the crowd, then shook his finger at the man. "And that would make every one of us unemployed murderers."

"Maybe that ain't so bad, Bowman," Fremont said.

"If your goal is to be an unemployed murderer, then you don't need us to achieve that. This meeting is exactly the opposite. We don't want anyone to get hurt," Turner shouted.

The judge studied the crowd's reaction. Some were muttering to each other, others listened attentively to their young spokesman. *That just might be the most important thing you will say tonight, Mr. Bowman.*

"If they keep cuttin' my pay, someone is going to get hurt," another man at the back hollered.

"If you think this can be settled by violence, then you'll end up no better than that Arizona bunch back there." Turner pointed toward Carson City.

Straining his eyes in the firelight, Judge Kingston spotted Ritter Crosley and five other shadowy figures mounted on horseback in moonlit silhouette. They hovered on the bluff to the west of the river, their guns across their laps. *They rode up quiet, set for trouble. Is this Mr. Grimshaw's contingency plan?*

"We ain't scared of them," Fremont shouted.

A short man with a double-barreled shotgun waved it at Crosley and the men with him. The judge recognized him as Mac McDonald, a year behind Roberta and Turner in school; he'd always had to defend himself because of his size. "This ain't your fight," he yelled at the Arizona men.

Ritter Crosley pulled off his hat and ran his fingers through his hair. Campfire light reflected off the nickel-plated receiver of his '73 Winchester carbine. "Boys, we heard this was an open meeting to discuss jobs. We ain't lookin' for no fight. 'Course, we ain't never backed down from one neither. Our funds are runnin' a little tight and we thought we'd come find out what the prospects are for work."

Fremont pushed through the crowd and stalked toward the bluff. "What's the matter, ain't Consolidated Milling payin' you enough, either?"

Above the crackling of the flames the judge heard the hammer of Crosley's carbine click twice. Fremont halted.

"We don't work for the Mill . . . yet," Crosley reported.

"You just waitin' to see who offers the highest wages?" Mac McDonald shouted.

Crosley kept his finger on the trigger. "Yep. Ain't that what you all are doin'?"

Turner Bowman jammed two fingers in his mouth and whistled loudly. Everyone immediately fell quiet. "It's an open meeting, boys. But that doesn't mean we don't have business to take care of. I don't have any intention of hiring out to the highest bidder. Not with my mind, my back . . . or my gun. What I want is good, fair wages for a hard day's work. That's all. I want us to make enough money so that a man can buy a house, settle down, and raise a family."

"You fixin' to get married, Turner?" shouted a blond man wearing a fleece longcoat and bowler hat. The others snickered.

"Everybody plans on getting married someday. That's the point. The way things are going now, I'd have to marry a rich widow just to pay rent," Turner replied.

"I wouldn't mind findin' a rich widow myself," a round-chested man said.

Again, Turner quieted the crowd. "I invited the judge out here just in case someone tried to make claims about us that weren't true. I wanted a fair witness. But maybe he'd do us the honor of instructing us a little concerning our legal options."

The judge glared at Turner. "You set me up," he muttered under his breath. "This is not what I agreed to do. You should have asked me about this ahead of time."

"You would have turned me down," Turner said with a shrug.

"How do you know I won't sink your ship now?"

Turner jumped off his podium. "I'll take that chance, Judge."

Judge Hollis Kingston carefully mounted the large round of tree trunk. He felt like he towered over the men below him. "I had no intention of addressing this crowd, but given the opportunity, I want to caution you. The state and federal courts will come down on the side of the laws of the land."

"Are you threatenin' us, Judge?" a voice

boomed from the shadows.

"I believe strongly that a man ought to get a good day's wages for a good day's work," he said, ignoring the man, "and that employers should not lower wages just to maintain their profit levels."

"You tell 'em, Judge," Fremont shouted.

"No, I'm telling *you*. If you violate state and federal laws, you will be punished. And I don't want any of you to face that." The judge pulled off his wire-frame glasses and rubbed the bridge of his long, narrow nose. "If an employer wants to fire an employee, they may do so. In the same manner, you have the right to quit anytime you feel you are being cheated."

The crowd edged closer to him. He could see clearly every intent face.

"Jobs are scarce, Judge, you know that," a gray-headed man declared. "So what kin we do?"

The judge crossed his arms. "You can quit and move to some other town and look for a new job. Or you can keep working for Consolidated, and on the side, seek some other solutions."

"Like what?" Turner demanded.

"Well, you could hire yourselves a good mining attorney to look after your legal interests."

"We cain't afford that," the gray-haired man said.

"Then encourage men like Turner Bowman to read the law. Keep yourself legally alert at every turn. Explore new directions."

"You got something in mind, Judge?" Turner called out.

The judge rubbed his goatee. He noticed that the Arizona bunch were no longer on the sandy, sage-covered bluff. "You might want to consider building your own milling company, or buying one out and running it yourselves."

"Where would we get the money to do a thing like that?" someone yelled.

The judge jammed his leather-gloved hands into the deep pockets of his wool overcoat. "Go to the mine owners. Maybe some of them don't like Consolidated's practices either. Perhaps they would finance a new mill. I'm not saying they will, but what I am saying is that you have to find a legal way to address your problems. I don't want to see any of you in court on account of violence. That kind of behavior will not bring peace and prosperity to you or your family." The judge nodded to Turner and said, "I heard Turner say he was mighty concerned about starting a family right away."

"I said sooner or later," Turner amended.

As everyone began to talk at once, the judge jumped down off the stump. He put his hand on Bowman's shoulder. "Are you planning on including my daughter in that family?"

Bowman's firm face got sterner. "No, Sir. She already turned me down two years ago."

Turned you down? You asked my daughter to marry you, and she didn't even talk to me about it?

After a half-hour of shouted debate, Turner Bowman declared the meeting officially over. He walked the judge to his carriage and blew into his hands to warm them. "Sorry, Judge, to call on you like that."

The judge fastened the top button on his overcoat. "Mr. Bowman, you acted in deceit. You tried to use my position and our friendship for your own advantage. I do not think lightly of such matters."

"Yes Sir, I did do that. But at the time I thought it the best solution. That way the crowd would get the benefit of your wisdom, which is very much respected by every man out here. And by doing it this way, you can always tell the folks at Consolidated that you were forced into it by an impertinent young man." Turner's smile was infectious.

The judge couldn't help but grin to himself as he climbed into his carriage and took the reins of the prancing black horse. "Turner, take care of yourself. Whenever men begin to argue over who gets the biggest share of the pot, someone gets hurt. Make sure the cause you give yourself to is worth the sacrifices it will take."

Bowman leaned up against the carriage wheel. "You sayin' this isn't worth the fight?"

The judge untied the lead lines. "That's your decision. Only you can determine how noble this battle is in your estimation."

Turner punched the side of the carriage. "A man hardly knows how many injustices he'll be called on to defend in his lifetime. This may be my only one."

"Turner, one thing I know . . . in twenty or thirty years there probably won't be a mine or milling company still operating in the Comstock."

"Even so, how does a fella know when a once-in-a-lifetime opportunity comes along?"

"Are you talking about choosing a vocation or choosing a wife?"

81

Turner shoved his hands in his back pockets and rocked back on his heels. His canvas coat opened and revealed a revolver tucked in his belt. "Maybe a little of both. Anyway, thanks for coming out, Judge. Tell Roberta I'll see her Saturday night."

The judge gave him a questioning look.

"I'm comin' over for supper."

"I didn't know that."

"Do you think Judith will mind?"

"You'd better check with her," the judge said.

Judith Kingston pulled open the front door of the Presbyterian Church and stepped inside the narthex. She brushed her bangs out of her eyes and unfastened the top button on her long wool double cape. *It does seem unfitting to come into the church without a hat.*

A young woman with a dark heavy cloak slipped in behind her. "I feel funny visitin' with you here," Fidora said.

Judith straightened a stack of hymnbooks on a small table near the entrance. "Why does it seem strange? It's a very nice, quiet place. Sometimes I come in here by myself just to think and pray things through. Let's sit down in one of the pews."

"Do you think he'll mind?" Fidora asked.

"The reverend?"

"No, God."

"Heavens, no. I guarantee the Lord won't mind. It just seemed that with Marthellen and Willie Jane baking in the kitchen, it would be more peaceful and secluded here — to talk about that private matter."

Fidora's shoulders slumped. "It's about the shootin'."

"Such an awful thing to go through. Is it giving you nightmares?"

Fidora shrugged. "I don't sleep much anyway."

"Tell me about it. What happened that day?"

"That's just the thing. I didn't see any of it. Not the stabbing. Not the shooting. All I heard was cursing and shots fired. I was afraid someone was shooting at me, so I kept running."

"Was Rudy Boca cursing the major?" Judith tilted her head and tried to peer into Fidora's lowered eyes.

"They both called each other some names. After the second shot, when I didn't hear any more sounds, I snuck back up the alley to see what happened. The

83

major was bleeding, but he gave me this." Fidora opened up her gloved hand and revealed a gold coin.

"A double eagle? What did he give you twenty dollars for?"

Fidora stared across the empty pews toward the pulpit. "He just said, 'I'm sure you saw exactly what happened.' "

"That's all?"

"Yes. I was still in shock at seeing the other man lying in the alley. He really did look dead."

"Why didn't you tell the sheriff about the twenty dollars?"

"Because I wanted the money. I figured the sheriff would take it away from me. I didn't do wrong by keeping the money, did I, Judith? It's been nagging at me and I don't know why. I didn't lie to the sheriff. Not one bit. I just didn't offer information he didn't ask about."

"If the major gave the money to you freely, then it belongs to you. But I'm not sure why he gave it. Perhaps he was afraid you would concoct some wild story about him murdering your boyfriend, just to extort him for more money."

"That man wasn't my boyfriend."

"But the major didn't know it."

Fidora sat stiffly in the dark wooden

pew. "I'm not the type that would do that."

"But Major Lansford doesn't know that either."

"Maybe you're right. Perhaps he was scared and didn't want me to make up some story that would get him in more trouble."

Judith patted Fidora's hands. "That's one possibility."

The younger woman let out a deep sigh and stared through the afternoon shadows at the communion table. "I hope you're right. I just got worried about it. Thanks for talking with me, Judith. I've never had someone to talk to . . . you know, about important matters."

Both ladies stood.

"Fidora, you know how I feel about your job."

"You hate it."

"And you know how I feel about you."

"You like me, don't ya?"

"Yes, I do. So that means you come talk to me anytime you want."

"Maybe we could come back in here sometime?" Fidora asked.

"I have a key to the front door. That would be no problem."

When she stepped into the center aisle, Fidora turned to the front of the sanctuary.

She bowed her head and recited, "O Lamb of God, who taketh away the sins of the world, have mercy upon me. O Lamb of God, who taketh away the sins of the world, grant me thy peace."

"Amen," Judith whispered.

"I used to go to church," Fidora admitted as they strolled toward the door.

"I can see that. You're welcome to come here as my guest anytime," Judith said.

"Sunday mornin' is about the only sleep I get on a weekend." Fidora pointed at a slotted, wooden box. "Is that the poor box?"

"The donations go to the needy."

Fidora reached over and dropped the gold double eagle into the slot. "I reckon there are some folks needier than me."

Abe Murdock and Toady Scott were perched on opposite ends of the unpainted wooden bench, staring at a chessboard, when Judge Kingston entered the small Second Street barber shop. Murdock jumped to his feet and grabbed his apron. "Need a trim today, Judge? Or you got a tooth that's ailing you?"

The judge hung his hat on the oak coat rack and unbuttoned his overcoat. "Judith says it's time for a haircut, Abe."

"You've got to keep the wife happy, that's what I say." Murdock stared at an oval-framed picture of a large unsmiling woman with braids tightly wound on her head. "Of course, some women is tougher to please than others."

Judge Kingston plopped down in Murdock's oak swivel chair as the barber stropped his scissors. "You having any luck with that game, Toady?" Judge asked.

The delicate man with canvas coveralls and weak eyes looked up. "Abe seems to take delight in humiliatin' me."

Murdock tied a large white linen cloth around the judge's neck. "Now, Toady, I'm only challenging you so you can improve your skills."

"I don't think it's workin'. I ain't won a game since October."

"It was September 21," Murdock corrected.

"Duffy Day is lookin' for you, Judge," Toady said. "Says he has secret information that could be of great help to you. What do you reckon that is?"

The judge stared into the large mirror and examined Murdock's every snip. "No telling. Most all of Duffy's information is a mystery."

The barber paused for a moment.

"Duffy's touched, but he's a good man in spite of it."

"Yep," the judge replied. "But I do wish he'd build a cabin. Some day he's going to freeze to death."

"Maybe he ought to move to southern Arizona," Toady suggested. "I hear even the winters is warm down there."

"Provided he doesn't get scalped by the Apaches," Murdock said.

Levi Boyer burst through the door, his wide-brimmed felt hat pulled low in front. "Judge, is Judith home?"

"I suppose so."

"Good. I need to talk to her. Me and Marcy just had a big argument."

The judge kept a close eye on the barber's actions. "I think she and Marthellen were going to bake today."

"That's an even better reason for visitin'. Duffy is lookin' for you." Levi slammed the door behind him.

"Say," Murdock began, "what do you think of this sanatorium that Major Lansford wants to build? Wouldn't that be something?"

"It sounds ambitious," the judge admitted. "I guess I'll learn a little more tonight."

"The major was in here not an hour ago.

He's got mighty clean fingernails." Toady Scott held up his hands in front of him. "You ever look at his fingernails, Judge?"

The judge reached out from under the sheet and flipped a clump of graying hair off his neck. "I don't believe I have."

Toady maneuvered his queen into checkmate. "I think I got you beat, Murdock."

"You can't move when I'm clear over here," Murdock said. "Say, Judge, did you hear what Major Lansford promised me?"

"No, I don't believe I did."

"He said that when they get that sanatorium up and running they will have so many guests they will need a barber right on the premises. Can you imagine that? A resort so large they need their own barber!"

"Did he want you to go work for him?"

"Even better than that. He said I could rent shop space and keep all the profit myself. Said he'd build whatever kind of shop I wanted. Ain't that something?"

"Trim that a little higher around the ears," the judge ordered. "Is it going to be very expensive?"

Murdock shoved his bifocals higher on his nose. "The buyin' or the monthly rent?"

"You have to come up with earnest money?"

"Said he'd need a thousand dollars guarantee up front, but he'd chop the rent in half until the money had been covered. That don't sound so bad, does it, Judge?"

"You're the only one who can decide that, Abe. The major sounds very ambitious. Has he already collected your money?"

"Shoot, no. He refused to take a penny until the patent deed clears and his Eastern backing is all committed."

The judge reached back and pointed at the right side of his collar. "A little more off there." The judge turned his head to the right side. "But be careful. I don't have a lot of hair left, and I don't intend for all of it to end up on your floor."

"Judge, I heard you gave a mighty fine speech down at the river last night," Toady declared.

"Who told you that?"

"Ritter Crosley. Him and that Arizona bunch went down jist to hear your talk."

The judge watched Toady in the mirror. "Are they behaving themselves down at Jack's?"

"They ain't causin' no ruckus, if that's what you mean. Of course, they got plenty of money to spend."

"I heard they might be running short of funds."

"You heard wrong. I was there for lunch and they had gold coins by the pockets full."

Judge Kingston plucked up a tuft of hair from the sheet draped across his lap and rolled it between his fingers. *Why did they say their funds were running low last night? Either they were lying or they got a job all of a sudden that pays well.*

Murdock pointed to a row of corked bottles on the shelf. "I've got some colorin' here that would take away that gray of yours in five minutes."

"I like the color of my hair," the judge said. "Comes with the territory. I'm getting old."

"You ain't old. That girl of yours is barely —"

"Twenty. And before she became a teenager I had no gray hair at all."

Mr. Murdock took a shaving mug and brushed the soap until it lathered. "How about David? Does he get to come home this year?"

"The last letter we received said they might have to wait until spring. Patricia was ill. They wanted to wait until she recuperates."

"She ain't got dysentery, has she? My first wife got dysentery in Indiana and up and died from it."

"They don't know what she has. But they're in India, not Indiana."

"Is that there India close to China, Judge?" Toady asked.

"I believe they do share a common border. China's a very large country."

"And you know what's funny? I ain't never seen a large Chinaman."

Tray Weston poked his head in the door of the barber shop. "How many ahead of me, Abe?"

"Just the judge, and he's almost finished."

"What happened to your eye, Tray?" the judge asked.

"I had a little trouble down at the Abalone Inn."

"Deputy business?"

"This was personal." He looked around the shop, then lowered his voice. "A teamster was makin' disparaging remarks about Willie Jane. I told him if he couldn't control his tongue, I could."

"So he gave you a black eye?"

"Shoot, no, Judge. I got this when two of his pals jumped me in the alley. But it don't hurt too much." Tray stuck his fingers inside his mouth. "And these loose teeth ought to firm up in a day or two. Right, Mr. Murdock?"

"You gargle with some bitters three times a day," Murdock said. "That will help."

"Judge, have you seen Willie Jane? Mr. Cheney said he gave her the afternoon off."

"Check the house, Tray. Judith and Marthellen are baking, and Willie Jane always wants to learn new recipes."

"She's goin' to make some lucky man a mighty good wife, ain't she?"

"Do you know a man lookin' for the job?" the judge asked.

Tray grinned. "Did you say they was bakin' cookies?"

"I think I heard talk of plum pudding, too."

"In that case, I reckon I better wait on that haircut and take a little stroll."

Toady Scott stood, stretched his arms, then pulled on his jacket. "I do believe I need to stretch my legs. Mind if I walk with you, Deputy?"

"You wouldn't be taggin' along to get some homebaked plum puddin', would ya?" Tray challenged.

"Well, thank ya," Toady replied, "don't mind if I do."

Tray paused at the door. "Oh, Judge, I almost forgot to tell you —"

"Duffy Day's looking for me?"

"No, it was Mrs. Emory. She acted like it was a real emergency."

After Toady and Tray left, there was no noise except the razor scraping across the judge's whiskers.

After his face had felt the ministrations of towel and tonic, the judge examined his reflection in the large mirror. *You're looking older by the week, Hollis Kingston. Lord, where have all those years gone?*

"What do you think, Judge?"

"Looks fine, Abe." He pulled a coin from his vest pocket and tossed it on a shelf next to an assortment of colored bottles. "Looks like you got some customers."

Murdock turned to survey the two scraggly-bearded Washburn brothers. "You boys know I can't give you any credit."

"We got cash money," Twig boasted.

"And we got jobs," Lester added.

"That's great, boys, where are you working?"

"We're going to be guards at that there new sanitation resort the major's buildin'," Twig announced.

Murdock chuckled. "Sanitation resort?"

"Who knows?" the judge said as he pulled on his coat. "They might be right."

The judge cut diagonally across the state

capitol grounds toward Carson Street. All the ash and box elder trees lining the black iron fence and the walkways were winter bare, exposing the capitol and any intruders to all passersby. *I never could understand why the Lord made some deciduous trees naked in the cold days and full of foliage in the heat of summer,* the judge mused.

As he got halfway across, he noticed a small campfire in the northwest corner of the grounds.

Duffy Day, hunched over like a small wagon wheel, huddled near the fire.

"Did you get permission to do this?" the judge asked.

"Governor John H. Kinkead himself told me so. He said if I cleaned out all of these prunings, I could have the firewood."

"I think he meant you could haul it back to your place."

"Why would I want to do that? I've got plenty of wood out there."

"Did you want to see me, Duffy?"

"Yes, Sir. I wanted to tell you about that spy." He continued to squat, his long arms stretched over the small fire.

The judge crouched down next to him, his knees cracking as he lowered himself. "What spy?"

"The one hidin' in the poplars at that

95

meetin' at the river last night."

"How do you know someone was hiding?"

" 'Cause I was spyin' out that meetin', too."

"You were spying on the spy?"

A big grin broke across Duffy's face. He chuckled for a moment, his expression like a boy who had played a good trick.

The judge grimaced as he slowly stood up. He slipped his gloved hands into his overcoat pockets and turned his back to the west wind. "Who was in the poplars, Duffy?"

"I don't know, but he smelled nice."

"Smelled nice?"

"It was too dark to see any face. I told you he was hid. But after he left I went over and looked, and it smelled like tonic water. Sort of like you do right now, only sweeter."

"Like a man after a haircut?" the judge quizzed.

"And that ain't all. I went back and looked this mornin' and found a name that had been written in the dirt beside them poplars. This one . . ." Duffy took a stick and scratched out T-U-R-N-E . . .

"Turner Bowman?"

Duffy looked up, wide-eyed. "How did you know?"

"So someone was spying out the meeting and wrote Turner's name down?"

"Turner didn't do it," Duffy insisted. "He was up there on that stump with you."

"Perhaps it was someone from Consolidated Milling," the judge said.

Duffy uncurled himself, stood up, and pulled his knit sailor's hat over his ears. "It was someone who smelled purdy."

The judge studied Duffy's wandering eyes. *It could have been a "purdy"-smelling woman, I suppose.* "Thanks, Duffy, I'll tell Turner to be on the lookout."

"What for?"

"In case someone spies on him again."

"Wild Bill Hickok used to spy on me. Did I ever tell you about that?"

"I believe you did."

"He's dead now, but I didn't kill him." Duffy began to kick out the fire.

"You going home now?" the judge asked.

"Think I'll hike over to see Judith. She invited me to stop by sometime for a cup of hot chocolate. My mama said it ain't polite to refuse an honest woman."

Spafford Gabbs met the judge at his office, briefcase under his arm. "I'm going across to the capitol and research those mining claims in the Washoes. There's a weepy woman waiting for you."

"Marthellen's here?" the judge asked.

"No, it's Peachy Denair."

"Are you sure she doesn't want to see Judith instead?"

"She said she desperately needed to talk to Judge Kingston."

"Why don't I go research those mining claims and you visit with Peachy?"

"You're the judge. I'm just the lowly clerk."

As Judith returned from her meeting with Fidora, heavy, dark gray clouds drifted like breaking surf over the top of the Sierras while the bright sun shone overhead. A brisk wind chilled her bones.

Two men hunkered on the Nevada Street porch of her home.

"I reckon I'd better accept that cup of hot chocolate you been wantin' to give me," Duffy said.

"And you, Toady, would you like some chocolate?" Judith asked.

Toady grinned. "I heared it goes real well with plum puddin'."

"What a coincidence. Would you like to come in?"

Duffy shook his head before Toady could reply. "My mama told me to never

98

enter a house with muddy boots."

"You could leave them on the porch," Judith suggested.

"I ain't got on no socks."

"How about you, Toady?"

Toady Scott sat down on a nearby wooden bench. "I kin wait out here with Duffy. I'm afraid I might get somethin' dirty. Besides, it's kind of crowded in there."

Judith opened the front door. "Well, meanwhile, why don't you and Toady go burn the trash for me? Put a log in the fire if you'd like. I don't want you freezing out here. Looks like a storm coming."

Duffy hopped up. "My mama said I should always do the chores whenever asked."

Toady Scott tugged at his worn wool gloves. "Judith, I always keep warm when I split wood. Do you reckon the judge would mind if I split and stacked some of his firewood for him?"

"I think the judge would be quite happy to allow you to warm up," Judith said. "But don't split it all or you'll spoil him."

She slipped into the house, hung her hooded cape on a peg at the back porch, and pulled on her full-length blue calico apron. The aroma of cinnamon, cloves, nutmeg, and mace filled the house.

In the kitchen, Tray Weston clutched half a raw, peeled potato to his left eye. Levi Boyer was drinking coffee at the breakfast table, and Willie Jane was drying her hands on an embroidered tea towel. Everyone watched Marthellen slide a pan of rich plum pudding off the cooling rack near the slightly open window.

"It's got lots of raisins and currants," Marthellen explained. "But I used walnuts instead of pecans. Otherwise, it's just like my mother used to make."

"I made the lemon sauce, and Judith made hard sauce with vanilla," Willie Jane said.

Judith helped Marthellen pull out the Blue Willow dessert plates. "What happened to your eye, Tray?" she asked.

"He got in a fight with some men who called me names," Willie Jane announced.

"Again?" Judith lifted the potato off Tray's eye and inspected the damage.

"They make me real mad," he said. "I jist can't hold back."

"It takes time to change people's minds," Willie Jane said. "Every one of those words used to be true. You know they were."

"But they ain't anymore. That's the point."

Willie Jane touched his shoulder. "And I don't want you hurt one more time on my account. I don't care what they say about me. The Lord has changed all that."

"I care what they say. It drives me crazy." Tray turned to Judith. "What am I going to do?"

"Marry Willie Jane and move to a new place where no one knows you."

The room fell suddenly still.

"But I don't want to leave Carson City," Willie Jane said. "There's lots of folks who are nice to me, like Mr. Cheney and all of you."

"I don't want you to leave, either," Judith said. "But that's about the only way I know to keep this from happening again. There's a reputation to live down and people will talk."

Marthellen sliced squares of cake. "It takes time for a town to forget one's past," she said, "but it gets dimmer over the years. I ought to know."

"You used to be a crib girl?" Tray choked out the words.

Marthellen didn't laugh. "What I did was even worse."

Levi dipped warm lemon sauce over the pudding. "What was it?"

"You don't have to answer that, Marthellen," Judith said.

Marthellen shrugged. "For the first time in my life, I realize it doesn't matter anymore. It's not what you used to be but what God makes out of you that matters."

"What did you used to be?" Levi pressed.

"I killed a man and was sentenced to prison for it. I am extremely sorry for what I did, but I have to go on and live my life."

"Eh, how did you kill him?" Levi asked.

"I poisoned him with plum pudding."

Levi gasped. "She's joking, right?"

"She's been stringing us along the whole time," Tray hooted.

"Well, she surely pulled it over on me. I was gettin' ready to bolt out the door," Levi admitted.

Judith giggled. "Did you ever see two men with wider eyes?"

"Forgive me for baiting you boys so," Marthellen said. "I don't know why I feel in such a teasing mood today."

"Could it have anything to do with your dinner engagement tonight?" Willie Jane said.

Marthellen blushed. "Oh, that? I hardly gave it a thought."

"You've been planning your wardrobe for hours."

"Say, is any part of that big windy you told us true?" Levi asked.

Marthellen grinned. "Yes."

Judith studied her housekeeper. *Major Fallon Lansford, whatever your weaknesses might be, you've put a lilt in this woman's heart and she's very dear to me. She looks ten years younger today.*

A knock at the front door sent Judith toward the living room. "Willie Jane," she called, "take some hot chocolate and plum pudding out back to Duffy and Toady."

Daisie Belle Emory's charcoal-gray silk coat seemed to catch and reflect the sunlight. Her light gray hat was tilted to the right, its alligator hatband sporting an ivory cameo. She marched in and paced the living room as if inspecting every item. "I just spent the afternoon with Major Lansford. He's such a dear man. I thought it would be nice for us to throw a New Year's Eve gala as sort of a fund-raiser for the new sanatorium. What do you think?"

"A fund-raiser? I thought this was a private business."

"Oh, that's right. You haven't heard the presentation yet. That comes tonight for the rest of you."

103

"I take it you got a sneak preview?"

Daisie Belle nodded. "You might say that. Anyway, if we have the fund-raiser, I was wondering if Marthellen could supervise the dinner. Like I told Major Lansford, Marthellen Farnsworth is the best cook in Carson City. You know, I don't think that man knew Marthellen was your housekeeper."

Well, he does now.

"The major, besides being so chivalrous, is such a gentleman in every way. Did you ever see such immaculate hands?"

"I think I missed that part," Judith said.

"Would you check with Marthellen about supervising the New Year's gala meal? It will be a costume party, of course. I thought about coming dressed as Lady Liberty. Do you think that would be too pretentious?" Daisie Belle prattled on. "Perhaps I should dress as an angel."

"Daisie Belle, why don't you go ask Marthellen?"

"I didn't want to bother the chef in her kitchen. It smells very busy in there."

"Perhaps you could ask her tonight, at the dinner."

Daisie Belle stared out the window toward Musser Street. "That's the point. One of the reasons I talked to the major today is that I got the sense that tonight's meeting was for couples only. I didn't want to stick out like a sore goose's neck."

"You are an important part of every civic meeting and you know it. We need you there," Judith protested.

Daisie Belle's face softened. "You are very kind."

"You know I mean it."

Daisie Belle's eyes watered as she clutched Judith's hand. "I know you do, dear Judith. You're the most honest friend I've ever had."

"I want you to be there tonight . . . please."

Daisie Belle's eyes dropped to the tied rug on the floor. "Sometimes . . . sometimes I get quite lonely."

Judith slipped her arm around the woman's shoulders. *Lord, I wish others could know this very vulnerable widow like I know her.*

She heard a noise on the porch and whirled around to peer through the sheer curtain of the glass and oak door. A square-chinned man with a thick, drooping mustache loomed on the porch.

Daisie Belle stepped behind her and said in a low voice. "Judith Kingston, I've never known a woman who could attract so many men with so little effort. There are men in your backyard, men in your kitchen, and a most becoming man banging on your door."

"Excuse me, are you Marthellen Farnsworth?" asked a deep baritone voice when Judith opened the door.

"Marthellen's in the kitchen. I'm Judith Kingston, and this is Daisie Belle . . . eh, the widow, Mrs. Emory. Do come in."

The man marched into the room as if inspecting a barracks, much like Daisie Belle had done earlier.

"Whom shall I tell her is calling?" Judith asked.

"Colonel Arthur Jacobs."

"Doctor Jacobs' brother?" Daisie Belle asked.

"At your service."

"We were expecting you last Saturday," Judith remarked.

"That's why I owe the widow Farnsworth an apology. I was delayed by the storm and then by the governor of California on some military matters."

Daisie Belle Emory slipped her arm into his and led him toward the kitchen. "Colonel Jacobs, do you have any dinner plans for this evening?"

CHAPTER FOUR

The judge didn't realize the fire had died down until his ears got cold. For two hours he'd been poring over maps of Washoe, Ormsby, and Storey counties at the roll-top oak desk in his home office. He pulled off his wire-frame glasses, loosened his tie, and unfastened the top button on his starched white shirt.

He toted several pieces of firewood from the side entry to the living room, then stooped to shove them into the glowing embers of the fireplace. As the flames perked up and warmed his face, he rose and spotted two brown eyes peeking at him from under a heavy comforter on the couch.

"I thought you were going to bed," he said.

Judith pulled the comforter down. "I decided to wait up."

"For me? Or for Marthellen?"

"For both of you."

The judge turned his back to the fire.

His long shadow stretched across the length of the room. "She'll be all right."

"I know. It's just that she hasn't been out this late in ten years." Judith stuck her stocking-covered feet out from under the comforter and wiggled her toes.

The judge looped his thumbs in the pockets of his vest. "She's forty-eight years old."

"What difference does that make? Tonight she was acting twenty." Judith tucked her legs under her again and patted the sofa.

The judge sat next to her and reached out his hand to clasp hers. They stared into the flames for several moments, then he said, "Did I ever tell you that you have the best holding hands in the entire world?" He gave her hand a squeeze.

"You've mentioned that. But I was never sure on what empirical evidence you made that judgment."

"One does not need to examine inferior diamonds in order to recognize a rare gem. Its own beauty and radiance establishes its worth beyond all reasonable doubt."

"Bravo. Case dismissed." Judith pushed the comforter lower, then retied the ribbon on her flannel gown.

The judge leaned against the back of the

velvet sofa and closed his eyes. "Which are you worried about most — Marthellen's late hour or Major Fallon Lansford's intentions?"

"He troubles me," she admitted.

"He's a promoter and a speculator. That type should always elicit caution."

Judith reached over and took his hand again. "I don't want Marthellen to get hurt."

"She didn't look hurt tonight at the dinner."

Judith sat up next to the judge and spread the comforter over both their laps. "No, she looked radiant. What do you suppose they're doing now?"

A sly grin crept across the judge's face.

"Don't you answer that. You're right. She's mature enough to make her own decisions."

His eyes were still closed. "And live her own life?"

"Provided she tells me everything when she gets home." She laid her head on his shoulder and he immediately put his arm around her.

"Is that the real reason why you are waiting up?"

"I suppose," she murmured, stretching her arm across his chest. "What's your excuse?"

He glanced down at her. "I'm still pondering the major's proposal for the sanatorium."

She fiddled with the button on his vest. "That was quite a presentation. I thought the scale model layout was very effective. It's an impressive plan."

"But remember, that model was all three phases of construction. It won't be that vast at first." The judge ran his hand gently through her unpinned curly hair.

"And what about the scientific analysis of the mineral content of Humboldt Springs? It matches up with other mineral health springs around the country."

He kissed the top of her head. "I was curious about how he got that analysis. It seems strange that a scientific team could slip into the hills last summer and no one even knew they were there."

"He said they dressed like prospectors. If so, they could wander through the hills without drawing suspicion. Were you able to locate the springs on the maps?" Judith unfastened the top button on his vest.

"No, but at least I did find the township and section. I look forward to riding up there and scouting out the land."

"Did it surprise you how much he expected from the city, county, and state?"

He began to rub her back. "It didn't surprise me as much as it did Governor Kinkead."

"Do you think they'll agree to it?"

"At least some of it. I think he deliberately requested a tremendous amount so he'd have some compromise and bargaining power."

"The state will have to build the roads and bridges, or it won't work." She unfastened the second button on his vest.

"I suppose so, but this wild idea about an electric current generator and electricity is far too experimental."

"I read that Mr. Edison thinks it's working well."

"In his laboratory in New Jersey, but it's much too expensive to think of in a practical way," the judge said.

"What about the landscaping? The major wants five miles of poplars to border the wide drive up to the springs." Judith reached back and pulled her hair to the top of her head so the judge could rub her shoulders.

"That's absurd. Those trees won't grow without water."

"But he says the overflow from the springs will irrigate them."

"It would take a flow the size of the

Carson River to grow those trees. But even if he gets the county to come up with a mile of trees, that's more than he has now."

Judith let her hair fall back down and slipped her arm around his neck. "Do you think he'll change his mind about using the sandstone? The prices from the state quarry should be tempting."

"He may be right. Easterners won't want to come clear out here only to discover a place that looks like an institution."

"His one-story central building with shaded, private cabins would certainly have a homey feel." She tucked her legs over his lap and he began massaging her feet. "And he even has Hank Munk signed up to run the custom carriage from the train station to the springs. Do you think there will ever be a narrow-gauge railway hookup like he wants?"

"Not if he's relying on state money. But who knows what his Eastern backers might want? As far as I can tell, he has a barber, a doctor, a grocer, a dry-goods merchant, and a druggist all lined up. It will be a veritable village out there." The judge reached down and unfastened the last button on his vest. The comforter dropped to the floor.

"Did you know any of the men he mentioned as potential financiers?" Judith asked.

"A few of the names sounded familiar."

"I heard they have reserved twelve rooms at the Ormsby House."

"Are you ready to retire, Mrs. Kingston?" he whispered.

Judith glanced at the front door. "I think I'll stay up a little longer. You go on to bed."

"Nonsense." The judge leaned back and tugged off his tie. "I presume we're waiting up until Marthellen returns, no matter what the hour might be." He folded the tie and laid it on the mahogany end table.

"I think so." She reached down to lift the comforter, then let it drop back and snuggled closer to the judge. "It sort of feels like when we waited up for Roberta, doesn't it?"

"Are you getting anxious for our daughter to be home?"

"I try not to think about it. But I actually caught myself counting the hours this morning."

He hugged her tighter. "Do you have any last prediction on what her big news might be?"

"I really think it has to do with changing her studies again. I say she's decided to become a lawyer."

"She knows better than that. I absolutely forbid her to do that."

"That's exactly why she'll do it," Judith said. "Her father said it was a field too difficult for a woman to enter, so she'll decide to prove him wrong. How about you, Judge Kingston? What grand news do you think your daughter brings?"

"I've eliminated one thing. She's not coming home to tell us that she and Turner Bowman are getting married. I asked him flat out the other night and he just laughed. He said she turned him down two years ago." He stared down into her dark, innocent eyes. "Do you know anything about that?"

"Why, of course."

She could feel his entire body stiffen. "You mean a man asked my daughter to marry him and I wasn't told?"

She ran her hand across his chest. "It would only have made you mad."

"That's preposterous," he fumed.

"Roberta turned him down on the spot without consulting either one of us. By the time it got to me, it was old news."

"Is there any other 'old news' I don't know about?" The judge began to relax as she continued to rub his chest.

"Perhaps. But don't count Turner out

yet." Judith yawned and stretched her arms. She could detect a hint of pine scent in the flame-warmed air. "He invited himself to supper on Saturday night."

"So did Peachy," the judge added.

"Now, tell me again, what did she say when she came to your office today?"

"She said she felt like you and I were trying to push Roberta and Turner together and it gave her an unfair disadvantage."

"Just how are we doing that? We sent our daughter away to an Eastern college."

"She got word of my teasing Turner about Roberta at the bonfire rally," the judge said. *I wonder if Peachy smelled sweet that night?*

"I think she's being too sensitive."

"She came to my office in tears."

"So you invited her to our house for Saturday supper?"

"It seemed like the right thing at the time."

"We will have a table full. I invited Willie Jane and Tray, too."

He patted her knee. "So much for a quiet, private family reunion." He left his hand on her leg.

"Since when was anything quiet that involves your daughter?" Judith reached up and brushed his gray hair back off his ear, then rubbed the back of his neck.

A narrow smile broke across his thin lips. "*My* daughter?"

"She's her daddy's little girl, remember?"

The judge shook his head and sighed. "It's been a long time since she was little." He leaned down and kissed Judith's forehead. "She's twenty years old." He stared at the flames for a moment, then reached up and rubbed the corner of his eye. "Do you really think that young Bowman still has a chance with her?"

"He's the only man in Nevada who does."

"Why is that?"

"Because he's the only man under thirty in the entire state who isn't scared out of his wits by Judge Hollis A. Kingston."

He rubbed his mustache and goatee. "Are you saying I'm a harsh man?"

She walked her fingers up the button row on his white shirt and tapped them on his chin. "Roberta and I both know you are a soft-hearted pushover. But most of the young men around town don't know that."

"Does Roberta hold that against me?"

"I don't think so. She just laughs and says any boy who won't talk to her daddy face-to-face is certainly not worthy of her undivided attention."

"Judith, am I a stern man?" He tried to lift his hand from her knee, but she clutched his wrist.

"You are a principled man. An honest man. A direct man." She raised herself up and kissed his cleanshaven cheek.

"You're making me out to sound like Colonel Jacobs."

"Wasn't he something? So military. So . . . so . . ."

"All that man ever wanted to talk about was the war. My word, the war's been over fifteen years."

Judith kicked at the fallen comforter. "I was glad Major Lansford tried to shut him up. If he and the colonel had started trading Gettysburg stories, we'd never have heard about the sanatorium plans. I thought the colonel a bit pushy, asking the major about this battle and that, although Daisie Belle didn't seem to mind his stories. There could be a romance there."

"Maybe so, but I doubt she would ever remarry," the judge observed. "It would cramp her style."

"What do you mean by that?" She traced a circle around each button on his shirt.

He patted her knee. "She loves to flirt with men and make wives jealous, but that's as far as it goes."

117

"Oh? Are you speaking from personal experience?"

"That's obvious, isn't it?"

"I hardly noticed," Judith said, then immediately pushed his hand off her leg.

"By the way, she did twist my arm to be in the pageant again this year."

"The Christmas or the New Year's pageant?"

"What New Year's pageant?"

"She's sponsoring a New Year's Ball to raise funds for the sanatorium. We're on the committee."

"What does that mean?"

"It means that you get to dress in a costume and serve punch."

"No, not a costume ball!"

"Daisie said she will either go as Miss Liberty or an angel." Judith took his hand and began to rub it up and down her calf. "What part do you have in the Christmas pageant?"

"Good King Wenceslaus."

She sat up and burst out laughing.

The judge's blue-gray eyes flashed. "I don't find it humorous."

"It's a perfect part for you. That's why I'm laughing. For once, Daisie Belle did a good job of casting."

"You haven't heard the entire cast. She

118

decided to add a princess to the story." He stared up at the flickering shadows on the ceiling. "She said the play lacked drama."

"Don't tell me. Mrs. Daisie Belle Emory stars as the princess."

"So it seems."

"So, you have the male lead and she has the female lead. How charming."

He refused to look at her as he said, "I'm certainly glad it doesn't bother you."

They heard voices coming from the front step and Judith raised her lips close to his ear. "Can you hear what they are saying?"

"I'm fortunate to hear you," he murmured. "Do you want to move closer to the door?"

"Of course not."

"That's what you used to do when it was Turner and Roberta on the front step."

"You knew about that?"

"Yes, and so did Roberta."

"She did not!"

"Ask her."

Judith's voice rose several levels above a whisper. "I have no intention of asking my daughter if she knew I was spying on her."

Now his lips were at her ear. "We could go to the door and invite them in."

"We will not. They should have some

privacy. I wonder what they're doing."

"Maybe they're doing this . . ." The judge tilted her chin and kissed her.

Her arm circled his neck and held him close until a voice startled them from just inside the front door.

"Well, I see you two are busy," Marthellen said, "so I'll just go on to bed."

They broke apart and looked at her mutely.

"I had quite an evening," Marthellen offered. "I'll tell you all about it tomorrow. Thanks for waiting up for me."

"But . . . but . . . ," Judith began. "You didn't tell me one thing about the major."

"He has nice lips and I'm exhausted." Marthellen stumbled against the couch for emphasis. She weaved toward the kitchen and her living quarters.

Judith stood up, brushing down her long flannel gown. "I'm going to talk to Marthellen."

The judge grabbed her arm and tugged her back to the couch. "No, you aren't."

"And why not?"

"Because, my dear Judith, . . ." he grinned, "you, too, have nice lips."

Judith scooped the raspberry jam out of the shallow china bowl and back into the glass jar. "Where are you and the major going tonight?"

Marthellen carried a stack of dirty breakfast dishes toward the sink. "He wants to see the Boisset family and their great parlor posturing act and the melodrama *Murder Will Out,* in Virginia City. We'll come back on the late train."

Judith carried the jam jar to the pantry. "You've been a busy girl this week."

Marthellen began scrubbing white china rimmed with tiny handpainted violets. "I don't know what to say. It's been so long since I've spent this much time with a man."

Judith filled her cup with hot chamomile tea and said, "A handsome man at that."

Marthellen grinned. "For a man our age, you mean?"

"There are plenty of women in Carson who would agree with you about the handsome part regardless of age."

"That's what makes all of this so incredible," Marthellen said. "That he would choose me. I keep thinking I'm going to wake up and find it all a dream."

Judith took a sip of tea. *Even if it is a dream, my dear friend, I guess you can enjoy it while it lasts.*

"He's so kind, so sensitive. I would take

that without the good looks," Marthellen said.

"You deserve a good man. I pray for a long and satisfying relationship for you someday."

"Oh, don't worry," Marthellen quickly added. "I'm not going to quit you and the judge. No matter what, I would never do that."

"Nonsense. If the Lord ever leads you to get married, you know you have our blessing. We have always wanted your happiness."

Marthellen stared into the soapy water. "That's exactly why I could never leave you."

"Well, until the situation actually presents itself, we don't have to worry about it." Judith picked up a cotton towel embroidered with red and green apples. "The situation hasn't presented itself, has it?"

"Not yet, but I do have some errands to run for the major this morning. Perhaps we could catch up with our Bible study and prayer later?"

"I'll read for both of us and give you a report," Judith said.

"I have been rather lax this week," Marthellen admitted. "What's the verse we were to memorize?"

"Jeremiah 4:13: 'Behold, he shall come up as clouds, and his chariots shall be as a whirlwind: his horses are swifter than eagles. Woe unto us! for we are spoiled.' "

Marthellen dipped a plate in the basin of hot water, then stacked it on the wooden counter. "I like the first part. It sounds like the major. That's the way this week has felt."

"Like a whirlwind?"

"Yes, but I'm not sure what 'Woe unto us! for we are spoiled' means."

Judith gulped down the rest of her tea. "There's a lot to meditate on."

"Judith, may I borrow your gray felt hat, the one with the burgundy bow and jetted black flowers?"

"Why, yes, of course. You mean for the theater tonight?"

Marthellen retrieved a handful of silverware from the bottom of the soapy sink. "No, for this morning."

"And what errands does the major have for you today?"

"I'm making arrangements at the Ormsby House for the Eastern backers."

"I thought he had already reserved the rooms."

"He has. But there's a long list of extras each room should have."

"Like what?"

"Some of the men like Cuban cigars. Some want caviar. One wants a bathtub right in his room. Another loves chocolates. That kind of thing."

"The major seems intent on making an impression."

"He's a very thorough man. Everything he does has a purpose."

Judith stacked the dry plates on the edge of the breakfast table to be toted to the hutch later. She stood there for a moment, thinking, *And just what is the purpose of having Marthellen Farnsworth as your unpaid errand girl, Major Lansford?*

Judge Hollis A. Kingston had just hung up his heavy black judicial robe when Sheriff Hill burst through the door. "You through with that court case already?"

"They settled out of court," the judge declared.

"What did they decide?"

"She gets the hotel. He gets the gold mine."

The sheriff pulled off his hat and smoothed his hand over his balding head. "Is that fair?"

"Neither will own anything within six months if their attorneys have anything to do with it. It's out of my hands now."

"Good, that means you have the after-noon with nothin' on your docket. That's divine providence, I say."

The judge tugged on the square-cornered cuffs of his gray-striped French flannel shirt. "What do you have planned for me?"

"A trip to Consolidated Milling. They sent word that one of their workers dyna-mited the buildin' and ruined the cam on their California stamp mill. Their guards have the suspect cornered. They want me to come out and arrest him."

"Is it Turner Bowman?"

"That's what the message said."

"Turner wouldn't do that. They're trying to oust him."

"It looks like they might have a case," the sheriff said. "Maybe you can help me figure out what's goin' on."

The judge pulled on his black suit jacket, mackintosh overcoat, fur-lined kid gloves, and rubber cover over his hat. "It doesn't look good, Sheriff, whatever happened."

"You got your shotgun?"

Kingston stared at the sheriff's stern eyes, then pulled a handgun from a desk drawer.

"You can use one of mine," the sheriff said. "Consolidated brought in a couple dozen Bay area loafers and armed them all

125

with '73s a couple days ago. I didn't know about it until today. Besides that, they've got a dozen amalgamation tables covered with gold flakes, and the whole line is shut down. I expect some tension."

The two men hurried across the marble foyer of the courthouse. The judge climbed into the sheriff's carriage and pulled his hat down against the frigid wind. They headed northeast on Washington Street, then broke into a trot when they passed the racetrack. The Sierras and the cold wind were now at their backs.

Full clouds dragged across the mountaintop, leaving a deposit of white glitter. Rain drizzled on the valley floor. Near the mill road, tufts of yellow-brown grass and weeds circled piles of boulders, looking like memorial markers. Mice skittered across the road in front of them. They passed a straggly outcrop of small, leafless cottonwoods and bushes in pale gold and rusty rose swaying in the wind.

The sheriff slapped the lead lines and raised his voice. "What did you tell those workers out at the bonfire the other night?"

"Not to break the law. Not to do anything dumb that would get them arrested."

"You weren't very convincin', I guess."

126

"I don't suppose this state will ever really settle down until every bit of gold and silver is dug out of the ground."

The sporadic rain mixed with sleet. Soon, snowflakes stuck to sage and creosote, brightening the mounds of small sand dunes.

"Did you ever wonder what Nevada would be like if there had never been any mineral discoveries?" Sheriff Hill asked.

The judge cracked open the sheriff's double-barreled shotgun and checked the chambers. "I suppose it would just be another county in Mr. Brigham Young's empire."

"If so, sheriffin' would be a whole lot different."

The Consolidated Milling facilities covered twenty acres of riverfront property just off the bluff at Empire, about four miles east of Carson City. The village was located on the Carson River at the Virginia City and Truckee Railroad crossing and consisted of ten houses, a post office, four saloons, a brothel, and three reduction mills: the Mexican Mill, the Meads Mill, and the newest, Consolidated Milling and Reduction Works, which had cost $202,000 to build in 1875.

Three men armed with '73 Winchesters

stopped them at the entrance to the mill.

"I hear you got some trouble out here," the sheriff called out as they slowed down. He opened his coat to reveal his sheriff's badge.

A thin man, standing six-foot-six, a carbine across his shoulder, sauntered up to the carriage. "Who's that with you?"

"First District Judge Hollis A. Kingston."

"What do we need a judge for?" The man stared back up the road toward the bluff and spit out tobacco juice. "Where's your posse?"

"What do I need a posse for?"

The man pointed his carbine toward the reduction plant. "There's goin' to be some shootin' if things don't settle down fast."

Armed men loitered behind wagons and barricades, staring toward a huge metal-sided building.

Mill superintendent D. B. Stevens rushed up to the carriage. "Sheriff, you have to do something quick."

The sheriff tied off the lead lines to the hand brake. "What's goin' on, Stevens?"

The superintendent tried to hug his fleece-lined coat tighter as one hand clamped down on his bowler. "Where's the rest of your men, Sheriff?"

"I got a message that one man was to be

arrested and you had him cornered. Why in the world does everyone keep tellin' me I need more men?"

"I guess the second message didn't get to you. Things have taken a turn."

The sheriff and the judge climbed down from the carriage, and Stevens led them toward the barricade. "Sometime during the morning, Turner Bowman slipped several sticks of dynamite along the cam of stamp mill number two. While everyone was eating at noon, he lit the fuses and destroyed the rigging and the cam."

"Was anyone hurt?" the judge asked.

"No."

"Did anyone see Turner do this?"

"As shift foreman, we know he was the only one with access up there."

"The only one?" the judge asked. "You mean, you can't get up there, Stevens?"

"Of course I can! I meant, he's the only worker that has access." The superintendent pulled off his spectacles and wiped his forehead on his sleeve.

The judge studied the twelve-foot-high double front doors of the mill about fifty yards away. "Then you're saying that no one saw him do it?"

Stevens replaced his spectacles. "I haven't questioned everyone yet."

The judge kept his eye on the mill. "Who have you questioned?"

Stevens shrugged. "Turner Bowman."

"What did he say?"

"He denied it, of course."

The sheriff pulled out his Colt .44 revolver, opened the cylinder, and slipped one more cartridge into the chamber, then reholstered his gun. "How does the situation stand now?"

"We were holding Turner in the shift foreman's office for your arrival when the mutiny hit. The rest of the men on the shift chased us out of the mill."

"They have guns in there?" the sheriff asked.

"Not only that, they have dynamite. They say if we start shooting or try to take Bowman, they'll blow up the entire mill. How much more proof do you want that they sabotaged the cam?"

The sheriff looked at the judge. "I reckon we ought to go talk to the boys inside."

"Don't you need some backup help?" Stevens asked. "Perhaps we should send for the army?"

Sheriff Hill brushed the shoulders of his coat even though it had stopped snowing. "He don't have much confidence in us, does he, Judge?"

Stevens' hands made frantic circles. "But they could be looting the amalgamation tables."

The sheriff pulled a sulphur stick match out of his vest pocket to chew on. "That they could. Or they could just be tyin' dynamite to ever' beam in the whole building. That's what we aim to find out."

The sheriff crouched down beside a guard who had stationed himself behind a weathered buckboard. He cupped his hand around his mouth and shouted. "Turner, this is Sheriff Hill. I need to talk to you, Son."

"We ain't goin' to let you arrest him, Sheriff," someone at the door shouted back.

"I didn't say I was or I wasn't. Me and Judge Kingston are here and we got to find out what's goin' on, to get the whole story."

"You won't get it out there," the man at the door hollered.

"That's precisely why I need to talk to you."

"Sheriff," Bowman yelled. "Send the judge in. We'll talk to him. You stay out there."

Sheriff Hill poked his head out from behind the wagon. "This is a law matter. You've got to talk to me."

"If it's a law matter, we want to talk to the judge," Turner called out. "The boys are afraid you'll try to arrest me if you come in, and some of them are about to cut loose as it is. Send in the judge. They know he'll listen, and I know they'll pay attention to him."

The sheriff looked at the judge.

"I'll go in," Judge Kingston said and handed the sheriff his shotgun.

"You don't need a weapon?" one of the guards asked.

"Nope. Someone could get hurt that way." The judge strolled out from behind the barricade. A huge brown hawk circled above him. His legs felt heavy and stiff as he plowed against the brisk wind. He crunched on dry grass and pushed past a poplar, a few dead leaves still hanging on.

Inside the thirty-foot-high tin-sided building were racks and racks of twelve-foot steam-heated pans that stretched the length of the building. Behind them loomed giant pulleys and cams, rods and stamps that usually roared so loudly you could hear them in Carson City. Many were now busted and twisted. All were silent.

The judge recognized many of the worried and defiant faces from the bonfire rally, including Mac McDonald and Fremont. A scratched and bruised Turner Bowman, wearing torn canvas ducking trousers and vest, stretched out a hand. "It's a mess, Judge."

"What happened to your face?"

"Them dockworkers jumped him," Fremont said.

"I suppose you heard the mill's side of the story," Bowman said.

"They said you planted dynamite and sabotaged the mill. What really happened?"

"Before I tell you, have you got a gun?"

"No, I left it out there. Why?"

" 'Cause I'd surely like to fire a shot over their heads if they decide to charge the place."

"There aren't any guns in here?"

"No. They don't allow them inside the mill."

The judge pulled out his spectacles and slipped them on his nose. "They said you had guns and dynamite in here."

"We don't have anything," Turner admitted. "I just said we had guns to bluff them."

"They believe you." Once again, the judge surveyed all the men in the huge room. One unarmed man guarded the door. The rest clustered close to him and Turner. "Don't stretch any lies out for me. There's no way I can help you unless I know what happened."

"They decided to shut down everything at noon for a safety check," Turner said. "Everyone went out to the cook shack to eat, except me. They wanted me on the inspection team."

"How many on the team?" the judge asked.

"Six," one man called out.

"There were seven, counting me," Turner said. "It was Stevens, Henderson, and the others from the office. But a few I'd never seen. I was told they were some members from the board of directors from San Francisco. I wouldn't know."

The judge pulled off his hat and stared back at the twisted cam. "How did the inspection go?"

"Fine. I don't know what they were looking for, but everything checked out. We wrapped up the inspection about 12:45 p.m. and were standing around the door talking. I excused myself and hurried over to get a bite before we had to crank her back up again. I had just sat down when the bosses sauntered by."

"But there was only five of 'em," pint-sized Mac McDonald interrupted.

"Let Turner tell it," Fremont shouted.

"I figured one of the trustees was wandering around and got stuck up on a platform or something," Turner said. "So I left my lunch and trotted back inside."

The judge jammed his hat on the back of his head. "Did you find him?"

"I called around but couldn't find him, so I figured on finishing my sandwich. I had just trotted out the door about ten or twenty feet when the explosion went off."

"It knocked him plum to the ground," Fremont said. "We saw it all from the cook shack."

"By the time my head cleared up, they had me in the shift foreman's office, threatening to hang me if I didn't confess."

"That's when we threw them out," Fremont boasted.

The judge looked at him sharply. "What do you mean, threw them out?"

"We picked them up and threw them out the door." There were shouts of agreement from the rest of the men.

"Even the longshoremen?" the judge asked.

"They don't allow them inside the building," Fremont said. "Afraid they'll scoop up some gold flakes, I reckon."

Turner shook his head. "Like I said, Judge, it's a mess."

"You reckon they'll fire all of us?" someone asked.

The judge waved his hand toward the back of the building. "With that cam busted, you don't have jobs anyway."

"They have to hire a crew to fix it," Mac McDonald said.

"But they don't have to hire *us*," Fremont boomed.

The judge held up his hands. "Turner, I've got to know two things, and this will make all the difference in the world. First, did you set off that dynamite or know of someone who did? Tell me the truth."

"No, Sir."

The judge surveyed each of the men. They all denied involvement.

"OK, second, did any of you scrape any gold off the amalgamation table and highgrade it?"

"You mean, today?" someone blustered.

"Yes, I mean today."

"I threatened to personally whip anyone who went close to them tables," Turner said.

The judge peered toward the doorway at the lone watchman. "The first thing we've got to do is get all of you out of here and safely back to Carson City."

"What about our jobs?" Fremont asked.

"Let's deal with your lives first. We'll worry about jobs later. Those guards are looking for a fight and they will use any excuse to pull a trigger, especially if they find out you can't shoot back."

"What about Turner?" Mac McDonald said.

The judge could smell the bitter aroma of black powder in the air. "I especially want to get Turner home safely. He's supposed to have supper with my daughter tomorrow night. Now, let me go back outside and make some arrangements."

"Don't let 'em charge us, Judge," Mac McDonald said.

Judge Kingston turned back to face the men. "You be praying for me, because if those armed men want to make a run at this building, I couldn't do a thing to stop them."

He slipped out into the cold December air and hiked to the barricade. The dark clouds had flattened out across the valley, making a purple swath of shadows over the frosty landscape. The brown hawk now eyed him from a fence post.

"You have any luck?" Stevens called out. "Where's Bowman?"

"I think I might have found a plan to

settle this," the judge said.

"How many guns do they have in there, Judge?" one of the armed guards called out.

"Innumerable." The judge waved the other men off. "I need to talk to the sheriff, alone."

"Why?" Stevens demanded.

"Because I'm the judge, that's why."

Judge Kingston and Sheriff Hill huddled near the carriage.

"These guards look like thugs right off the Embarcadero. It's as if they're countin' on trouble," the sheriff said. "What's happenin' inside?"

The judge leaned closer. "They are totally unarmed and fear for their lives. Turner's been beaten up."

"But you said they had a bunch of guns."

"I said their guns were without number. Zero is without number." The judge squirmed under the half-truth.

"What's your plan, Judge?"

Kingston waved his arm north. "You go out there and stop the three o'clock V & T coming down from Virginia City."

"Then what?"

"Then you and I march them out of here as our prisoners — unarmed, of course — right onto the train that'll take them into Carson City."

"And turn them loose?"

The judge shoved his glasses back and nodded.

"How about Turner?"

"They can come and press charges if they want to. I'll set bail at $100 and post it myself, if I must. Turner won't run. You and I both know that."

"You think these Frisco longshoremen are going to let all of them just walk away from the mill? They were hired to fight, and they're lookin' for a scrape."

The judge plucked the shotgun from the carriage seat. "We'll have to bluff our way through."

The sheriff ran his hand across his fleshy lips. "Will the men inside accept this deal?"

Stripes of light filtered through the overcast sky, a keyhole crack in the clouds. The judge tugged his hat low over his eyes. "If you and I guarantee their safety, I think so."

"But what if one of these guys takes a potshot?"

"Then God help us all."

It took twenty minutes to explain the plan to Superintendent Stevens, and nearly as long to get all the hired guards to back away and provide a corridor to walk the men out. It took the judge even longer to convince the men inside.

"If we had guns, it wouldn't be so bad, Judge," Fremont complained.

"If you had guns, you would have been shooting it out by now," the judge reminded him. "I'm giving you my word that I'll walk you to the train."

"And we go straight home?" Mac McDonald said.

"As soon as we reach Carson City."

"Even Turner?" Fremont asked.

"If they press charges, he might have to post bail, but that has already been arranged."

Turner Bowman pulled the judge aside. "If I pleaded guilty, would these men get to keep their jobs?"

"Turner, justice won't be served by confessing to something you didn't do."

"But these are family men, and Christmas is coming on. It's getting colder every day. They can't lose their jobs now. Even poor pay is better than no pay."

The judge glanced back at the ruined millworks. "That bridge has been burned, or I should say dynamited. Let's get everyone home safely and figure things out from there."

"When do we march out, Judge?" Fremont demanded.

"As soon as Sheriff Hill gets back."

Judge Kingston had the men lined up single file inside the refraction building when the sheriff approached.

"How's the mood out there?" the judge asked.

"The longshoremen are drinking pretty heavy. I don't know if Stevens can control them."

"I don't know if he wants to," the judge said. He turned to the column of men. "Let's go."

"Yea, though I walk through the valley of the shadow of death I will fear no evil," one man prayed.

"Finish the verse," the judge called out.

"I don't know the rest," the man said.

"For thou art with me," the judge added, "thy rod and thy staff, they comfort me."

Turner Bowman and the judge led the procession out of the building. At a distance the judge could see horseback riders fanned out on the bluff beyond the mill, behind the longshoremen.

Sheriff Hill marched beside the middle of the column, revolver in hand, hammer cocked. The parade had cleared the building when the judge and Bowman reached the gate. Three of the carbine-toting guards blocked the entrance.

"Where do you think you're goin', Bowman?" one of them demanded.

"We're goin' home," Fremont shouted.

The judge groaned and hoped the sheriff would shut him up.

"So you're runnin' to your Marys?" the gate guard snarled.

"Yeah, we don't live in no cathouse like you waterfront bums," Fremont said.

The guard threw the carbine to his shoulder, and Judge Kingston shoved his shotgun barrel into the man's ribs. "Put down the gun," he commanded.

"We got you outnumbered, Judge," the man said.

"They do. You don't."

"What do you mean?" He kept the carbine at his shoulder. "If you pull that trigger, the others will shoot you and you'll be waltzin' through pearly gates."

"And you'll drop into the pit of hell. These two barrels will blow you in half, mister. You know that."

"You ain't goin' to pull the trigger."

The judge shoved the barrel harder against the man's stomach.

"Put the gun down, Tommy," Superintendent Stevens ordered.

The tall man lowered his carbine, angry eyes glaring at the judge. "We want

Bowman left here for questioning," he said.

"Any questioning can be done in my chambers or the sheriff's office," the judge said.

"That ain't the way we see it," Tommy said.

"Call off your dogs, Stevens," the sheriff shouted.

"Sorry, Sheriff, the men believe they have a better way of getting Bowman to confess than you do. Maybe they're right."

"Are you refusing my order?"

"Oh, no. I'm trying. Tommy, let everyone go. Even Mr. Bowman."

"Nope, and you cain't talk me into it."

"Sorry, Sheriff, they won't listen to me," Stevens announced. "Now, I surmise you'll have to go along with *our* plan."

"You surmise wrong." The judge pointed to the rim where the riders sat with carbines across their laps. "Turner, whistle a signal to the posse."

Tommy and the other guards spun around.

Bowman's whistle and the judge's waving arm brought one of the riders down off the bluff toward the gate. The man trotted within twenty feet of the judge.

"Mr. Crosley," the judge called, "it seems like you get an opportunity to take sides after all."

"You payin' top wages, Judge?" Ritter Crosley yelled back.

"I guarantee you will get what you're worth," the judge promised.

"I'll double his offer," Stevens shouted. "All you have to do is ride off."

Crosley stared at the mill superintendent. "Last week you didn't want to hire us, Stevens. You said you could get better men for half the price. Besides, we didn't ride all the way up here from Arizona to get paid for riding away from a fight. The judge is a friend of mine, so this time I think we'll side with the law."

"There's only six of them; we can take 'em on," Tommy said to the other guards.

"You may want to put that up to a vote," the judge said. "My good friend, Stuart Brannon, said these are some of the toughest fighters in the territory and he'd arrest the whole bunch of them on sight."

A smile broke across Ritter Crosley's face. "Yep, that's Brannon, all right." He circled his carbine above his head. The other men began to ride down the bluff. Then he turned to Tommy. "Well, Mr. Gate Guarder. It's your move. If you're

144

going to shoot someone, now would be a good time. When my friends get closer they'll drop you all dead in your tracks."

"We ain't professional gunmen," one of the guards mumbled as he backed away.

"If Stuart Brannon says they're tough, I ain't goin' to test 'em," a second guard said. "I don't get more pay when I'm dead."

Tommy waved his hands. "Wait," he bellowed.

The judge began to move forward and Crosley spoke up. "If I were you, boys, I'd hide behind a barrier. My gang may get itchy and shoot you anyway."

One by one, the armed guards disappeared.

CHAPTER FIVE

The young woman wore an emerald-colored French sateen wrapper dress with black sateen robe edged in point d'Venise lace. A beaded Medici collar gathered around the neck. Her ruche-trimmed hat swept up in the back with layers of black roses, a French gold leaf pin, and ostrich feathers.

She waited for the train door to open. Her face was narrow, her small nose upturned, her chin firm. Sable brown eyebrows arched like her father's. Brown eyes flashed with barely contained energy, just like her mother's. Curly hair that rebelled against its confinement under the stylish hat gave the only clue of the girl still becoming a woman.

Judith's gloved hand reached up and covered her mouth. *She is so grown-up, Lord, and so beautiful. I always forget. I keep thinking that I'm waiting for my little girl. Oh my, where has she gone?*

Judith quickly dabbed her eyes and blew her nose on the handkerchief Roberta had stitched for her ten years ago. *I am not going to cry. She has only been gone five months. I am an adult. She is an adult. There is no cause for tears.*

Roberta was the first person off the train. She swayed across the worn wooden platform of the Virginia City and Truckee Station and stopped a yard shy of Judith, then did a slow twirl.

The sweet, melodic voice sang out, "It's straight from Paris, a one-of-a-kind original."

Judith held her breath. *It is the loveliest travel dress I've ever seen in my life. And she . . . she fills it out so well. I should have a photograph of this scene. "Homecoming," we could call it.* She dabbed her eyes again. *I am not going to cry!*

Roberta threw her arms around her mother. Their cheeks pressed together like soft magnets. A hint of lilac scented the air, mixed with something much stronger and bolder, like orchids. "Oh, Mama, I'm so glad to see you."

Judith clutched her daughter's shoulders and began to sob.

A tall, dignified man with wool longcoat and crisp felt hat cleared his throat. The women parted and Roberta rushed to his arms. "Oh, Daddy, it feels so good to be home."

147

His long arms hugged her tight.

This time, Roberta was the one who sobbed.

The judge rocked his daughter gently back and forth. "My word, ladies, it's only the end of the fall term."

Roberta kissed her father's cheek. "You can't imagine how many nights I've gone to bed wishing I had this hug and could hear this voice."

"It must be contagious," he grumbled as he tugged off his black leather gloves and wiped the creased corners of his eyes. "Perhaps we should save a few of these emotions for the privacy of home."

Roberta tucked her chin low and tried to speak in a husky voice. "Yes, your Honor."

The judge's face lightened and his eyes softened. "And I have missed your teasing."

Judith dabbed at her eyes. "The outfit is gorgeous. You had it tailored?"

"They altered it a little, but not much."

"I understand that Paris fashions are expensive," the judge commented.

"I paid for it myself, Daddy. I told you about my part-time employment."

"I had no idea that working in a confectionery factory was so lucrative," Judith said.

"I got a Christmas bonus."

"Someone was very generous with a beautiful young woman," the judge added.

"Yes, indeed," Roberta chattered. "I have a million things to tell you."

"And one big important thing, right?" Judith pressed.

Roberta's smile dropped. Her chin quivered and her eyes narrowed.

"What's the matter, Roberta? What is it?"

She clutched her fingers under her chin as though she were praying. "I . . . I have two important things to tell you."

"What are they?" Judith prodded.

"I can't tell you here. I promised myself I'd wait until we got home. Let's have a cup of tea, sit down, and relax first. I don't want to spoil everything by having this conversation on the platform. Trust me, this is something we must discuss at home."

The drive from the V & T Railroad Station seemed much longer than eight blocks.

Judith insisted that Roberta sit in the back seat with her father while she sat in the front with Chug Conly, the hack driver. Her mind buzzed. *She has two things to tell us and at least one of them is not good. A dress like that is much too expensive for clerk's wages. Someone bought it for her. And if someone bought it for her, then he would have wanted something in return. Now, Lord, I have prayed about Roberta and her virtue. This would not be a good time to let me down.*

Though it was clear sky above them, the mountains were barely visible, hidden behind a sheet of precipitation. That morning a squall had blown through the valley.

Roberta leaned against her father's shoulder. "Daddy, do you think we'll have snow for Christmas? I have been counting on snow."

The judge slipped his arm around her. "We've had some flakes, and it's cold enough, Darling, but so little moisture seems to make it over the Sierras. Did you have snow in New York yet?"

"A few flurries, but nothing that stuck."

Judith stared straight ahead and pulled up the wool lap blanket. *How can they sit there and talk about the weather? I am dying up here. My heart is so worried and troubled it could burst, and they talk of snow?*

"Daddy, what do you think about *Holter v Department of War*? Do you think he has a chance before the Supreme Court?"

The judge pulled off his wire-frame

spectacles and folded them into a leather case, then slipped them into the inner pocket of his overcoat. "So, you've been following the case?"

"You know me, I scan the newspaper every day. I get the impression it's complicated and important."

Judith glanced back at her daughter. Her eyes danced. *Still begging for your daddy's approval. Young lady, you have him permanently wrapped around your finger.*

The judge rubbed his mustache and goatee. "I would say, given the present makeup of the court and the number of veterans elected to Congress, he won't have much of a chance. However, give the issue another ten years . . ."

She kissed his cheek. "Will you be on the Supreme Court in ten years, Daddy?"

"I doubt it. Carson City is our home now." He stared at the courthouse as the carriage slowly moved south. "I'll either be First District Judge or a Second Street lawyer."

Roberta brushed out a wrinkle in her cloak. "You could do better. Everyone tells me that."

"I'm serving where I am needed. There's no way to place a value on that. There are thousands of judges, attorneys, and politicians in the country who are confident they could do a better job than the present members of the Supreme Court. And not a one of them wants to move to Nevada. As long as there's someone here who needs us, we won't consider moving. Isn't that right, Mama?"

Judith turned around. "Did you tell her about Turner?"

Roberta retied her hat ribbon. "What about Turner?"

"Perhaps we should wait until we're home," the judge said.

"And have had our tea," Judith added.

Roberta brushed wayward bangs out of her eyes. "Did he do something really dumb again?"

Judith reached back and patted Roberta's knee. "That really is a beautiful dress, dear. It will make Peachy jealous."

"What about Turner?"

"It will turn his head, too, I'm sure."

"That's not what I asked," Roberta said, her voice rising.

"Your mother's just a bit edgy, waiting for you to tell us your news," the judge mediated.

Roberta gazed at the back of the hack driver's head. "I just can't talk now," she whispered. "Please tell me about Turner."

152

"Have you written to him recently?" Judith inquired.

"I haven't written to him in over a year. But he's been writing to me."

Judith reached back and brushed a straw sliver off Roberta's dress. "He writes to you, but you don't write back?"

"I hear from him almost every week." Roberta reached up and brushed a stray strand of graying hair back over her father's ear. She held on to the black iron frame of the carriage as they turned west on Musser Street.

Judith braced herself on the leather cushion as Chug Conly stopped the carriage at the alley and waited for a six-up freight wagon to park. "And you never write back?" she prodded.

"I told him I wouldn't." Roberta's pale nose seemed to sweep up toward the Sierras. "And he said that was fine, he would write anyway."

"And you always read his letters?"

"Of course. Now, what is this you hinted about Peachy?"

"She just got a nice job in the governor's office. Records clerk, I believe," Judith said.

"That's not what I meant."

"And she's still sweet on Turner."

"I've been gone most of the past two years. Why doesn't she get him to marry her?" Roberta huffed.

"I don't suppose he's asked," Judith replied.

Roberta leaned far to the right so she could view the house as they pulled up. "That sort of thing never stopped Peachy before."

Chug Conly parked the hack at the concrete step near the Musser Street gate. The judge climbed down and held his hand up for Roberta. Conly offered his hand to Judith, but she waited for the judge.

While Chug Conly and Judith unloaded the valises, Roberta clutched her father's arm and seemed to study every detail of her childhood home, from the white picket fence to the New England windows. Marthellen's room was the newest addition on the side and had made her a permanent addition to the family. The American Holland shade with damask covering that Roberta and her mother had picked out together in San Francisco, on her thirteenth birthday, was raised up on her upstairs room window.

"This is the perfect house to come home to. I'm glad you and mother will never, ever move. No matter where I am in the world, I always want this house to come home to."

The judge glanced back at Judith. "My word, let me carry those things. You ladies go in." He grabbed several of Roberta's trunks and bags.

As soon as they stepped inside the door, Roberta said, "Tell me about Turner."

Judith eyed her daughter. "He's been accused of bombing the reduction mill, for one thing."

Roberta's face tightened. "He wouldn't bomb the mill."

"Your father thinks it's Consolidated's way of getting rid of Turner. But your daddy and the sheriff had to go out there and put their lives on the line to get the workers back to town safely. It was tense for awhile."

The judge burst through the door along with a young man in ducking trousers and white cotton boiled shirt and suspenders, swinging luggage behind him.

"Turner," Roberta called out.

His square jaw and clean-shaven chin looked as solid as the concrete step. "Miss Roberta, now you truly do look New York."

She spun around the way she had at the depot. "Paris," she corrected.

He cocked his head to the side, revealing dark bruises at his neck and ear. "You surely don't look Nevada anymore."

"That is a compliment, I presume?"

Turner slammed the door with his boot. "There was no moral value attached, if that's what you mean."

"I hear you got yourself in a fix, and Daddy and the sheriff had to come out and save your skin."

"I am grateful for their assistance," Turner said, "but I was fully prepared to pay the cost of supporting righteousness and standing against evil." He stomped up the stairs, banging a canvas traveling case and steamer trunk as he went.

"You seem to be taking up where you left off last summer," Judith noted.

"I'll tell you what's the same since last summer . . . this room. You haven't changed a thing."

Judith glanced around at the carved rosewood china cabinet, the Genoa velvet chairs, the Chesterfield settee, and the Louis XVI print sofa. *Marthellen must help me rearrange this furniture. Maybe we should add a wallpaper border and a little draping at the mantel like Daisie Belle has. Everything's too cozy, too routine.* "Sit down, Roberta, we've got other very important matters to . . ."

The Nevada Street side door swung open. Marthellen scurried into the living room, draped in a long fringed wool shawl. " 'Berta, darling, what a delight!" She paused before she gave the young woman a hug. "Did you ever in your life see such a pretty dress? Other than on Daisie Belle Emory, that is," Marthellen gushed. "Did you tell your mother your big news? We've all been anxiously waiting."

"Not yet. Mother was telling me about the happenings around here."

Marthellen blushed. "About the major? Isn't that something? It has been such a year. Bence coming home, then his death. Charlotte having a baby, and now my Major Lansford."

Roberta glanced at her mother and then stared at Marthellen. "I'm sorry, I didn't know about your major."

"We just walked in," Judith explained.

"Do come sit in the kitchen while I start supper," Marthellen said. "I'll tell you everything."

"You haven't started supper yet?" Judith blurted out.

"I had a quick errand to run for the major."

A blonde, curly-haired, felt-hatted head popped through the door before anyone could respond. "I'm early. Can I come in?"

"Peachy!" Roberta squealed.

"I saw Mr. Conly. He said you were home, and I couldn't wait." Peachy Denair, attired in sky blue challis trimmed in velvet bows, entered. "You aren't allowed to wear that in Carson City," she said, staring at Roberta's finery. "It isn't fair. Did you tell your mother yet?"

"I really haven't had a chance . . ."

Turner Bowman galloped down the stairway. "Roberta, I put your things on your bed. Is that where you want them?"

Peachy swirled around. "You've been home only minutes and he's in your bedroom?"

"The judge and I carried her satchels up to her room," Turner explained.

"I told you it would be this way," Peachy muttered. "I'll go see if I can help Marthellen with supper." She marched into the kitchen.

The judge strolled down the stairs. "I know how you like a little fresh air, Darling, but I couldn't get your window open. It must have swollen shut. I'll try again later." He pulled back the iron grate of the fireplace and stoked the fire with pine logs.

Roberta pulled off her silk cape, then

walked over to Turner. "Mother said you got arrested for anarchy."

"I did not! There have been no charges filed as of today."

She arched her dark brows over teasing eyes. "You seem quite defensive, Turner Bowman."

His reply was so low that Judith could barely hear it. "We need to talk."

Roberta untied her hat and tossed it on a green velvet chair. "We will. But tonight I want a quiet dinner with —"

"Turner's staying for dinner, dear, and that's not all . . ." Judith announced as she plucked up the coats and hats and carried them to the mahogany hall tree.

"Who else?" Roberta asked.

"Remember I wrote to you that wonderful story about Willie Jane marrying Bence only an hour before he died? Since then, Willie Jane has been seeing Tray Weston, and they're —"

"Tray Weston? The one who set off all the fireworks at once and almost ruined Farmer Treadway's picnic?"

"That was years ago. He's grown up now, like you all have."

"Like some of us have," Roberta said. "Turner, I really must talk to my parents."

"You go right ahead. I'll be quiet." He

plopped down on an overstuffed side chair, plucked up a cut-crystal glass egg, and rolled it in his hand.

"I need to talk alone," Roberta commanded.

Turner sprang to his feet, dropping the egg back into its hand-painted ceramic nest. "Oh, sure, I'll go see what's happening in the kitchen."

"Why don't you go into the judge's office and read some law books or something?" Judith suggested.

Turner's face brightened. "Say, Judge, do you have the ruling on *Storey County v The Blackwidow Mine*? I've been wanting to read it."

The judge replaced the fireplace grate. "If you ladies will excuse me for a moment, I'll find that brief for Turner."

Roberta let out a deep sigh as Judith reached up to rub her taller daughter's shoulders and back.

"It's a little hectic," Judith said.

"You mean, the way it always is."

"Only when you are home. Your father and I have many quiet evenings, especially since Marthellen met the major."

Roberta leaned back and whispered. "Who is the man? The only majors I ever heard of are Daisie Belle's husband and

Major Ormsby, and both of them are dead."

Another knock at the door interrupted them. Willie Jane entered with Tray Weston, who was wearing a suit. "Tray insisted on coming around to the front," Willie Jane explained. "I don't know if I've ever come into your house through this door."

Tray tipped his hat.

The couple waltzed into the living room and Judith closed the door behind them. Roberta sailed over to Willie Jane. "Mother's written to me all about you. I almost feel like we're related." Roberta skirted past Willie Jane's outstretched hand and gave her a tight squeeze. "We're a hugging family," she said. "I'm sure you know that."

"You're just like your mother," Willie Jane said with obvious delight. "What your parents did for me goes way beyond belief. I had no idea in the world what real love was like until I met them. They're solid gold, but I reckon you know that."

Roberta stepped back. "They'll spoil you rotten if you don't watch out."

"We did not spoil you or David," Judith insisted.

Roberta slipped her arm around her

mother's shoulder. "And then they'll deny it."

"We'll go help Marthellen," Willie Jane offered.

"Peachy's in there. It might be crowded," Judith warned.

"I'll wait out here," Tray said, twirling his hat.

"Turner's in the judge's office. Perhaps you'd like to go in there and visit."

"Oh, no, this is fine." Tray plopped down on the sofa, but Judith's glance brought him back to his feet. "Come to think of it, I do want to see Turner."

The judge met him at the office door.

"Did the sheriff find you this afternoon?" Tray asked.

"No, is something new?"

"Things is poppin' all over."

"What kind of things?"

"First off, Stevens ain't come in to press charges against Turner."

The judge pushed back his wire-frame spectacles. "They could still do it Monday."

"The sheriff was talkin' about ridin' out to the mill in the afternoon, just to find out their intentions. But I don't know if he did it or not."

"That might be wise . . . as long as he's cautious."

Tray Weston tugged at his tight shirt collar. "And he wanted to tell you about Rudy Boca."

"Did the county bury him?"

"No, that's the thing. The sheriff found some relatives of his over in Pagosa Springs, Colorado. Seems they want a signed warrant concerning his death."

"They don't take the sheriff's word for it?"

"I guess not. He wanted you to write them a letter."

"When is the body going to be shipped?"

"On Monday, I understand."

"I'll draft a letter by then."

"That's about it. Reckon I'll mosey in and visit with Turner." Tray disappeared into the room crammed with shelves and books.

The judge tugged down the cuffs of his stiff white shirt, then loosened his tie. The office door swung open. "Say, Judge, I heard Duffy Day is lookin' for you," Tray called out.

"Duffy is always looking for me."

"Did you invite Duffy to supper, too?" Roberta asked.

"Not until Christmas," Judith said.

The office door closed again. Laughter streamed out from the kitchen. Roberta glanced out the front window. "Who else is coming to dinner?" she asked.

"This is it," Judith said. "Why do you ask?"

"Mrs. Emory and a man as stiff as a tree are walking up your sidewalk."

Judith turned to the judge. "Did you invite Daisie Belle and the colonel to supper?"

"I most certainly did not."

Roberta nodded toward the front door. "Well, they're on the porch."

Both Judith and the judge headed to the door. Judith tugged it open before the knock.

"There they are," Daisie Belle beamed. "The most handsome older couple in the state."

Judith ushered them into the living room. *Older couple? I will never be as old as you, Mrs. Emory.*

Daisie Belle danced over to Roberta. "Oh, my dear, the dress is exquisite. I must have one. I have to have one. Wherever did you get it?"

"Jordan Marsh and Company brought it in from Paris."

"Then I'll have to go to Boston and find one for myself."

"They have a New York emporium now," Roberta said.

164

"How very convenient of them. But I don't have any plans to go to New York," Daisie Belle replied. "Do you have business in New York anytime soon, Colonel Jacobs?"

The tall, thin man with plumb-line posture rubbed his mustache. "No plans whatsoever."

"That's too bad. I do hate to travel alone." She gently rubbed the lace on Roberta's dress. "You look absolutely wonderful. Now I know what Judith looked like when she was younger."

"I looked nothing like that," Judith said.

"Can you stay for supper?" Roberta asked.

Judith forced a smile and folded her hands in front of her. *Lord, somewhere there is a limit to my ability to play hostess.*

"Thank you so much, but I'm afraid we have plans to go down to Genoa this evening," Daisie Belle was saying.

Judith rubbed the back of her neck and felt the muscles begin to relax, just a little. "That's nice," she murmured.

"We'll spend the night down there. But don't worry, we are taking a chaperon," Daisie Belle announced. "Doctor Jacobs will be going down with us."

The colonel stood to attention. "A

family friend sent word that he has just moved to Genoa from Stockton. We were neighbors back in Ohio as youngsters. He and I served together in the war. But I haven't seen him in ten years."

"Doctor Jacobs went down to Benton's to rent a carriage. He's going to meet us here in a moment," Daisie Belle said.

The judge motioned to the sofa. "Would you like to sit down?"

"I'll be sitting in that carriage compressed between two handsome men for several hours," Daisie Belle said. "I believe I'll just stand." She touched Judith's arm. "I'll miss church tomorrow. I was hoping I could impose on you to make an announcement for me."

"Of course."

Daisie Belle turned toward the colonel. "Arthur, do you have my list?"

He reached into his pocket and removed a folded piece of heavy cream notepaper.

"Thank you, my dear colonel," she purred. "This is a casting list for the Christmas pageant. I promised to have it announced by tomorrow."

"I'll take care of it," Judith said.

Daisie Belle spun around toward Roberta. "You will be here for the pageant, won't you, Roberta?"

"Yes, I believe so."

"Wonderful, wonderful. I was counting on it. I wrote a delightful short scene perfect for you. There are two squirrels conversing about their favorite dish during the feast of Stephen. And I've cast you and your dear mother in the roles. I wouldn't be surprised if it steals the show."

Judith's mouth dropped open. *I will not play a talking squirrel!*

"I don't have a squirrel costume," Roberta protested.

"I have all you need," Daisie Belle insisted. "A dear little hat with ears and a round, black nose."

Judith looked down and saw that her clenched knuckles had turned white.

Daisie Belle pulled back the floral dado chenille drapes at the front window. "Dr. Jacobs must be delayed."

"Shall I go look for him?" the colonel offered.

"Oh, no, Arthur, let's just enjoy the Kingstons' hospitality. Don't you love their home? If I ever needed to live in a smaller place, this is exactly the one I would choose." Daisie Belle floated to the sofa, towing the colonel behind her. "Now, dear Roberta, while your mother and father are busy with their chores, tell me all about college life in the East."

Judith scurried toward Roberta and latched on to her arm. "Daisie Belle, Colonel Jacobs, please make yourselves at home, but you must excuse us. The three of us have something to attend to upstairs. We'll be right back."

Daisie Belle shooed them with her hand. "Go on. The colonel and I can certainly amuse each other for a few moments, can't we, Arthur?"

The colonel snapped a quick, "Quite so."

It was the first time Judith had seen him smile.

When they reached the second floor landing, Judith said, "I am not going to be a talking squirrel."

"Oh, Mother, it will be amusing."

"Only to Daisie Belle Emory." Judith closed the bedroom door behind them.

The room was small and full of richly inlaid furniture with a cabbage rose design that matched the flounced valance over the window and over the bed. Roberta marched toward the four-poster and sorted through her black valise.

The judge sat down on the edge of the quilted spread. "I believe the point of this meeting is to have a quiet moment to discuss some important things," he said.

"I know, but there's something I need to find." Roberta searched the valise.

Judith strolled over to the combination dresser and wardrobe and straightened a pale pink starched lace doily that had lain untouched for five months.

"Here," Roberta announced. She took a deep breath. "I think you both should sit down."

"My word, this is serious," the judge said.

"Please, this is going to be difficult for me, and in my mind I have you two seated."

The judge got up and led Judith to the cretonne-covered loveseat, upholstered in a smaller rose pattern like the wallpaper. The judge sat down on the edge of the tucked cushion, his back straight, his neck rigid. *She's going to quit college. Poor thing thinks I will be crushed. I suppose I'll be disappointed, but she did quite well to attend two years. Well, one and a half years. Perhaps I can convince her to stay until this year is completed. It seems more logical to have two complete years of study.*

Judith dropped her hands in her lap. She glanced up at the anxious face of her twenty-year-old daughter. *Lord, she's preg-*

nant. How did this happen? We never should have sent her so far away to school. A girl gets lonely. She makes the wrong kind of friends, then someone persuades her to drink a little champagne. Oh, poor dear, what will the judge say? This will crush him.

" 'Berta!" the word seemed to explode from the judge.

"OK, here goes. But you look stunned already and I haven't even told you the news."

Judith tried to stay calm. "If you don't tell us soon, I will die on this very spot of a heart attack."

"Remember? I telegraphed you. I wanted to come home and tell you, but you said stick it out until Christmas."

"We know that, dear. Go on."

"Since David's not able to come home this Christmas, I wrote to him a few weeks ago and told him everything."

Judith gripped her fingers tight. *So big brother gets to know before mother and father?*

"He cabled me this reply; I received it the day before I came home."

"He sent a telegram from India?" The judge scratched the back of his neck. "I didn't even know you could do that."

"He has a friend with the British Foreign Office. They telegrammed England, then it came over to me."

Judith sat up. "What did David say? We haven't had a letter in weeks. The last one was mailed in September."

Roberta took a deep breath, then began.

Dear Roberta,
Don't do it. I'll write later . . .

"Don't do what?" the judge quizzed.

"I'll tell you that later. Let me finish the telegram. He goes on to say . . ." Roberta's chin began to quiver.

Patricia is dying. Malaria. One more week at most. Tell Mom and Dad face to face. I'll write later. It hurts too much now. Love, David

"Lord Jesus, no . . ." The judge rose to his feet. "This can't be . . . this isn't right . . . not Patricia . . ."

Judith wanted to get up and hug Roberta. She wanted desperately to feel the judge's strong arms around her. She wanted to say something. But she felt frozen to the spot.

Roberta flung her arms around her father's neck. "I thought I was all cried out. I've known this for more than a week and hardly an hour's gone by that I wasn't in tears."

The judge cradled his daughter, tears flowing down his cheeks. "I never should have let him go. I should have insisted they remain in the States."

"It was never your decision, Daddy."

"I know. But he's so far away. I need to be there. My word, a father is supposed to be there. What's the use of having family if they aren't there to support you?" The judge turned and held out his hand to Judith.

When she saw his outstretched arm, she rose to her feet and rushed to his side. "What about Timothy and Alicia?" she moaned. "Oh, dear Lord, what about the children?"

Judith's eyes were closed and pressed tight against the judge's tear-stained vest when she felt the soothing texture of a cool, damp cloth. She turned and Roberta gently began washing her face. *My daughter is taking care of me? I should be the one who is strong. I should be the one taking care of her.*

Then Roberta turned to the judge. "Hold still, Daddy. I've had a whole week to get over some of the pain. Let me do this, please."

Judith took the towel from Roberta's arm and wiped her face. "One more week? That would have been yesterday. We don't know if Patricia is alive or not." She walked over and plucked one of Roberta's old hats from a peg on the wall and placed it on her head.

"What are you doing, Mother?"

"David needs me to help him with the children. I have to go."

"David's in India, Mama . . ." Roberta lifted the hat from her mother's head and put it back on the peg.

"We don't even know if she's alive or dead," Judith mumbled, "and my hair is a mess."

The judge grabbed her hand and Roberta's and led them to the side of the bed, then dropped to his knees. Through tears he led them in prayer for their missionary son, his wife, and children.

Once again, Roberta brought the basin and washcloth.

Judith stood up and brushed down her skirt. "I believe you had some other important news," she said, her voice clear again.

"Mother, it's not that critical. Let's wait."

"Whatever it is, it can't be more crushing than what we've just heard."

"Really, Mother, I need more time . . . when we aren't grieving over Patricia, and when there's not a house full of guests."

"After supper we'll shoo them all out," the judge said. "Then you, Mama, and I will sit by the fire and have a long talk."

"I'd really like that, Daddy."

Judith moved toward the door. "Shall we go back down?"

"I'd like to change first. I've worn this same dress all the way from Omaha," Roberta said.

The judge offered Judith his arm. "Are you ready, Mother?"

"How do my eyes look?"

"Like you've been crying."

"There's no way to hide it."

"There's no reason to try. They will all understand."

Judith and the judge walked down the stairs, arm in arm.

"We should tell everyone," the judge said.

"I'll bring them to the living room. You make the announcement. I don't think I'm ready to say it out loud."

Daisie Belle Emory and Colonel Jacobs perched on the sofa. Tray and Turner, their ties loosened, stood behind them. At the end of the sofa, next to the mahogany table and stained-glass lantern, Marthellen,

Willie Jane, and Peachy waited in long flowered aprons.

Peachy bounced on her toes. "Where's Roberta? She's getting married, isn't she? I was right," she twittered.

The judge raised his hand. "We don't wish to bring sadness into this evening, but our hearts are heavy and we thought it only fair that you all knew. Roberta brought us news from David. He telegraphed Roberta to say that his wife, our precious Patricia . . ." He stopped to catch his breath. Judith squeezed his hand.

"He said that Patricia is dying of malaria and not expected to finish the week. That's all we know."

Willie Jane hugged a sobbing Marthellen.

Peachy burst into tears and ran up the stairs to Roberta's room.

Daisie Belle Emory leaped to her feet and marched to Judith's side.

Turner leaned over and said to Tray, "That's just the way her folks died, too. Remember? They were crossing the Isthmus and never made it back to Virginia."

Colonel Jacobs rose and held out his hand. "My heartfelt sympathy, Judge. What a sorrowful tragedy."

There was banging at the front door. A nervous Levi Boyer shifted his weight from one foot to the other until the judge trudged over.

"Excuse me, Judge. I know you were havin' a big doin's on account of Miss Roberta, but this was kind of an emergency."

Judith moved to the judge's side. "What is it, Levi?" she said.

"Doc Jacobs sent me —"

"Where in blazes is he?" the colonel pressed.

"Duffy came and got him."

"Is Duffy ill?" the judge asked.

"No, it's his brother, Drake."

"Drake made it home?" Judith asked.

"He showed up this afternoon, so I hear. But he's sick, Judith, real sick."

She raised her clasped hands to her chin. "What's the matter with him?"

"Doc says it's that . . . well, I cain't pronounce it . . . it's that terpen . . ."

"Tuberculosis?" the judge said.

"Yeah, and it's real advanced."

Judith tugged on the judge's arm. "Drake can't live out there in Duffy's tent. He'll die for sure."

Levi pulled off his hat and held it in his hand. "Doc sent me in to see if you and the judge could put him up at your house until some other arrangements can be made."

"Without question," the judge replied.

"Yes," Judith said. "We'll . . . we'll put him in . . . David's room."

Daisie Belle Emory came up behind Judith. "You will do no such thing," she said.

"What? Of course he can . . ."

"Levi, the Kingstons have just received sobering news and need time to reflect. Tell Doctor Jacobs to bring Drake Day straight to my house. I will hurry right home and have Clarice and Rodney prepare one of the guest rooms."

"You might want to prepare two," Levi suggested.

"Duffy won't come inside a house. You know that," Daisie Belle replied.

Levi nodded. "You're right. He'll pitch a tent in your yard, but he won't step inside."

"By all means, tell Duffy to bring his tent."

Levi stared down at his black boots. "But we still need another room . . . for the boy."

"What boy?" Judith asked.

"Drake's boy. He showed up with a five-year-old son."

Judith glanced at Daisie Belle. "We will prepare a second guest room," Daisie Belle announced. "Don't just stand there, Mr.

Boyer. Go and help the doctor bring him in."

"I'll go along, too," Tray offered.

"So will I," Turner said as he grabbed his hat.

"I say, Daisie Belle, my sweet," the colonel began. "All of this is well and good, but what about my friends who are waiting for us in Genoa?"

Daisie Belle Emory spun on her heel and narrowed her eyes at the tall military man. "We're talking about a critically ill man here, Colonel, not supper with an old army buddy."

The colonel raised his chin. "The family is certainly more than just an old army buddy."

"Colonel Jacobs, they are your friends, not mine. Why don't you drive on down and have supper with them? Duffy is my friend. In Carson City we take care of our friends, thank you."

She hugged Judith and planted a quick kiss on her cheek. "You take care of the judge and Roberta tonight. I'll send Rodney over with word of how Drake and the lad are doing as soon as I get them tucked in."

Daisie Belle Emory strutted down the painted wooden stairs and out into the chilly December night.

CHAPTER SIX

The bright December sun lost heat long before its rays touched Judith's face. Only her brown eyes peeked out at the Sunday afternoon splashes of yellow and sage green scenery as she rode next to the judge in the one-horse carriage. Water puddled the road, unable to sink or soak into the alkaline soil.

A buffalo robe covered her lap. Two wool blankets surrounded her shoulders. A thick black knit muffler encircled her neck and covered most of her face while the judge's floppy felt hunting hat was pulled low over her ears. A heavy tin box of warm coals rested under her boots.

"Lovely day for a drive," she called out.

The blanketed judge rubbed his whiskered chin with his gloved hand and slapped the lead lines on the horse's rump. "It's a little tense at home. I needed to clear my head."

"Do you have any idea where we are going?"

He patted the buffalo robe in the general

area of her knee. "Does it matter?"

"Not really, just as long as we aren't going up to Lake Tahoe for a swim."

"Last summer seems like a decade ago," he said.

"I needed to get away, too. It was all I could do to keep from bawling in church."

The judge rubbed his numb ears. "So I noticed, but the reverend's sermon wasn't that emotional. Which news were you crying over?"

Judith huddled closer to him on the carriage seat. "Both."

"I'm afraid the Lord supposes us to be much stronger than we are. How else can you account for so much shocking news to hit us all at once?" The judge kicked his right boot up on the firebox. Instantly, the leather sole began to warm. "How do you think Roberta's doing? She would hardly talk to me this morning."

Judith's breath fogged out in front of her. "She's crushed, of course."

"Judith, I just wasn't emotionally strong enough for her news. I don't believe I've ever been so overwhelmed. I wasn't prepared. I lost control. The news about Patricia seemed to have weakened my wisdom and prudence. I would like to have reacted more nobly. I do say, you were amazingly strong."

Judith's words came out in rhythm to the bouncing of the carriage. "I was too stunned to move. Too shocked to speak. Too drained to cry. I don't think I slept for an hour all night."

"Well, I know I have to go back and apologize to Roberta. There was no excuse for my behavior," the judge admitted. "But after that debacle last night in the living room, I felt I needed to collect my thoughts and weigh my words carefully. And now I'm sure she feels like we've run off on her."

Judith moved her boots off the firebox. "Marthellen said she would help explain it to her. We both have some thinking and apologizing to do."

The judge's normally erect posture slumped. "We really have no say in the matter, do we?"

"I hope we can calmly help her see the ramifications. It's all we can do. She will have to make her own decision and live with it."

"But why didn't she talk to us before?"

"She tried. We insisted she stay in school," Judith reminded him.

"It is that thought that kept me awake

most of the night. I have relived that decision over and over. Why didn't I have her come home immediately? Judith, you know how desperately I try to do the right thing."

"I know, dear Judge. Perhaps we have done the right thing. In the long view of her life, how can we claim omniscience?"

"The right thing?" he fumed. "If I had done the right thing, my twenty-year-old daughter would not be engaged to marry a forty-year-old divorced man with three teenage children. My own words shock me."

"Now, Judge, she's *our* daughter. We are in this together. Besides, they aren't engaged, not until she accepts the ring. And the youngest boy is only eleven."

"That's not the point."

"I know, I know. I trust this will be a long drive," she added.

"This is what I can't figure. What makes some . . . some middle-aged lecher like that want to marry our Roberta?"

"She's young, beautiful, vibrant, intelligent, and a delight to be around," Judith declared. "Frankly, I can't imagine any man of any age not wanting to marry her."

"That's the point. Out of all the men on the face of the earth, why this one? He's forty, almost our age."

"You are over fifty, Judge Kingston . . ."

"But he divorced his first wife. And she lives in the same city and comes to visit the children once a month. He's not even a widower."

Judith pulled her wool muffler closer around her neck. "How much better would you feel if he were?"

The judge ran his tongue across his chapped lips. "A little bit."

"She says he's rich, handsome, kind, and generous to her. And he moves among the highest rung of Eastern society." Judith slipped a gloved hand out from under the buffalo robe and plucked gray hairs off the judge's upturned coat collar. "Roberta will become an instant socialite."

"Kingstons are Kentucky lawyers and frontier judges. That's always been social enough for this family."

"Things change, dear Judge."

"Yes, and now she can be out from under 'the suffocating cloud of Judith and the Judge.' Isn't that what she said?"

"She was upset, dear."

"We were all upset."

"I suppose it is difficult to find your own way when your parents are so . . ."

The judge slapped the reins. "She used the word *dominant.* Do you really think that's why David went off to India, like she said?"

Judith slid a hand up and brushed the corner of her eye. "I pray not. I think she was hurting immensely and just lashed out with that."

"It hit the mark. It stabbed me to the heart."

"There wasn't a whole lot of peaceful wisdom from either side last night," Judith said.

"Do you think she'll stay with us until the first of the year?"

Judith's reply was barely above a whisper. "I don't honestly know if she'll be home when we return this afternoon."

"That thought is far too crushing for me to even contemplate," he said.

She slid the firebox back under her boots. "What are we going to do?"

"Finish our ride."

"I mean, beyond that?"

"I don't know anything beyond that." His sigh was so deep that it brought more tears to Judith's eyes. "For the past seventeen years in Nevada we have been consumed with other people's problems. Day and night, week after week, month after month, year after year they have needed our help and attention. But now, we're the ones who are overwhelmed. Whom do we turn to?"

"We have good friends here. They sense our struggle."

"Did Daisie Belle's act of mercy surprise you as much as it did me?" the judge asked.

"Not really. I had momentarily forgotten what it was in her that I liked so much. She has always been that way. As much as she swaggers around town, when the need arises, her generosity is legendary."

"Do you think it comes from her modest beginnings in Nevada?" the judge ventured.

"I think she's never forgotten those late '50s, with the one-room dirt cabin, snow up to the eaves, eating tree bark and pack mules and watching babies die. Sometimes I think Daisie Belle's entire act is just to drive the pain in her life far back in her memory."

"Then something like a sick Drake Day comes along and she reverts back to the pioneer woman, struggling to keep a family alive? Maybe that's the real Daisie Belle," the judge said.

Judith brushed her curly bangs back and reset the hat low on her head. "No, they are both the real Daisie Belle. People are complicated. No one is easy to box into one label."

He glanced down at her. "Not even the highly predictable Judge Kingston?"

"He's a very complex man. But at the moment, he's desperately trying to focus on a way to reestablish himself with his daughter, who is the light of his life."

"One of the three lights of my life," he said.

"Do you have any great new wisdom?"

"I know some things I can't do." He stared out at the yellow tints of dry, frozen bushes covering the desert like a jaundice. Clouds hovered over the hills, breaking away and crossing the valley in small patches. Some were stacking up above them. "Maybe if I eliminate some choices, the direction will become clearer."

Judith leaned against his arm. "Such as?"

"We can't kick her out, disown her, or banish her from our presence."

"Heavens," she gasped, "I didn't know those were options."

"They weren't. But I needed to be reminded."

"And we can't cut off communication," Judith added.

The judge brushed his chin whiskers.

His cheeks had lost all feeling, and his words came out stiffly. "Nor can we cut off visits. We will have to invite her and her family to come and stay with us."

"We can't stop praying for her. If she goes ahead with this, we have to pray that it will be a wonderful marriage and a deeply satisfying relationship."

The judge glanced down at her. "Judith, what are you staring at?"

"I'm not staring."

"You most certainly are."

"No, this cold has frozen my tears, and my eyelashes are stuck to my eyebrows and I'm too cold to reach up and brush the frost off my face."

The judge reached over with his gloved hands and rubbed her eyebrows.

Judith blinked. "Thank you." She pulled his arm under the buffalo robe and clutched it with both hands. "It dawned on me during the sermon this morning that I was so upset with Roberta that I hadn't prayed for David. That's horrible, isn't it?"

"I must confess to the same neglect," he said. "What was the sermon about this morning?"

"I haven't the slightest idea."

"I hope it wasn't Revelation 11:14."

She wanted to close her eyes but was

afraid they might freeze shut. "What is that verse?"

" 'The second woe is past; and, behold, the third woe cometh quickly.' "

She burst out laughing. "Three woes, huh? What could that third woe be? We don't have any more children."

Suddenly she began to sob.

"My word, are you crying or laughing?"

"I just realized you are my third woe," she said with a sniffle.

"There's nothing wrong with me."

"But what if something happened to you? I would go mad. I would be one of those crazy women who staggers out into the blizzard and freezes to death."

"You are much too strong for that foolishness."

"No, I'm not. And that's what scares me. My strength, what there is of it, depends upon you and the children. As long as family life is peaceful, stable, predictable, I can venture out to help others. Without you three, I'm not much better than Duffy Day."

"Judith, you and I both know that our strength comes from the Lord. Speaking of Duffy, can you imagine what will happen if Drake dies? His brother's impending return has sustained Duffy for seven years."

"He will be crushed."

"And the lad? What will happen to little Douglas?"

"Duffy will want to raise him," Judith said.

"But someone will complain about a boy living in a tent and not fed or bathed properly. He'll be sent to the orphans' asylum."

"Would you sign the papers to place him there?"

"What choice would I have?"

"Our whole existence suddenly seems to be spinning out of control like a Chinese pinwheel on the Fourth of July," Judith said. "A few days ago the only problem we faced was Marthellen's fascination with the major. Now that seems minor. I haven't even thought about those two lately. Have you?"

The judge stared at the leafless row of poplars and sycamores running across the horizon. Beyond them two huge clouds loped over the mountain summits, as though dropping out of the sky. "Only in-directly."

"In what way?"

"Where do you think we're going?" he asked.

"Jack's Valley?"

"Nine-Mile Butte. To a small, flat-

189

topped mountain just west of Williams Canyon. I understand there is a mineral springs there."

Judith tried to sit up and scoot back as they rambled along the roadway turned trail. "The major's mineral spring?"

"I thought it could be a possible destination. But the ride is really about clearing our minds."

"He's so secretive. I didn't think you'd be able to find it."

"I picked up a clue or two at the Surveyor General's office."

"So, have you been investigating Marthellen's major?"

"Not the major, just the mineral springs. Before any local folks start buying store space and franchises, I want to see the site, at least."

Judith studied the monotonous terrain of a few leafless trees, scattered gray sage, and sparse clumps of thick dead grass and dirt. She spotted man-made tailings from unsuccessful prospect holes. "I presume it's undeveloped," she commented.

Thin ice cracked as they rolled over a shallow mud hole. "There must be something to see. He's bringing Eastern investors out here."

Judith clutched her arms close to her

chest under the wool blankets. "I hope he has a campfire."

"If we don't find any trace of the mineral springs, we'll swing over to Farmer Treadway's and warm up before driving home," he promised.

To the right, the alkaline flatland looked almost snow-covered. "Is this trail where he wants the road built?" Judith asked.

"This gets so swampy in the spring that the river can only be forded about six months of the year," the judge pointed out. "He'll need the roadbed built up and the bridge finished before construction of the sanatorium."

"If he's serious, he should build the road this winter, while the ground is still firm. I suppose he could build it himself and put in a toll road."

The judge brushed the fine, stinging alkaline dust from the corners of his eyes. "He says county and state funds for the road would provide the commitment that will make the enterprise work. He claims he won't do it any other way."

"He certainly knows what he wants and how he means to get it."

"Major Lansford reminds me of Adolph Sutro and his tunnel," the judge declared.

"Sutro did get the tunnel built."

"A few years too late to do much good."

"But it still made him a fortune."

"That's what I keep wondering. Exactly who is going to make a fortune out of this sanatorium?"

Judith reached up and pinched her earlobes, trying to stimulate circulation. "He's got the whole town believing they will be a part of the wealth."

When they reached the Carson River crossing, Judith clutched the judge's arm with both of hers as they bounced and sloshed their way across the two-foot-deep water. Across the river, the road turned into two narrow, freshly used ruts and a few horse prints. Judith laid her head on the judge's shoulder as they bounced along the sage-scattered high desert.

Exhausted emotionally and physically, she soon fell asleep and dreamed.

It was summer. A gentle breeze wafted from Lake Tahoe. David was twelve. He and the judge led the hunt through the steep forest hillside for mushrooms. Five-year-old Roberta dawdled at her mother's side. Then a large bull elk crashed through felled timbers fifty feet downhill. Judith turned to grab Roberta. But she wasn't there.

Panicked, Judith rose up and hollered her name.

Far down the hillside, a tiny brown-haired ball, wrapped in a long white dress, tumbled toward the elk and the rocks below.

Fear froze Judith's legs, but not her mouth. "Judge," she screamed. "Save your daughter."

A gentle squeeze from a familiar strong arm woke her. She sat up, feeling the sweat beginning to freeze on her forehead.

"I've just had a horrid dream."

"Real life is troubling enough," the judge said. "However, you slept long enough for me to figure out a few things."

She wiped her forehead on the wool muffler, then tried to straighten the pain out of the small of her back.

The judge pointed straight ahead of them. "You see the smoke up on that butte?"

"Do you think it's the hot springs?"

"Either that, or Indians."

"Paiutes?"

"Most likely, but I don't expect trouble."

Judith pulled a white linen handkerchief from her coat pocket to wipe grit off her lips.

"Here's what I decided," the judge said. "At the moment, we can't do a thing for poor David and the children, besides pray.

So I thought you and I should have a regular prayer time for him every night until we hear some specifics. There is no reason for me to fume and fuss the rest of the day, because it brings him no comfort and us no peace. He will write to us when he can, then we will do what needs to be done."

"Have you thought about what we should tell him?" she asked.

"If Patricia has died, we'll tell him to come home with the children. He can live with us until he has some further direction. We are still operating with temporary pulpit supply at the church. Perhaps he could become our pastor."

"I think it would be best to suggest what he might do, rather than tell him," she said.

"You're right. You should write the letter."

"It could be we will have two grandchildren running through the house by summer."

"I can think of worse fates," he said.

The carriage began a slow incline. The judge slapped the line on the horse's rump to pick up the speed. "I thought through this matter with Roberta, as well."

"Was that the 'worse fate' you were thinking of?"

194

"No, but I must tell her honestly and bluntly that this proposed marriage doesn't seem to be in her best interests or follow a biblical pattern. But I also will tell her that at age twenty, I cannot forbid her to do anything. She must use her best Christian wisdom and accept the consequences of her decision. Then, I want to tell her that nothing will ever diminish my love for her."

"And that we will host the wedding and welcome her husband and his children into our home as our own?" Judith challenged.

"You didn't sleep long enough for me to come to that point. But I'm working on it."

"A ride does make a difference."

"Yes, now I'm getting in a hurry to go back and talk to Roberta."

"Do you want to turn around?"

"Just as soon as we check out the column of smoke on Nine-Mile Butte."

"Which one?" she asked.

"There's only one."

"Put on your spectacles, dear Judge."

He pulled out his wire-frame glasses and looped them around his ears. "You're right. There are two columns of smoke."

"I hope they have extra coals. My feet are beyond cold."

The wagon tracks they followed swung

to the right at the base of the butte. Gigantic boulders sat like shoulders on either side of the trail. A newly raised wooden gate blocked passage. Its sign read, "H.S.N.S., No Trespassing Without Permission."

"H.S.N.S.?" Judith inquired.

"Humboldt Springs National Sanatorium," the judge said. "At least we found the correct mountain."

"I don't remember ever hearing about a hot springs out here," Judith said.

"It was on the Surveyor General's map. But he said the only report they had was that the mountain was rough to climb, the springs were small and up on the mesa, and in the summer the hillside was thick with rattlesnakes."

Judith peered around.

"It's too cold for snakes now." The judge handed her the lead lines, then rolled the buffalo robe off his lap. He climbed down to the near-frozen ground, then tugged down his hat and turned up the collar of his heavy wool longcoat.

"What are you going to do?"

"Open the gate."

"But it says, 'Keep out.' "

"There's a fire up there, Judith. We need a few more coals."

"But this is private property."

"Not yet, it isn't."

"What do you mean?"

"As of Friday, no patent deeds had been issued on any property on Nine-Mile Butte. So, this gate is illegal."

"Perhaps you should tell that to the men with the guns."

The judge glanced up the hill. A man wearing a heavy ducking duster cradled a Winchester '73 carbine across his arm.

"Is that you, Judge?"

"Mr. Crosley, has the Arizona bunch taken a new job?"

"Yep. The reduction mill's closed and you and the sheriff didn't need a permanent posse. What's a fella to do?"

"Do you know this barricade is illegal? This property still belongs to the state of Nevada."

Crosley strolled down the grade toward the gate. "Don't know a thing about what's legal or not. But me and the boys was paid good cash money to stand out here and look like regulars, then keep anyone from followin' 'em up the hill."

"The major and his backers are already up at the springs?" the judge asked.

Crosley reached inside his coat and yanked a watch out of his vest pocket. "They've been up there about three hours."

"How many are there?" Judith called out from the carriage.

Crosley looked surprised and tipped his hat. "Afternoon, ma'am, sorry to act impolite. With them robes and blanket and that flop hat pulled down, I couldn't tell if you was a woman or not. A grievous error on my part."

"The judge told me all about your great assistance last Friday, Mr. Crosley. Please accept my thanks, too."

"It's about the only fun we've had since we left Arizona. Your husband is a brave man. It's the kind of trait I admire." He turned to the judge. "I hope you ain't wantin' to go on up the trail, 'cause the major made it plain we couldn't let no one pass."

"Not even a district judge and his wife?" Judith called out.

Crosley tipped his hat again. "I'm sorry, but with the kind of work I do, if I cain't back up my promise, I ain't worth nothin'."

"Just what kind of work are you in, Mr. Crosley?" Judith asked.

He grinned. "Mostly bank work."

Even from the carriage Judith could see his dark eyes sparkle.

"My, that does sound challenging," she said.

"Sorry, Judge," Crosley said, "but you know it ain't personal."

The judge leaned over on one leg. "I'm sure the major has his reasons for secrecy, but I thought the Osburn brothers were going to be guards out here."

Crosley plucked a cigar out of his pocket and jammed it into the corner of his mouth. "Are they those two dimwits that float in and out of the saloons?"

"They aren't too deep of thinkers, if that's what you mean."

Crosley chewed on the unlit cigar. "Maybe they're coming out after we're gone."

Judith leaned forward in the carriage to hear better as the wind began to pick up.

"How long are you hired for?" the judge asked.

"Two weeks. Major Lansford wants two of us out here twenty-four hours, so we decided to rotate in and out."

"I wonder why they're up there so long?" the judge said. "Can't be too much to see."

"Jist a hole in the ground."

"And a mineral spring," the judge added.

"Eh, yeah . . . and a mineral spring. But they brought in a big dinner in several picnic baskets, and a couple of kits of scientific gear. I reckon it will take a spell."

The judge glanced back at Judith. "I suppose we should turn around."

Crosley put a match to the cigar. "Thanks, Judge, for not pushing it. I kind of liked us being on the same side the other day. I didn't want to have to back you down." Crosley tossed the carbine across his shoulder.

"I understand loyalty, Mr. Crosley. But you should know this is an illegal gate," the judge reminded him.

A sly grin broke across the Arizona gunman's face. "I'll take that under advisement."

"Have you got a fire on the other side of the boulders, Mr. Crosley?" Judith called out.

"Why, yes, ma'am. Are you cold?"

"Our firepan has all but gone out."

Crosley glanced around behind him. "Judge, why don't you park that rig over behind those boulders, then hike up to the fire. We'll warm your hands and your firebox. That way I haven't opened the gate for no one, and yet I can be neighborly. The major don't even have to know you've been here."

Behind boulders the size of train cars, they discovered a small, straight-walled white canvas army tent and a blazing fire.

A wiry, dark-skinned man with criss-crossed bullet belts on the outside of his fleece-lined ducking coat squatted near the flames.

"This here is Señor Nadie," Crosley introduced.

"Mr. Nobody?" the judge said.

The man flashed perfectly straight white teeth. "That's me, Mr. Nobody. Of course it isn't my real name."

Judith stooped next to the fire. She was still wrapped in a dark wool blanket and wore the judge's hat over her ears, hair pinned up inside.

Crosley rolled over two rounds of firewood. "You can use these for chairs," he offered. "We aim to bring a load of firewood out with every shift change. Ain't nothin' to burn out here."

"Can I get you some coffee?" Nadie asked. "We do have a couple more cups somewhere. I do not think they are very dirty yet."

The flames and the hot liquid soon warmed Judith's face. She could feel perspiration forming on her face.

Crosley slurped his coffee. "Do you really know Stuart Brannon, Judge?"

"We served on a California, Nevada, and Arizona Territory boundary commission together. How do you know him?"

"He arrested me . . . twice."

"Oh, dear," Judith murmured. "What did you do?"

"Well, first time, me and five of the boys walked into a bank in Prescott."

"Were you making a withdrawal?" she asked.

"Yes, ma'am. The boys fanned out to cover the crowd and I hiked straight up to one of the tellers. I'd heard of Brannon. Shoot, who hasn't? But I'd never met him. He was standing in line at another teller's window. I set a little satchel on the counter and reached for my gun. Before I cleared leather, Brannon grabbed my hair, yanked my head back, and jammed the barrel of his .44 halfway into my ear. He told me that there satchel better be full of money to be deposited, because if it was empty, he'd shoot me on sight for attempted bank robbery.

"It was empty, all right, but he didn't shoot me. He bluffed my buddies right out of the bank and marched me down to the jail house. The next morning, the judge threw the case out. He said folks can't be arrested in anticipation that they might commit a crime."

"And the second time?" Judith asked.

Crosley spit on the ground. "I don't want to talk about it."

"Does it have something to do with your departure from Arizona?" she asked.

The Mexican man at the fire snorted. He had two bottom teeth missing. "You are a very smart lady, Señora."

"Thank you. And I believe I'm quite warm now," she said.

The judge pulled on his gloves. "I forgot the firepan. I'll go get it."

"I'll go with you," Crosley offered. "I need to ask you something."

The judge retrieved the firepan and dumped out the dead coals near the rear wheel. Ritter Crosley leaned against the carriage seat. "What do you know about Major Lansford?" he asked.

"Just met him a little over a week ago," the judge replied. "He seems quite ambitious."

"You think he's on the square?"

"He has some impressive letters of recommendation. Have you got a beef with him?"

"At ten dollars a day, there's no complaint. But he surely keeps things secret for a businessman. I know bank robbers that cain't keep things that tight."

The judge looked him in the eye. "My

suggestion is, if you have any extra money, don't invest it in Humboldt Springs Sanatorium. At least, not yet."

"You don't think he's going to build it?"

"Oh, we may get a sanatorium. However, it will probably be a long time before there's much return on the investment."

"I told him we needed to be paid daily," Crosley said.

"That was a wise move."

"I reckon we'll pull out at the end of two weeks."

"Where will you go?" the judge asked.

"Probably spend the winter in California . . . or Mexico." Crosley glanced up toward the mesa.

"Sounds like some carriages coming down the hill," the judge said.

"Let's wait here, Judge. The major is just expectin' two guards at the gate. I don't want him to start askin' questions."

Nadie heard the wagons first. "Stay low and keep your back to the wagons, Mrs. Kingston. With your hat pulled low like that and the blanket, the major will never recognize you. I don't think he would be happy to find you and the judge at our fire."

Nadie hiked to the gate and waited for

the two wagons to approach.

Judith heard the major's voice. "Everything all right here, Señor Nadie?"

"Yessir, just cold. Pepe is a little under the weather."

Judith leaned further over the fire. *Pepe? I get to be Pepe?*

"Tell Pepe if he stays off crib row at night, he will be in better condition to work the next day."

"I will tell him, Señor."

"And inform Crosley I will see him at the hotel in the morning about breakfast time."

"He will be there."

As the second wagon rolled close, Judith strained to hear some of the excited conversation behind her.

A man's high-pitched voice reported, "The minute I get Tiffany's appraisal, I'll let you know."

The reply was a deep baritone. "The minute that appraisal hits the streets of New York, it will be too late."

"True . . . how true . . ."

"You thinking about a little earnest money up front?" another man asked.

"If we don't nail it down, Hearst and the others will move in again."

Tiffany's? Hearst? Appraisal? Mineral water appraisal?

The fire snapped and popped. Wagon wheels creaked.

Soon the voices faded and there was nothing left but a lump in Judith's stomach and a grinning, dark-skinned man looking at her across the fire.

Judith poised on the love seat in Roberta's room with dry, clear eyes. "Did you and your father talk things out?"

Roberta lay on the rose-covered comforter wearing only a muslin chemise with Hamburg lace and ribbons. Her arms surrounded a thick, goosedown pillow clutched to her stomach. "Yes, but it was difficult for him, I know."

"Darling, since the day you were born that man has prayed about and worked hard to provide for your future happiness. Don't expect him to let go easily."

"How about you, Mama?"

"I had your wedding planned before you were a year old."

"Really?"

"That's part of being a mother."

"I know divorce is not the Lord's perfect plan, but even sinners need to be forgiven."

"You're right about that."

"Anyone I marry would be a sinner of some sort," Roberta said.

"That's true, too."

"I could never find a man like Daddy. You told me that when I was little."

"I did?"

"You said that God only made one man in the whole world like the judge."

"The judge is certainly perfect . . . for me. But I think the Lord has made someone perfect for you, too."

"And you don't think it's Wilton Longbake?"

"My first reaction was absolutely not. I told you that. But now that I've had time to think and pray, I have to admit I just don't know him enough to say that. I didn't have the right to tell you that before I've even met the man. Forgive me."

"I knew it would come as a shock. But I just don't know why you and Daddy don't think it will work out."

"Darling, I will pray every day for it to work out. But it will be difficult, no matter what. You face the added burdens of a great difference in ages and suddenly having children only a few years younger than yourself, a first wife who is still around town, and a spiritual battle with the Lord over marrying a man who could, someday, potentially reestablish his relationship with his children's mother."

"You're as sweetly pessimistic as Daddy."

"You just take all of those factors that we've presented, add them to your sacrificial love for him and his sacrificial love for you, and then —"

"What do you mean, 'sacrificial love'?"

"I mean, the kind of love that makes a marriage work. Sacrifice. Giving something up for the other person. You're going to sacrifice your college, your hometown, your freedom to be his wife and the main caretaker of his children. He will need to sacrifice for you as well."

Roberta sat up, flopped her legs over the side of the mattress, and, still gripping the pillow, said, "What kind of things should he sacrifice?"

"I'm not sure. He'll certainly have to give up his unmarried lifestyle. Perhaps there's a partnership in his business."

"No, we've talked about that. The way the business is set up, he owns half. The other half belongs to the children in a trust. I won't enter into that."

Judith gently pressed her hands together. "He told you this already?"

"Yes, but what does that have to do with love?"

"Trust and commitment are a large part of it. But all I'm going to say is that I want you to take all of these things to the Lord and pray about it. If you believe he is leading you to go ahead with the marriage, I will not say another disparaging word. Meanwhile, when will we get to meet Mr. Longbake?"

"Next Saturday."

Judith rose to her feet. "He's coming here?"

"He has some business to do. He wants to invest in Nevada mining. Isn't that wonderful? That means we'd have another reason for coming to Carson City."

Judge Kingston lounged at the window of his office, staring out on Carson Street. Freight wagons rolled by. Horses pranced. Pedestrians scurried. Dogs barked. Dark, heavy clouds stacked up against Pine Nut Range to the east. The flag at the state capitol building unfurled in the wind.

But the judge's mind was on other scenes, torn between wondering about David and family in India and concern for a young woman making the most important decision of her life. *Lord, I am in over my head. Give me a complicated mining law case. Or a gruesome murder. Or a property rights ruling. But now, with David and Roberta, I'm reduced to a spectator. All I can do is just wait and watch and pray.*

Spafford Gabbs barged into the office, letter in hand. "Judge, are you busy? I need to talk to you . . . about a personal matter."

There was a commotion behind him. "There you are," Sheriff Hill said. "You disappeared yesterday and no one knew where. Did you hear about the trouble at the mill?"

The judge peered at the sheriff. "More trouble?"

The sheriff slammed his hat on the judge's desk. "It's those armed guards that Stevens brought in. It seems —"

Spafford Gabbs backed up to the door and bumped into Doctor Jacobs.

"Judge, have you got a minute?"

"Join the party, Doc . . ." Sheriff Hill said.

"Did you tell him about Consolidated?" Jacobs asked.

The sheriff looped his thumbs in his coat pocket. "I was just beginning."

Turner Bowman strolled into the room, wearing a new coat, a smile, and a weltering bruise over his left eye. "Is this a closed meeting?"

"Closer to a mob," the judge declared.

"You'll never guess what kind of contract I just worked out," Bowman said.

"Does it have to do with Consolidated?" the judge asked.

"No. But did you hear about —"

"I was just tellin' him," the sheriff reported.

"My word," the mayor sputtered as he strolled into the room. "Is everyone in town here?"

The judge scowled around his crowded office. "Welcome aboard, Mayor Cary. Do you have rumors to hint at, or are you going to actually tell me something?"

The mayor pulled off his hat and spun it around. His curly hair bushed out on the sides. "Nine-Mile Butte. That's what I'll tell you."

The judge tugged his starched white shirt cuffs down below his suit-coat sleeves. "I was there yesterday."

"You were? And you didn't tell me?" the sheriff sputtered.

"I just did." The judge surveyed the men in his office. "Gentlemen, this can be done in the good old Presbyterian way, decently and in order. Spafford, you're first in line."

The clerk glanced at the others. "Mine can wait, Judge."

"No, please. What can I do for you?"

Mr. Gabbs scooted up close to the judge and spoke in a soft voice. "Did you know

211

that Isaiah McKensie is retiring?"

"I heard his wife wanted to move back home to California," the judge replied, gazing into the clerk's steady, trusting eyes. "That means there's an opening for Chief Clerk of the Nevada State Supreme Court. It's perfect for you. You have my permission to apply."

The clerk looked down and unfolded a piece of paper. "Well, you see, Judge, I already applied. And they hired me."

The judge never flinched. "When do you start?"

"January 1 . . . I just wanted to give you notice."

The judge looked around the room again. "Then I'll need a new clerk . . ."

"Sorry to leave you, Judge," Spafford Gabbs stuttered.

"Nonsense. You are too qualified to be stuck in this office. You'll have to tell me all about it later."

"Perhaps this afternoon. I'll be at my desk if you need me." Spafford gave a quick bow and wound his way out of the room, shaking hands and receiving congratulations.

"That's too bad about losing Gabbs," the sheriff began.

"I'll have to train someone else," the

judge said. "Now, what in the world went on out at the mill?"

"With the reduction plant shut down and Bowman and workers led off to town, Stevens fired all those Bay Area bums," Sheriff Hill reported.

"And they weren't too happy?"

"That's an understatement. They turned on Stevens and tied him up, along with Henderson and the cook shack crew. Then they raided the amalgamation tables and rode off into the Sierras. I found Stevens and the rest still tied up, dehydrated and freezing, yesterday afternoon."

The judge walked over to the window. "Where is Stevens now?"

"He left for Sacramento to get the authorities there to arrest them."

The judge spun around. "What about the charges against Turner?"

"He said they would decide what to do about that within thirty days. It seems the only ones who claimed to witness Bowman setting the dynamite were a couple of those armed guards."

"Who are now fugitives." The judge marched back to the desk. "It might be tough to sell a jury with their testimony."

"But they said they still might press charges later."

"So what's the future of the mill?" the judge asked.

"Stevens mentioned they may sell it."

"Who would want to buy a bombed-out reduction plant?" Mayor Cary commented.

"Someone willing to rebuild," the judge said.

"Speaking of building," Doc Jacobs broke in, "I just came from seeing Drake Day at Daisie Belle's."

The judge plopped down in his oak swivel chair. "How's he doing?"

"Better than I figured when I first saw him. Daisie Belle hovers around him with soup and home remedies. He's not going to get rid of the TB, but at least his breathing has stabilized."

The judge leaned forward. "That's some of the best news I've heard in days. How about the boy?"

"He follows Uncle Duffy around like a stray puppy."

"I imagine Duffy doesn't mind."

"He eats it up. That's the reason I came by," Doc Jacobs said. "Duffy wants to borrow $500."

"What for?" the mayor sputtered.

"He wants to build a house . . . out at his place . . . for Drake, the boy, and him to live in."

The judge pulled off his glasses and rubbed the bridge of his nose. "Duffy wants a house?"

"This thing with Drake seems to have stirred him up. He even shaved this morning," the doctor said.

"Did you lend him the $500?" Turner asked.

"No, but the bank will loan it to him against his place, provided the court rules that he's competent to enter into a legal agreement."

The judge banged his clenched fist on the desk. "If Duffy wants a house, he should get a house."

"Is that the ruling of the court?" the sheriff said.

"It will be, as soon as the papers are filed."

"Daisie Belle is really something," the mayor added.

"Which reminds me," the judge said, looking over at the doctor. "How is your brother dealing with this matter with Drake?"

"He hasn't come back from Genoa, which is probably just as well. It's hectic enough without dealing with a military stuffed shirt. Say, I heard Miss Roberta's getting married."

The judge glanced over at Turner Bowman. His face was blank, his body stiff. "She's making plans that way."

"Whoever he is, he's a lucky man, I'll say that much," the mayor said. "Isn't that right, Turner?"

"Luckier than he'll ever know," Bowman muttered.

"What kind of contract did you work out, Turner?" the judge asked.

"I signed a contract with Major Lansford to be foreman of the crew and supply the workers for building the road and bridges out to the sanatorium. I can hire everyone who lost a job at the mill. Looks like we'll have some work, after all."

"Wait a minute," the judge said. "The major is building the road? I thought he wanted it to be a public road."

"That's what I stopped by to tell you," the mayor said. "The major seems to have done quite well with the Eastern backers. He said he got them to agree to finance 40 percent of the road expense."

"They're going to just donate their part to the county?" the judge asked.

"Yes, all we have to do is landscape that last mile up to Nine-Mile Butte."

"But he's retaining the job as road contractor?" the judge pressed.

216

"That was part of the agreement. I didn't see anything wrong with that. He'll use the state road engineer just like anyone else," Mayor Cary said, his face reddening.

The judge shook his head. "This is the fastest moving government project in history."

The mayor nodded. "Isn't that something? Sort of like divine providence, if you ask me."

The judge rubbed the back of his neck. *That wasn't exactly what I was thinking.*

Mayor Cary tapped his hat back on. "Well, I need to go talk to Mr. Tjader at the bank. Lansford needs the city and county to put some earnest money in the account."

"He's already collecting the money?" the judge asked as he brushed down his mustache with his fingertips.

"Seems the Eastern backers want a tangible commitment from the community before they deposit their capital. They want to make sure the road will be built. Can't rightly blame them for that."

"I bet I know something about the sanatorium you fellows don't," Doc Jacobs said. "The major's going to build a wing just for children. It will be the only sanatorium west of the Mississippi like that."

"Sounds wonderful," the mayor said, beaming. "They are going to name it in memory of Jennie Clemens, Orion's daughter and Mark Twain's niece," the doctor said. "Seems like the major got some substantial contributions from the Clemens family."

"Times are changing," Mayor Cary said. "Progress has come to Eagle Valley. That sanatorium is just exactly what this economy needs. I think it will bring many more positive changes to our area."

"Think of all the changes in the past two weeks," the sheriff said.

The judge stared out the window to Carson Street. *Not to mention the changes in our family.*

"Well," Turner blurted out, "I've got to go tell a certain young lady about this road contract."

"You might want to wait until after lunch," the judge cautioned. "Judith and Roberta were going to be tied up this morning."

Bowman frowned. "The young lady I have in mind is Peachy Denair."

CHAPTER SEVEN

A dollop of snow-white clouds floated across Eagle Valley, followed by thin, striated wisps. Then the sky cleared.

Judith enjoyed the unexpected sunshine and warmth of the December morning. She wore her coat and a straw hat and gloves, but the coat was unbuttoned. Roberta strolled beside her, carrying a bundle of neatly folded clothes tied with a black ribbon.

"Do you think Daddy's things will fit Drake?"

"I think they'll be close. Drake's not as tall, but he can roll up the cuffs. Of course, your father might be a little surprised to find his closet picked through."

"Daddy won't care. As long as he has his suits and ties, he's content. I think men look especially handsome in suit, vest, and tie, don't you?"

Judith tilted her head toward her daughter. "Your father is a handsome man, no matter what he wears."

The ostrich feathers in Roberta's hat made her look taller than usual. "I know you're crazy about him, Mama. You and Daddy have set a wonderful example for David and me. Of course, I worry that we will never be able to live up to such high standards."

"The world doesn't need another Judith and the Judge."

"What do you mean by that?"

"You just be the Roberta the Lord wants you to be. That's a goal you can reach." Judith slipped her arm in her daughter's. "Now I'm beginning to sound like Miss Hannah Clapp giving a lecture at her academy. Enough of that."

Roberta squeezed her mother's arm. "I can't wait until Saturday. I just know you're going to like Wil."

Judith brushed a strand of hair out of Roberta's face. "Should we call him Wilton . . . or Wil . . . or Mr. Longbake?"

Roberta's brown eyes danced. "Call him Wil. That's what I call him. Except at the factory, of course."

"What do you call him there?"

"Mr. Longbake." Roberta shifted the bundle to the other arm. "Everyone calls him that. Even men older than he is. He said it would be best for us to maintain professional decorum, so I never call him Wil at the factory."

A freight wagon full of empty beer barrels rattled past them. Judith waited for the noise to subside before saying, "I suppose that helps keep the other women from getting too jealous."

The smile dropped off Roberta's face. "What other women?"

"The other women workers. You do have other women working in the factory, don't you?"

"Well, yes, of course." Roberta turned up her small round nose. "But Wil's not interested in any of them."

"I meant professional jealousy, not social. They might begin to think you were being more favorably treated at work."

The tight muscles of Roberta's neck relaxed and a smile broke across her face. "That's why we don't even . . . you know . . . in public."

"You don't what?"

Roberta blushed. "Hold hands . . . kiss . . . all of that."

All of what? Judith lengthened her stride as they crossed Telegraph Street. "I'll call him Wil."

Roberta's step was light, almost skipping. "Everyone who knows him well calls him Wil, except Billy Astor."

"Of the famous Astor family?"

"Yes. He's William Waldorf Astor."

"How is he related to John Jacob Astor? Your father and I met him once in Washington."

"He's the son. Billy and Wil have been friends for years and Billy calls him Zeeb. Isn't that bizarre?"

Judith fussed with the hat ribbon tied under her chin. *I'll tell you what's bizarre: Roberta Louise Kingston from Carson City, Nevada, having nobby New York friends like Billy Astor.* "Why is he called Zeeb?"

"When they were younger, Billy used to tease Wil that he saw everything in black and white, yes or no, do or don't. So Billy nicknamed him Zebra. It just got shortened to Zeeb."

"You've had quite an exciting term. Did you ever go to class?"

"Of course, Mother."

"But you've also had time to go to affairs with the Astors and others like that?"

"Oh, yes. So many of those people I had only read about, like Cornelius Vanderbilt."

"I thought Mr. Vanderbilt died."

Roberta shifted her bundle to the other side. "That was his grandfather. The younger Cornelius is about Wil's age."

"New York night life is quite different

for you, I would imagine?"

"I don't want to sound like it was all parties," Roberta said. "There were just times when Wil needed me."

"It's nice to be needed." Judith refused to look at Roberta. She looked everywhere, up and down and sideways, but avoided a direct glance. *Lord, why am I so suspicious of this man? First, it was Major Lansford and now, Wil Longbake. Why can't I trust my friend and my daughter to make their own romantic choices? After all, not every man can be like the judge. And just because they're nothing like him doesn't mean they aren't decent men.*

"Wil needed me to oversee some of his parties," Roberta said.

"You acted as hostess?"

"Not really. I didn't stand around shaking people's hands and things like that. I supervised the staff. And I made sure the children were taken care of."

"His children live with him?"

"They live most of the time with their mother, but he does have them one weekend a month and all summer long. He has servants, of course, but sometimes you have to keep right on the staff. There aren't many servants like Marthellen in the world."

"Perhaps that's because I've never thought of Marthellen as a servant."

"Anyway, Wil says he doesn't know what he'd do without me. Can you imagine me organizing big New York parties? I've had to hire caterers and orchestras. I even brought in an opera singer for a birthday celebration."

Judith couldn't formalize pictures of this in her mind. "It sounds like you were an administrative assistant."

"Yes, it's quite thrilling. I don't mind helping wherever I can. It's been good training to see how well I'd do as his wife."

Judith dropped behind for just a moment. She studied her daughter, the brisk step, the straight back. Roberta knew where she was going and had the youth and strength to get there. "Roberta, when you were in the room with Mr. Astor, Mr. Vanderbilt, and the like, exactly how did Mr. Longbake introduce you?"

"What do you mean?"

"I was just curious. I know that you call him Wil in private and Mr. Longbake at the factory. But what does he call you? Does he say, this is my girlfriend, Roberta Kingston? Or does he call you his fiancée?"

"Oh, no, we aren't officially engaged, not until he talks to Daddy. Wil introduces me as Miss Kingston. But sometimes he's just too busy to introduce me to everyone."

"That seems a little rude."

"Don't judge him so quickly. I'm usually quite busy also, in and out of the kitchen, seeing that everything is ready to be served on time."

"Doesn't he have staff for that?"

"Of course, but he doesn't trust them too much. He loves it when I come over and supervise everything for him. I told you he's very charming. He has a lot of influential friends, but his business prospers because of his own natural talent."

"Does he pay you for doing all this?"

"Mother, you're talking about the man I'm going to marry. Of course he doesn't pay me."

The two ladies walked another block in silence. A cloud bank covered the sun. Judith shivered. "Did your father talk to you this morning?" she finally asked.

"I didn't see Daddy. I guess I slept late. What did he want to talk about?" There was no hint of a smile. She looked steadily forward, intent on her own view, her own thoughts.

"He wanted to know if you knew the name of the man in New York who received David's telegram from England."

Roberta shifted the bundle once again to her other arm. "I don't remember his name. Why did he want that?"

"He wants to find a way to send a telegram back to David, but no one seems to know how to get a message to India. Everyone says it's impossible."

"Well, I received a telegram. It can't be impossible."

Judith paused by the picket fence on the south side of Daisie Belle Emory's house. "Duffy's tent is gone. Now I wonder what that means?"

Roberta lowered her voice. "I can't believe that Mrs. Emory would have allowed such a thing in the first place."

"Never underestimate Daisie Belle Emory," Judith whispered back.

She knocked at the door and waited. "They must be busy."

"Oh, my," Roberta said. "That looks like one of Daisie Belle's cats outside. She's always had only house cats."

Judith knocked again. "I'm sure it has to do with a man with TB being nursed in her home."

Daisie Belle greeted them wearing an apple green, gingham-checked apron over soft yellow challis. She held an immaculately combed white cat in her arms. "How are my favorite talking squirrels? You look a little puzzled."

"I wasn't expecting you to open the door, Mrs. Emory," Roberta said.

"Look at me. Quite domestic, I should say. Please come in, I'll pour some tea. Rodney's helping Drake with a basin bath, and I sent Clarice to the store to buy some pomegranates. I read that pomegranate juice is good for respiratory problems. And she took little Douglas with her."

Judith took the bundle from Roberta and handed it to Daisie Belle. The cat slinked to a back room. "We brought Drake a few clothes. The judge had some nice items that he doesn't wear much anymore."

Daisie Belle set the bundle on a black marble inlaid table. "Please thank the judge for me. What is that dear man doing today?"

"Out judging about, I suppose," Judith replied.

Daisie Belle ushered them toward the high-ceilinged kitchen.

"Has Duffy gone home?" Judith asked.

"Yes. Isn't it exciting? He's actually going to build a house out there. I am so thrilled. I worry about Duffy every winter."

Roberta meandered to a spice rack that contained over two hundred different seasonings. Judith followed Daisie Belle toward the stove, where a large pot of meat was simmering. "I didn't realize he would get started so soon."

"The weather's not too bad. Perhaps they can get most of it built this week. It's just a modest cabin." Daisie Belle pulled the top off a porcelain canister shaped like a giant red apple.

"Who's helping him?" Roberta asked.

"Turner Bowman volunteered. But I guess you know all about that." Daisie Belle served them ginger tea from a white set with gilt handles and edging. "I have been so busy the past couple days, I've gotten quite behind on news. What is this I hear about a wedding at your house?"

Judith smiled to herself. *Even in self-inflicted confinement, Daisie Belle knows everything.* "I don't believe a wedding date has been set," Judith said.

"Of course not. I'm not officially engaged yet," Roberta said. "I think he intends to take care of that this weekend. He needs to talk with Father first."

Daisie Belle ceased pouring the tea. "Why on earth does he need to do that?"

Roberta untied her hat ribbon. "It's customary to talk to the father before asking a daughter to . . ."

"What?" Daisie Belle cried out. "You? Oh, my, I've really been out of things far too long. Oh, Roberta, Roberta . . . congratulations!"

Roberta blushed as Daisie Belle smothered her with hugs.

"Who did you think we were talking about?" Judith asked.

"Why, Marthellen, of course, and our Major Fallon Lansford. I understood they will be announcing soon."

"I don't think that has been decided yet," Judith said.

"Of course it has, dear Judith. And what a nice catch for her. I'm so tickled that she can improve her station like that."

Judith sipped the strong ginger tea. *Exactly what is wrong with her present station?*

"But enough about Marthellen, tell me about Roberta and Turner."

Roberta gasped and Judith shook her head.

Daisie Belle's hand flew to her mouth. "But I just assumed . . . I'm bewildered. You are dear, dear friends and I don't have the foggiest what's going on. Please, let me start this all over. Give me another chance." She cleared her throat. "Why, Roberta, dear, who is this man that I hear you're going to marry? Is he from New York?"

"Yes, I work for him. He's my boss. He owns the business, in fact."

"How nice." Daisie Belle nodded her approval. "And what's his name?"

"Wilton Longbake."

"Longbake? Now there's an old-line New York name. I'm not sure which one is Wilton." She turned to Judith. "They run with the Astors and that crowd. I have a dear friend who used to be married to one of the Longbakes. She and I toured Europe together the summer of her divorce. She was ten years younger than I, and oh, it made me feel young."

Judith's stomach began to churn. She was afraid she would lose her breakfast.

"This friend of mine was married to Zeeb Longbake, a rather impossible fellow to live with as it turned out . . . but enough of that. Every family has a black sheep."

Roberta stared down at her teacup. "I'm sorry, Mrs. Emory, I have a terrible headache. Mother, you stay and tell Mrs. Emory all about it. I must go home . . . now." Roberta moved to the side door, almost tripping over a cat.

Daisie Belle followed after Roberta and scooped up the cat. It jumped from her arms and up onto an end table, easing down on a large round crocheted doily.

"Oh, dear, what did I do? Did I say something wrong?" She walked back to Judith and hugged her close. "I do believe I've made more mistakes and uttered more careless words in this day than in my entire life. Judith, forgive me. I don't believe I will write any of this in my journal. You know I wish only great happiness for your Roberta. If any of my girls had lived, I would have wanted them to turn out exactly like her."

"It's all right, Daisie Belle. You said nothing out of spite or harm. It's something we will have to deal with. It's what the Lord has brought to us. Nothing has been set, but Mr. Longbake is coming here Saturday. His name is Zeeb, by the way."

"To Carson City? Why would he come this far from Manhattan?"

"To see Roberta, of course, and meet her family. Also, I believe he's interested in investing."

"Well, the treasure he finds at the Kingston home is much greater than any in the Comstock. You can be assured, dear Judith, that I will not say a word to anyone about this matter."

"I would appreciate your discretion until we find out what his intentions are."

"Most certainly."

A knock on the northside door drew both women to that direction.

"Clarice must be loaded down with packages," Daisie Belle said.

"And it's time I went home and checked on Roberta."

"If she hates me the rest of my life, I will certainly understand."

"She'll do nothing of the kind."

Daisie Belle raised her eyebrows. "I would, if I were her."

She swung open the door. A straight-backed Colonel Jacobs stood there. He promptly removed his hat. "Good day, ladies."

"Colonel Jacobs, if you'll excuse me, I was just on my way home," Judith said.

He stepped aside. "Certainly, Mrs. Kingston. I presume the judge is at his office or in his chambers today. I do need to talk to him."

"I believe he hoped to wrap up today's case by noon."

Daisie Belle tugged on Judith's arm. "Just a minute, dear Judith, I need to tell you one more thing. If you could just wait. What can I do for you, Colonel Jacobs?"

"Perhaps we could go inside?"

"Colonel Jacobs, I don't entertain men at this time of the morning. Besides, I am still very busy with nursing duties."

The colonel glanced over at Judith.

"I really need to scoot," she said.

Daisie Belle clutched her arm again. "As you were saying, Colonel Jacobs?"

"Yes . . . well . . ." he stammered. "I've been giving our relationship some thought over the past couple of days and . . ."

"I really feel like I'm imposing," Judith said. She tried to tug her arm away from Daisie Belle.

"Go on, Colonel," Mrs. Emory said.

"Heavens, this is not the proper forum." His face was more than red. It was mottled, like a permanent sunburn.

"Were you planning to give a formal speech?" Daisie Belle asked.

"Perhaps we could converse this evening. Would you care to attend the Virginia City Opera House with me?"

"I'm so sorry, but I have gentlemen guests for supper."

"Oh?"

"Drake, Duffy, and Douglas Day will be dining with me." Daisie Belle stuffed her hands in her apron pockets. "Would you like to come to supper?"

The cords in his narrow neck bulged. "I had hoped to have time to speak with you alone. Couldn't you leave the charity cases with your servants?"

Daisie Belle touched his arm. "I could, but I won't. They are not charity cases to me; they are my friends. Perhaps you could call on me tomorrow afternoon, after church."

"Indeed, I will." Colonel Jacobs jammed on his hat and marched to the sidewalk, three cats chasing in front and behind.

"Was I a little too harsh on the colonel?" Daisie Belle asked.

"Perhaps. I do believe he cares for you."

"He cares about only the things he sees on the surface of me. He hardly knows what I'm really like. Thank you for staying, Judith."

"What did you want to talk to me about?"

"About how wonderful it is to have a friend who will stick by me during a tight situation and give me a reason for sending a caller off in a hurry."

"Oh, that reason."

"You do understand?"

"Perfectly." Judith strolled toward the white picket gate and the cats stole back into the house.

When Judith entered her kitchen, Marthellen was sipping cinnamon tea and examining a stack of white paper notes.

"Is Roberta upstairs?" Judith asked as she hung up her navy double-layer cape and hat.

"She informed me about Daisie Belle knowing Mr. Longbake's former wife, then said she was going to get a hack and go help Duffy build his house."

"Help Duffy? She's become a carpenter?"

Marthellen's smile filled her whole face. "That's what she said."

Judith stood at the kitchen window and stared out to the north. The largest cloud bank had broken up. Pale blue edges showed all around. "She's going to talk to Turner."

"It reminds me of all those times when she was younger. We'd catch her and him in the woodshed. She'd always claim they were just talking, of course."

"Marthellen, this relationship with Mr. Longbake is getting complicated. I do hope she knows what she's doing."

"I've been wondering what you and the judge will do."

"So have I. But I need to get it off my mind, if even for a moment. Daisie Belle had lots of news for us."

A few wisps of Marthellen's hair kept falling in her face. She pulled it back, but it slowly fell down across her eyes and cheeks. "Don't tell me she said the major and I are getting married," she blurted out.

"That's exactly what she said." Judith moved to the stove and poured herself a mug of hot water, then sat down beside Marthellen.

"I've heard the same rumors. I don't know where they're coming from."

"Perhaps, since you have spent so much time together lately, people assume things."

"We have been rather thick."

"Are you bragging or complaining, Mrs. Farnsworth?"

Marthellen raised her hands to her cheeks. "Am I blushing?"

"Yes, you are."

"I haven't blushed in years."

"How does it feel?"

Marthellen rolled her eyes. "It feels really, really good."

"You look really good."

Marthellen smoothed down the white lace on her bodice. "It's your dress that does it."

"You look much better than I do in it."

"That, Judith Kingston, is a beautiful, wonderful lie. I love it. In fact, I've loved every minute of the last two weeks. The Lord has given me a good life since I found him. And I've always known that I have to live the life that my poor choices, years ago, dictate. But I never thought I'd know what it felt like again to have a man . . . a handsome man . . . hold my hand and kiss my lips and . . ."

"That's enough bragging," Judith said, laughing. "Now I'm the one who's blushing."

"What I'm saying is, I'll enjoy this time, this friendship, for as long as I can. But I could never leave you and the judge."

"Nonsense. It would break our hearts if you turned down happiness on our account."

"But you need me."

"Marthellen, all we have ever wanted for you was the abundant life Jesus promised to give all who believe. If you were to come to us and tell us the Lord is leading you to marry the major — or any man — we would be absolutely thrilled."

The housekeeper stared down at the notes scattered across the table. "Honestly?"

"Yes. Now you be honest with me. Has the major asked you to marry him?"

Marthellen closed her eyes and bit her lip.

"He did, didn't he? Daisie Belle is right."

"The major asked if I would marry him after the sanatorium is completed. He wants to have the wedding out at the facilities."

"And what did you tell him, Marthellen Farnsworth?"

"I told him I would have to think about it, that I needed to talk to you and the judge."

"So when is the projected date?"

"September 1."

"That does give you plenty of time to think it through."

"That was my idea. Fal wanted to get married on the day the foundation stone was set. But I told him he would be so busy with the road, bridges, and buildings that we should wait. I didn't want to sit in some big old house with a husband too busy for me."

"Is he planning to build you a house, too?"

"He said he's thinking about buying Audrey Adair McKensie's home."

Judith sat back in the chair. "My goodness, that is ambitious. That's one of Carson City's nicest mansions."

"I can't imagine living in such a house except as a housekeeper."

"You'd do very well. And I do believe it's

wise that you're waiting that long."

"You think I'll change my mind?"

"I would think that by September you will be confident beyond a shadow of a doubt."

"I'm confident now," Marthellen said.

"Well, then, by September, I'll be confident beyond a doubt," Judith announced.

Marthellen smiled to herself, then said aloud, "Do you know what Fal said? He said, 'Let's wait that long because maybe Judith will like me by then.' "

Judith covered Marthellen's hand with her own. "We did get off to a rough start. But I'll relax a lot more when the sanatorium is built and people begin to be helped. Drake Day could use it right now."

"How was he?" Marthellen asked.

"Daisie Belle insists he's improving." Judith gestured toward the papers on the table. "What in the world are all those notes?"

"They are messages to almost everyone of importance in Carson City, Ormsby County, and the state government."

"From the major?"

Marthellen stacked the notes in a single pile. "Yes, it takes quite a bit of organization to coordinate a project like this."

"He's lucky to have you to help him out.

Perhaps he should hire a staff."

"He's going to, just as soon as he gets definite commitments from the community. Fal said it wouldn't be fair to offer some assistant a position, then have the whole deal collapse. He wants the money in the bank before he starts hiring."

"What money in the bank?" Judith asked.

"The Eastern backers and the government, I presume. Anyway, I'm trying to sort these notes into some order to make the deliveries smoother. Fortunately, I've run enough errands for you and the judge to know my way around the courthouse and the capitol."

"You certainly have a pleasant day for it. It's quite nice out there for December."

"A pot of beans is soaking on the counter and there's a pork roast in the oven," Marthellen said. "If you get a chance, can you stir up the fire from time to time?"

"Certainly. Is there anything else I can do?"

"Tell me if you think I'm a foolish old lady."

"This week, you have not looked a day over thirty-five."

Suddenly, Marthellen looked lonely. "If

240

we lived in Audrey's house, you and I could still see each other every day."

"Most every day," Judith amended, then moved to the counter to stir the beans.

The judge left the state capitol and strolled toward Carson Street. To the west, the snow-capped peaks still reflected brilliant white from the sun as fresh clouds slowly piled on top. The foreground hills looked close enough to touch. A mild desert breeze drifted up from the south.

The judge felt pleasantly cool. Under his arm, he toted a packet of papers. *It might be a long time before we have another day this mild. Thank you, Lord. The storms and clouds in my mind have been quite sufficient lately.*

He stopped at the black iron front gate to watch two farm wagons pull over in front of him. Perched on top of a load of lumber was Duffy Day.

"I got me some help buildin' my house," Duffy called down.

The judge tipped his hat to Turner Bowman, who drove the first wagon. Levi Boyer and Tray Weston drove the second. "You've got a mighty fine quality crew," the judge acknowledged.

Duffy grinned. "Their quality remains to

241

be seen, Judge. I ain't seen 'em drive a nail or saw a board yet."

The judge stepped up to Turner. "Looks like you're going to have a tough taskmaster."

"If we can get him out of the cold this winter, it will be worth it," Turner said.

Judge Kingston pushed his hat back. "Looks like you're going to have to sleep indoors this winter, Duffy."

"I aim to do that, Judge. 'Course, I might put my bunk by a big old winder and leave it open. But Drake and little Douglas is goin' to need a warm place."

"They certainly will," the judge said.

"It's a good thing I never did sell our land, ain't it?"

"You're a smart businessman, Duffy."

"Ain't no one ever told me that before. Say, Judge, you'll have to come down to the place this evenin' and see what we've done."

"You don't intend to complete it in one day, do you?"

"Shoot, no. It's a three-room house. I reckon it will take a week."

Judge Kingston watched the two wagons roll south, then crossed Carson Street, which was the consistency of something between mud and dust. The city magis-

242

trate, Mayor Cary, waited for him at the curb.

"Just the man I need to see," the mayor said. "How about coming down to the bank and witnessing some documents?"

"Can't Mr. Tjader, the bank manager, do that?"

"Need two witness signatures on any transaction over $10,000."

The two men walked together along the wooden sidewalk.

"What's the city buying that's going to cost that amount?" the judge asked.

"A road to Nine-Mile Butte."

They hiked past Cheney's grocery store. John Cheney swung the double doors open. "Judge, are you headed home?" he asked.

"Not until noon."

"I have a jar of pickled eggplant wedges and pimento all the way from Siam for Judith. Willie Jane said she'd tote them over to your place this evening. Do you think that will be soon enough?"

"I assure you, Mr. Cheney, this evening will be quite soon enough."

The two men continued on. "So, the city's share in the sanatorium road project will be $10,000?" the judge asked. "That sounds a bit steep."

"But it's not just a common road. The state engineer said we'll have to raise the roadway at least four feet and build six limestone bridges. Not only that, the city's share includes landscaping with Italian cypress trees within the city limits. There'll be a shaded lane all the way out to the sanatorium. People will want to take stereoscopic photographs of the road itself, not to mention the sanatorium."

"How much are Ormsby County and the State of Nevada coming up with?" the judge asked.

"We divided it in thirds."

"Thirty thousand dollars for nine miles of road?"

"That includes the horse-drawn trolley system."

The judge scratched the back of his neck. "I thought Major Lansford was going to franchise out the trolley."

"He did. We bought it. We figured that by charging even a small amount, the road would pay for itself in five years."

"That sounds like a lot of customers."

"You've got to think big, Judge. This is a wonderful project for Nevada. It's a lasting monument. This sanatorium will be helping people a hundred years from now, long after all the mines have shut down and the mills close. There's going to be a bronze marker by the sanatorium flagpole with the names of government officials who helped with the project. It's a historical event."

"I suppose he's included the city magistrate?"

"My name will be right there after Governor Kinkead's. I didn't ask about judges' names."

"That's quite all right. Seeing sick people receive helpful treatment will be quite enough for me," the judge said. "With that money in the bank, I presume the major can start to work soon."

"This government money is just a drop in the bucket compared to his other financial backing," the mayor said.

"Oh?"

"This is between you and me, but Tjader says the major's development company already has funds of over $100,000."

The judge pulled off his felt hat, ran his fingers through his thinning hair, then jammed the hat back on. "That's more money than we spent on the state capitol."

"I told you, our sanatorium will be the envy of the country."

"When does construction begin?"

"The major said he thought he'd wait

until right after Christmas. He still has a few more backers coming in. I heard a New York big shot will be here this weekend."

The judge halted the mayor. "Does that man happen to be a Mr. Longbake?"

"I believe that's the name. Do you know him?"

The judge rubbed his chin whiskers. "No, but I'm going to get to know him real soon."

"Judge!"

Both men craned their necks as they looked up at the open window above the Paradise Hotel lobby. A woman with a scooped-neck blouse revealed more than her smile.

"It's a pretty day, Judge," Fidora called down.

He tipped his hat. "It certainly is, Fidora."

"I got me a new room."

"So I see."

"But I got a problem."

"A legal problem?"

"I don't know. I got a letter from the Boca family in New Mexico."

"I thought he came from Pagosa Springs, Colorado."

"He did. But his kin live across the border in New Mexico. They're coming to take that dead man home for burial and they want to talk to me. I'm scared they'll blame me for his death."

"Why don't you agree to meet with them in my office? I'll be there to mediate," the judge said.

"That would be swell, Judge. I just don't want no more violence."

The judge tipped his hat and walked on.

"Thanks, Judge," Fidora called after him. "Tell Judith I'll be up for that quilting lesson on Monday."

The men hiked on in warm sunlight to the corner. "What did Fidora mean, 'quilting lesson'?" the mayor asked. "Is Judith giving the crib girls quilting lessons?"

"Apparently so," the judge said. "I'm also hoping she feeds them pickled eggplant from Siam."

"With pimento," the mayor said, chuckling.

Roberta rushed toward them, holding her long dark skirt off the sidewalk as she hurried along.

"What's the matter, Darling?" the judge asked.

"Can you rent me a hack?" she said, breathing hard.

"Where are you going?"

She caught her breath and gently patted

her face with a gloved hand. "For a ride. I need to think."

The judge tilted his head. "Something upset you?"

"Not something, someone — Mrs. Emory."

"What did she tell you?"

Roberta glanced at the mayor, then back to her father. "The truth, probably."

"Perhaps you'd better explain."

She squeezed his fingers, then released his hand. "I've got to think it through first. I really need a hack."

"There's Chug Conly over by Kitzmeyer's. Have him drive you. Tell him I'll pay him later."

Roberta stood on her tiptoes and kissed his cheek. "Thanks, Daddy."

He held her head close. "Have you been crying?"

"Sort of."

He stared into her reddened eyes. *I have no idea in the world what that means.* "Where shall I tell your mother you are going?"

"Down by the river," she said.

"If you have a chance, stop by Duffy's and encourage him to move into that house when it's finished."

She scooted out into the roadway and

paused. "That's exactly where I'm headed." Then she scampered across Carson Street in front of the Bodie Stage.

"She's going to visit Duffy?" the mayor asked.

"I imagine there's someone else she wants to see."

After the radiant sunlight, the Ormsby County Bank lobby seemed dimly lit. The judge and the mayor lingered in the marble-floored lobby while Mr. Tjader met with another customer.

Abe Murdock strolled by. "You here to do a little investing, too, Judge?"

"I've got papers to sign. How about you, Abe?"

He sidled up close, then spoke loudly enough for everyone in the bank to hear. "I bought me that franchise on a barbershop at the sanatorium. It's a good thing I did. The major is just going to put in ten shops. He's got eight of them already leased out, even before a spade is turned."

"I hope it goes well for you, Abe," the judge said.

"It's the best and easiest deal I ever made. I've got to get back to the barbershop. I left Toady Scott at the chessboard, and I will have lost ten games by now."

The customer at the bank manager's desk stood up and turned around. It was Garrison Grimshaw.

"Counselor," the judge said in greeting.

Grimshaw walked over to them.

"Mr. Stevens hasn't pressed charges against Turner Bowman," the judge said. "What's the status of that matter?"

"The Board of Trustees voted to sell the mill," Grimshaw said. "The insurance company has settled up, and they feel that building a new mill in a different location would be wise."

"Where?" the mayor asked.

"In the Black Hills of Dakota."

The mayor pulled off his round hat. "You're just going to walk away from Nevada?"

"Without witnesses, the anarchist will undoubtedly go free," Grimshaw said. "But the trustees do want to sell the mill."

"Who's going to buy a busted mill?" the mayor challenged.

"That presents a problem. But the trustees have offered a very good price. You don't happen to know anyone looking for a reduction mill?"

The judge rubbed his fingers across chapped lips. "No, but there are good men looking for work."

"That is an unfortunate consequence of the fluctuating market conditions," Grimshaw said and left them without another word.

The paperwork signed, witnessed, and filed, the judge went back to his office where he found Colonel Jacobs pacing the floor next to his desk.

"I say, Judge Kingston, sorry to barge in like this. Your clerk, Gabbs, seemed to be nowhere in sight."

The judge hung up his hat. "He's probably at the Supreme Court."

Colonel Jacobs folded his arms across his chest. "Do you have five minutes to spare?"

The judge motioned to an oak side chair.

Jacobs shook his head. "If you don't mind, I think better on my feet." He paced the hardwood floor, his heels tapping a steady, constant rhythm.

"I was just down at Mrs. Emory's. Your wife said I might catch you here. I am extremely puzzled. I thought you might be the one man in town to clear it up for me."

The judge eased into the oak swivel chair behind his desk. "Don't tell me you're having a difficult time figuring out Daisie Belle Emory?"

The colonel halted and stood to attention. "I've never understood the female mind. That's probably why I've been a bachelor all these years. But then, I don't comprehend this frontier mentality. I don't fathom how my brother can work here for chickens and promissory notes. But those aren't the things that trouble me most."

The judge rearranged the pencils and papers on his desk. "What's the problem, Colonel?"

"As you know, I've spent the last few days in Genoa, visiting a family friend and comrade from the war." The colonel stood still in front of the desk. "One topic led to another and I explained to him Major Lansford's sanatorium project."

"Did he know something about it?" the judge asked.

"He said it was an interesting coincidence that he remembers reading about a man named Lansford Fallon during the war."

"That is unusual. I suppose the names could have been transposed," the judge suggested.

Once again the colonel began to pace. "The man my friend read about spent most of the war in the stockade."

"What for?"

"He was a quartermaster sergeant who was accused of misappropriation of cash and supplies."

"I suppose quite a bit of that went on during the war."

"I'm sure it did. Only, my friend remembers this case because the supplies and funds were intended for a hospital facility. A very dear friend of his died because of lack of proper medical equipment. He thought the man should have been hanged."

The judge leaned back in the chair. "Is he saying that our major is this man?"

"Not necessarily. But he was quite startled by the striking similarity of names."

The judge pulled his wire-frame spectacles out of their worn leather case and slipped them on. "Once, when I was a judge in Kentucky, I had to sentence a man named Kingston Hollis. It's a strange feeling to share names like that with another."

"Quite so, Judge. At the end of the war, there were at least a dozen different Colonel Jacobses. Still, it troubled me . . . about the major."

"I don't blame you. It's something we need to check out. I've never known a man who could get funds allocated as quickly as he." The judge leaned forward and jotted a note on a scrap of paper. "Why don't you invite your friend to Carson City and introduce him to the major? This could easily be confirmed or denied."

The colonel threw up his hands. "He never met the man. He wouldn't know him if he saw him. And the major seems unduly reluctant to talk about his war experiences."

"I've known many a man who felt the same," the judge said.

"Yes, quite so."

"Tell you what. I'll pay the expense if you want to telegraph Pennsylvania to find out what happened to this renegade, Sergeant Lansford Fallon."

"I believe I'll do that. But I feel uncomfortable around a man who won't talk about his war experience."

"I guess some just want to forget it."

"Till my dying day," the colonel said, "I will never get it out of my mind. But those who fight with honor have nothing for which to be ashamed." He straightened his tie and slid his hat on. "One more thing, Judge . . ."

"Yes?"

"About Daisie Belle Emory . . ."

Roberta stood on tiptoe at the edge of the Washington Street platform, gazing west, wearing the same emerald dress, black sateen laced robe, and black rose and ostrich hat she'd worn on her arrival.

"Isn't it a beautiful day? Not a cloud in the sky and it's mild again. I believe this is a sign from the Lord, don't you, Mother?"

Judith sat on the front half of the worn wooden bench and tugged at her beige gloves. "Every day is a sign from the Lord. Isn't it, Judge?"

The judge stretched his long legs out in front of him and leaned against the back of the bench. "Indeed, every day is God's gift."

"That's not what I meant," Roberta said.

Judith brushed her curly bangs back out of her eyes. "I'm very happy this is such a pleasant day for Mr. Longbake to arrive."

"You need to call him Wil."

"But I haven't even met him yet."

"The train should be here soon. What time is it, Daddy?"

"About sixty seconds later than the last time you asked."

"I'm nervous. I know I'm nervous. I so want you to like him."

"It will be difficult not to like a man our daughter simply adores," Judith said.

"This is so unbelievable. Five months ago, I didn't even know the man. Then,

Libby and the girls made that silly wager. After that, everything moved so rapidly."

"Wager? What wager?" Judith asked.

The judge leaned forward, eyes piercing into Roberta's.

"I told you about that, didn't I?" she said with an audible gulp.

"I don't believe so," Judith replied.

"That's one of the things I wanted to tell you when I came home in September, but I didn't come home in September."

"You can tell us now," the judge said.

"It was just a silly thing that girls do in a factory when things are slow. A couple of the girls wanted to make a wager about which one could get a date with Wil . . . I mean, Mr. Longbake, first. We had sort of a pool."

"You made bets on such a thing?" the judge asked.

"It seemed like a funny joke at the time."

"How many girls participated?" Judith asked.

"Twenty."

"And you won?" he said.

"No. That's the funny part. Libby won and she had a horrible time. She said he was so straight-laced and formal that she felt like she was at a funeral the whole time. She said he was perfect for me."

"What did she mean by that?" the judge asked.

"The girls know my Christian faith comes first and I don't do the kinds of things some of them do. So, Libby introduced me to Wil and things started happening fast." She walked over to the edge of the platform and stared west.

"Is the train late?" a woman's voice called out.

"Peachy!" Roberta exclaimed. "What are you doing here?"

"I'm hoping for a package on the train." Peachy plopped down next to Judith and the judge.

"Did you order something?" Judith asked, as she admired Peachy's light blue crepe de Chine tea gown and yellow and blue embroidered jacket.

"Oh, no, I was just hoping for a package."

Roberta's attention was on the tracks.

Two women strolled toward the station from Carson Street. The younger woman held the older woman's arm, gently tugging her along. The judge stood as the ladies approached.

"Marthellen! Willie Jane!" Judith called out.

The judge motioned to the bench. "Please sit down. I think I will nervously pace with my daughter."

"I'm surprised to see you two," Judith remarked.

Willie Jane shoved a jar of boiled chestnuts into her hands. "I brought you these. Mr. Cheney wanted me to deliver them to you."

"You could have left them at the house instead of trudging all the way to the station," Judith said.

"It's no bother. I saw Marthellen headed this way and thought I'd accompany her. It's such a beautiful day."

"I thought you were running errands for the major, Marthellen."

"I was, but I finished. I'm expecting that photograph of my granddaughter, so I thought I'd check the train freight."

"But Charlotte said she wouldn't send that until Christmas," Judith reminded her.

"Christmas is only a few weeks away."

"Look at this, will you? A whole welcoming party," Peachy said.

Turner Bowman and Duffy Day strolled up to the platform, hair slicked down, wearing clean shirts but dusty pants and shoes.

"I thought you guys were building a cabin," Peachy said, scowling.

"We needed a break. You know how

Duffy likes to watch the trains roll in," Turner said.

"Me?" Duffy slumped to the platform and sat cross-legged on worn wood. "This was your idea."

"This is quite a gathering," Judith declared. "If we had the city orchestra and the church choir we could present a pageant."

"Not without Daisie Belle," Roberta commented.

"Did someone mention me?"

Daisie Belle Emory, decked out in purple satin and red lipstick, strutted out of the waiting room, leading a scrubbed-clean Douglas Day at her side.

"Uncle Duffy," the boy squealed, jumping onto the grinning man's lap. He had the same narrow face and protruding ears of the Day brothers, but his eyebrows were thicker and his hair lighter.

"I'm his favorite uncle," Duffy said, beaming.

Daisie Belle squeezed in between Judith and Marthellen to wedge herself on the bench. She smelled of lilacs and something medicinal. "It's so exciting to watch trains come in. Little Douglas wanted to see the choo-choo and I know we won't have many more days this nice, so I said to myself . . ."

"Exactly what did you say?" Judith asked.

Daisie Belle leaned over and whispered, "I said that I will surely die if Wilton Longbake comes to town tonight and I don't get to see him until tomorrow, that's what I said. I so hope Roberta won't mind." She looked over at the young woman who was still absorbed in watching the tracks.

"My goodness, Judge," a man from the far end of the platform called out, "how did you manage to surround yourself with such beautiful women?"

The judge turned to wave at Doctor Jacobs and a somber Colonel Jacobs at his side.

"Don't tell me you two also wanted to catch sight of Roberta's beau?" the judge called out.

"The colonel and I are on our way to Virginia City to the Opera House."

Colonel Jacobs glanced down at Daisie Belle and commented, "Some others were too busy to attend."

"I see the choo-choo," Douglas yelled.

"The lad's right," the judge said. "It's making the turn at Two-Mile."

Roberta clutched his arm. "I'm really, really nervous, Daddy."

"Darling, it will be just fine. Don't worry."

"But all these people. It's like an inspection."

"It is, of course. Did you forget how frontier people are?"

"Maybe I did."

"Any man smart enough to nab you will not be intimidated by a crowd of well-wishers."

"Please, please like him, Daddy!"

"If you have truly captured his heart, I can't help but like him."

"At least he won't be as exhausted and dusty as I was. I'm sure he's riding first class," Roberta chattered. "They have plush seats that convert into beds, fresh daily linen, and everything."

Levi Boyer and Marcy Cipiro joined them on the platform. "Is this his train?" Marcy asked.

"It's supposed to be," Roberta said.

"Marcy said it would be good manners to meet your fella at the train, and I'm tryin' to learn manners as fast as I can," Levi said.

The locomotive whistle screeched at the edge of town. Smoke and cinders belched from the stack, and there was a steamy cough from the exhaust. Duffy Day stood and saluted as the iron horse braked into the station. And so did little Douglas.

The engine roared, the steel wheels shrieked on iron rails. When the noise died down, the judge felt someone thumping his shoulder.

"We're lookin' for the major. Have you seen him?" Sheriff Hill asked. Mayor Cary, curly hair sweaty and flying all over, was beside him.

The judge kept his sight on the train cars. "No. Is there trouble?"

"Rudy Boca's brother showed up to claim the body. He wants to talk to the major."

"Is he looking for revenge?" the judge asked.

"I don't know. That's why I wanted to warn the major."

"I'll tell him if I see him."

"Who we waiting for? The president?" the mayor asked.

"Roberta's fiancé."

"He's not my fiancé yet," she said. "Not for a few hours."

A few passengers began to disembark and Judith appeared at the judge's side. Their hands touched. He gave her a small pat, but that was all she needed.

Judith studied each suited man who

came to the door. *He'll have broad shoulders. Square chin. Dancing eyes. And a winsome smile. He'll be cleanshaven but have slightly ragged hair . . . No, I've just described Turner. Lord, I have no idea what he looks like. However, with Roberta at his side, they will be a handsome couple no matter what.*

The Saturday afternoon train emptied quickly. No one emerged looking like a rich New Yorker. No one ran to Roberta's arms. No one even seemed to notice two dozen people waiting for something or someone.

Finally, a pot-bellied man in a plaid suit struggled to get off the rail car as he dragged two heavy carpetbags. His round hat tumbled to the platform off his bald head. He retrieved the hat and called out, "Roberta? Roberta Kingston?"

"Is that him?" Marthellen whispered.

Judith clutched her hands in front of her. *Lord, I hope not. Forgive me, Lord. Not as I will, but thy will be done.*

Roberta led her father toward the rotund man and said, "Are you looking for me?"

He tipped his hat. "I'm Alexander McGee, dry goods and exotic fragrances. I have a message for you."

"Yes?"

"A written message." He searched his

pockets and pulled out a folded paper. "Mr. Wilton Longbake of New York City asked me to deliver this note."

"Where is he?"

The man pulled a silver watch from his plaid vest pocket. "I suppose by now he's almost in San Francisco."

CHAPTER EIGHT

Roberta paced the kitchen, barefoot, in a sleeveless muslin chemise. Her dark brown wavy hair was tousled, and bounced against her back.

"Mother, do you think I'm spoiled?"

Judith sprinkled a navy blue flannel dress with water from a small enamel can and plucked a sadiron off the woodstove.

"It depends on what you mean by spoiled."

"What do *you* mean by it?" Roberta slung a damp tea towel over the towel bar.

"When parents spoil a child of theirs, it means they give them better than they deserve. We all need that kind of love from time to time. It's the kind of love God shows for us." Judith dropped the iron back on the stove to warm and retrieved the other iron. "Why do you ask?"

"Wil told me once that I was acting like a spoiled child."

Judith looked up from the ironing board. "Were you?"

"You tell me. One Saturday, a few weeks ago, I took his children to the zoo all day . . ."

Judith traded irons again. "By yourself?"

"Yes. It was his time to have the children and he had some work at the factory. So, I volunteered to take the children. Wil promised he and I would have dinner that night at the Del Rio Hotel. I assumed it would be just the two of us and I looked forward to it all week. When we got there, it was a big party for Fiona DiFenes."

"The French dancer who uses ostrich feathers?"

"She is quite talented."

Judith raised her eyebrows. "So I've read."

"But Wil was so busy with some old college friends, I felt abandoned. He left me at a table by a post. I didn't know anyone in the room. When he took me home that night, I pitched a fit. That's when he called me a spoiled child." Roberta retrieved a cold biscuit from under a plaid tea cloth and spun around to face her mother. "Was I acting spoiled?"

Judith wiped perspiration off her forehead with a tea towel. "You two are of very disparate ages and from diverse backgrounds. It's natural for two humans to ob-

266

serve situations from different viewpoints."

Roberta placed the uneaten biscuit back under the plaid cloth, walked over to a shelf, and picked up Judith's Bible. "Why do you have this verse about being spoiled underlined? Were you thinking of me?"

" 'Woe unto us! for we are spoiled,' " Judith recited. "I hadn't thought of that in terms of being pampered or coddled. I interpreted the word as denoting being ruined or punished or even overwhelmed, as when God enacts his righteous judgments. It's the fear of the Lord. Or the people could be so full of sin they're spoiled like food gets, as in smelly and putrefied and of no use to anyone. It's a memory verse Marthellen and I are learning. At least, I'm learning it. She seems to be busy these days."

Roberta replaced the crocheted cross bookmark and closed the Bible. "Speaking of spoiled, you are probably the only woman in town with a hired housekeeper who still has to do her own pressing."

"I don't mind. I don't have to do it often. Besides, Marthellen is having more fun than she's had in her entire life. I want her to enjoy it." Judith winced as a pain shot up her right arm from her hand to her shoulder. She set the iron back on the stove.

"Mother, do you think I should pitch a fit when Wil shows up? Or would it just make me look even more spoiled?" Roberta grabbed another biscuit and took a bite.

Judith sprinkled more water on the dress. "Because he went to San Francisco?"

Roberta broke the biscuit in half and circled the kitchen. "Because he sent me a note by a drummer saying, 'Dear Roberta, I need to go immediately to San Francisco on business. See you soon. Be good. Sincerely, Wilton Longbake.'"

Judith brushed curly bangs out of her eyes. "What disturbs you most about the note?"

"One thing is the part about 'be good.' That's the kind of thing you say to your child or your dog."

"I assumed it was a little tease."

Roberta mashed a biscuit half into her chemise pocket. "Wil doesn't tease."

"Never?"

"No, never. The thing that bothers me most is that he wouldn't give up one little business deal to keep his appointment with me and my family."

"I assume it was a critical matter. Mr. Hearst is very wealthy and influential. Do you know about his involvement with the Ophir Mine up at Virginia City?"

Roberta sailed around the small breakfast table, then plopped in a chair. "Even so, he could have explained it all in person. How can I ever live down the embarrassment of having all my friends at the station and him not showing? I could never live in Carson City. It would be too humiliating."

Judith clanged the iron back on the stove. "Nonsense. It's just the opposite." She took a sip of tepid spice tea. "Everyone here knows every little thing about you and loves you anyway. In some other town you would have to wait for times of trouble and crisis to see where people's loyalties lie."

Roberta walked her fingers across the lace tablecloth on the breakfast table. "Remember the other day when you said marriage meant sacrificial love?"

Judith set the teacup down and rubbed her wrists. "Yes, I do."

"That's been nagging me ever since. I wish you had never said it."

"You don't think it's true?" Judith resumed ironing the dress.

"I know it's true. I see you and Daddy sacrifice for each other every day. But . . ." Roberta wiped the corner of her eyes. "But I don't see it . . ."

"Go on," Judith urged.

Roberta slumped her head in her hands. "You know what I'm going to say."

"I think you need to say it aloud."

Roberta took a deep breath and her body shook. "I don't see Wil making any sacrifices for me, whatsoever." One lone tear slid down Roberta's face.

"Honey, perhaps it's something you should talk to him about."

Wrinkles tightened across Roberta's forehead. "I could never do that."

"Why?"

"He would call me a spoiled child again. We can't talk like that."

"You should be able to talk to the man you marry about any subject," Judith said.

"Wil and I talk a lot. Really."

"I believe you, Dear."

"There are just a few subjects he doesn't like to discuss."

Judith stood straight. She felt a sharp ache at the base of her spine. "What are those?"

"His ex-wife . . . his business . . . his politics."

"That narrows things a bit. I can understand the pain of the first marriage. But no business or politics?"

"He doesn't think a woman should

trouble herself with her husband's business. Daddy doesn't come home and tell
you about every court case, does he?"

Judith looked up and smiled. "As a
matter of fact, he does."

Roberta's eyes widened. "But he never
talked about them when I was around."

"He thinks those things should be kept
in the privacy of marriage."

"Oh . . . well, I probably wouldn't understand Wil's business anyway."

Judith turned the dress over once again.
"And he never talks politics?"

"Oh, he talks politics all the time, just
not with me."

Judith slid the heavy iron carefully
around the lace cuffs and braid buttons.
"He doesn't think women should talk politics?"

"Wil supports suffrage. He thinks that
women should vote and run for office and
everything. But when we talk politics, we
usually argue because . . . now, don't tell
Daddy this." Roberta's voice dropped to
almost a whisper. "Wil's a Democrat. In
fact, he's an earnest campaigner in the
Democratic ranks. He has canvassed New
York state in the interests of the party
many times. He can be a most zealous and
untiring worker."

271

Judith chuckled and exchanged irons. "That's not a sin. Daisie Belle is a lifelong Democrat and we get along very well."

"Yes, but he's very stubborn in his ways and I'm . . ."

"And you are a Kingston, and Kingstons are known throughout Nevada and the rest of the country as staunch Lincolnesque Republicans."

"We get along fine with it as long as we don't discuss anything too serious," Roberta said. "But I do think I should warn Daddy."

"That might be nice." The bottoms of Judith's feet ached.

"Would you tell him?" Roberta asked.

"All right, if you want me to." Judith set both irons on the stove, then held the dress up. "I think I'm done. It's your turn."

"Oh," Roberta said, "I thought you were going to . . ."

"Heavens, no," Judith replied. "I wouldn't want to spoil you."

Turner Bowman and Levi Boyer were nailing cedar shakes to the roof when the judge stopped the carriage in front of the cabin. A dozen mallards skimmed along the Carson River. Each one swam close to the bank, took a quick flip of a turn, and crossed to the other side. The judge's face felt red and raw after the carriage trot. Dark, heavy clouds covered Eagle Valley from the Pine Nut Range to the river.

Duffy Day came up to meet him wearing coveralls and a flop hat that drooped down to his eyes. "Ain't it a beaut, Judge?"

The rough-cut cedar, board-and-bat structure was perched on half-buried river boulders. "It's a fine home, Duffy," the judge said as he climbed to the ground.

"I ain't never owned no cabin before, Judge, even when I was working the mines." Duffy danced from one foot to the other. "It surely does make a man feel permanent, don't it?"

Duffy looked grimy, but he smelled clean as the judge walked him to the cabin.

"Looks like your roofers will beat this storm," the judge said.

Duffy peered inside a square opening. "I was thinkin' of maybe sleepin' inside tonight. There ain't no windows, doors, or interior walls, but I ain't ever had much use for the like, anyway."

"That's a good idea, Duffy."

"You jist look around, Judge. I've got to get to work. Me and Tray is battening down the east side."

The judge slowly hiked around the

structure that sat like a new wood crate in the middle of all the barrels, boxes, tents, corrals, hog houses, and scattered, rusted mining equipment that was Duffy's domain.

On the north side, Turner Bowman scampered down a wobbly, homemade ladder, a three-day beard on his strong, square chin. He shoved his hat to the back of his head. "I've been aimin' to talk to you, Judge. Could we go over by the carriage? It's kind of private."

The judge, in dark, three-piece suit, tie, and overcoat, towered over the young man in rough duckings by three inches.

Turner yanked some roofing nails out of his mouth. "Have you talked to Doctor Jacobs today?"

"No, I haven't."

"I took Duffy to town this morning to visit Drake. Mrs. Emory said he had a very bad night. He could hardly get his breath and they were waiting for Doctor Jacobs to show up. I'm worried about him, Judge. I think that after that brief recovery, he's starting to slip."

The judge glanced toward the cabin. "How does Duffy feel about it?"

Turner dropped the nails into a pocket. "Duffy thinks Drake's going to move into the cabin and get well. I don't think he grasps the seriousness of his brother's condition."

"He might understand but doesn't want to acknowledge it," the judge said.

"I'm not sure we'll get this built in time for anyone to use it."

"Well, it's a fine cabin. Duffy needs it, no matter what happens to Drake."

"I know. But listen, there's something else. I have an idea about future employment."

The judge slipped his hands into his overcoat pockets. "That's a coincidence. That's what I came out here to talk to you about."

"Tell me your idea first," Turner said.

"You know Mr. Gabbs has tendered his resignation and is moving on to the state Supreme Court?" The judge pulled off his spectacles and rubbed the bridge of his nose. "When you complete construction on the road out to the sanatorium, I was wondering if I could hire you to be my new clerk."

Turner looked stunned. "You're kidding!"

"I think it's a good place for you to be employed and still learn the law." The judge folded his arms across his chest.

275

"Someday, of course, you'd want to pass the bar and go off on your own; I think you'd make a good lawyer."

"That's mighty tempting, Judge. Let me ponder on it. But that wasn't what I had in mind."

"What was your idea?"

Bowman pulled a hammer from his leather apron and waved it in front of him like a gavel. "I want to buy the Consolidated Milling reduction plant and rebuild it."

The judge rubbed his chin whiskers. "Now, that, Turner Bowman, is an ambitious idea."

"I know it sounds crazy. I don't mean I, personally, will buy it. I want to try and find some backers. Consolidated never had the plant running efficiently. They had Stevens, Henderson, and the others from the East that never got it right. I know how to do it right. Besides, I could hire back the old crew that way. A properly run mill should still be making money."

Judge Kingston leaned his backside against the carriage. "I have no doubt that you could do it, Turner. But Grimshaw told me they're asking $100,000 for the plant. How much would it take to get it back to operational level?"

"A minimum of $50,000. To do it best, $75,000."

"Do you have any idea where to come up with $175,000?"

"Back at that bonfire rally, you told me to go up and talk to the mine owners in Virginia City. I thought I'd start there."

The judge nodded. "There aren't many funds left around Carson City, I know. The major has latched on to most of the public investment money. It would have to be private funding."

"Tell me, Judge, do you think it's too wild an idea?"

The judge turned his back toward the northwest breeze. "I think it's absolutely crazy. However, if you don't try for it you will regret it until your dying day."

"That's what I thought. I have to at least try."

"A lot of folks get good ideas. But only a few act on them. Besides, if it doesn't work out, I know a boring clerk job you can have."

Turner's grin was wide and infectious. "Tell me one time when Judith or the Judge ever had a boring day."

"July 21, 1868," came the deadpan reply. "It does happen."

Turner laughed. "Thanks for the offer. I

truly appreciate it. You'll never know how much having your support means to me."

The judge climbed into the carriage and reached for the buffalo blanket. "Keep me up on your progress with the mill. If you need a letter of introduction, let me know."

"Hey, Judge," Levi called from the roof of the cabin. "We got an extra hammer if you're lookin' for work."

"Tell you what," he shouted back, "you go to town and meet with Rudy Boca's vengeful brother, and I'll stay here and roof the house."

"Think I'll pass, Judge. Standin' on a roof is dangerous enough for me."

Sergio Boca looked so much like his brother, the judge had to keep from staring when the man stormed into his office. Strapped to the outside of his dust-covered black suit was a two-holstered bullet belt and two silver inlaid .45 pistols.

The judge motioned to the east wall. "The rack is for your coat, hat, and guns."

Boca whacked his wide-brimmed felt hat against his leg. "My guns, too?"

"I allow no weapons in my office except those of law enforcement officers. It helps keep legal discussions at a professional level."

"I will respect that." Boca slapped each item on the rack while the judge studied him. *Lord, he is an angry man. Give me the wisdom to know how to tell the truth, and the patience to overlook his wrath.*

Sergio Boca stalked to the desk. "Where is the *puta?*"

The judge rubbed his temples. *Lord, he is not helping me with my patience.* "Mr. Boca, Fidora is a witness. She is the last person your brother talked to. Her occupation is of no consequence. Nor was your brother's. If you persist with such language, I will advise her not to meet with you at all. In my office, all women are treated with the respect God gave them at creation. Is that understood?"

Boca's dark eyes darted to his mud-baked brown boots. Then he looked up. A faint smile broke across his face. "You are correct. I understand. It is your rightful domain."

Spafford Gabbs stuck his head in the doorway. "Are you ready for Fidora?"

The judge peered at Boca over his spectacles, "Yes, we are."

To the judge's relief, Fidora wore one of Judith's dresses, a dark navy one with white lace cuffs and high neck and braided buttons. She strolled across the bare wooden floor in her high-heeled, side-laced black kid boots, trying to keep steady, balancing one foot and then the other. The judge knew she wore soft slippers most of the time, even when walking to town. Her long, narrow face, high dark eyebrows, and thin lips were taut and tense.

The judge tried to relax her. "Fidora, this is Señor Sergio Boca."

"You look a lot like your brother," she said.

"And you do not look as I imagined," he replied.

Besides a light coat of lip rouge, she wore very little makeup. Sergio seemed transfixed, watching her.

The judge studied her demeanor. *I believe Judith was giving you more than quilting lessons.*

"Mr. Boca," she said, "your brother, whom I met only once . . ."

The judge suppressed a smile. *Whom? Judith has Fidora using proper English?*

". . . was intoxicated and violent. He chased me down the hotel stairs and into the alley, brandishing a knife. I feared for my safety and my life. However, I in no way wanted the man shot, and I express my sympathy to you and his family on his death. If my panic contributed to his demise, I apologize. I was terrified and could do nothing else."

The judge watched as Fidora ran her tongue across her lips, then chewed on it in triumph. *Judith, that was one of the finest speeches you ever wrote.*

Boca sat speechless.

The judge broke the silence. "Mr. Boca, I believe Fidora offered her sympathy and apology."

Boca seemed to wake out of a daydream. "Oh, yes, for the family, I accept your apology, Miss . . . Miss Fidora."

"Will you need me for anything else, Judge? I do want to get back to my quilting."

"Mr. Boca?" the judge said. "Do you need to ask Fidora any questions?"

"I understand you witnessed my brother getting shot."

"I was running for my life. Running away from your brother. I heard the shots, but I saw nothing," she reported. "I realize I cannot offer you much information. I am sorry for that. As I said, I was very scared and was thinking only of my own safety."

"I am sorry for this inconvenience," Sergio Boca said, "but it was good to hear these things from your lips. I appreciate your indulgence."

"My what?" Fidora clutched the lace collar at her neck.

"He thanks you for taking time to stop by," the judge explained. He stood and walked around by her chair.

Fidora got up. "Can I go now?"

"Yes, and give my compliments to your quilting instructor." The judge walked her to the door.

When he returned, Sergio Boca was waving his hands in the air. "I had the notion that —"

"I presume you were expecting this meeting to go differently?" the judge challenged.

"I know that Miss Fidora did not kill my brother. I will be frank. Rudy was a lying, cheating, worthless brother. If he were drunk, he was certainly capable of pulling a knife on this woman, or any woman. As for his death, it came as no surprise to his family. Having said all of that, I am still concerned."

"What concerns you?" the judge asked.

"Normally, it is easy to disarm a drunk. I have done it many times myself. Second, my brother was not stupid. To lunge at a man with a gun pointed at your chest is stupid. Then, to have that man shoot not once, but twice, also puzzles me." Boca leaned forward in the chair. "I am not proud to say this, but I, too, have been in gunfights. My only desire was to keep the other man from killing me. To shoot a man who is holding a knife twice in the heart is not self-defense. It is murder."

The judge rapped his fingers on the desk. "People panic, Mr. Boca. Whenever there is the threat of death, some people overreact."

Boca scooted back in his chair. "That is true. But I would have expected more from a military man."

"I see your point. As Scripture states, 'The Lord is long-suffering to usward, not willing that any should perish, but that all should come to repentance.' I find no pleasure in the violent death of any person. However, any man who pulls a knife and threatens others opens himself up to such a response."

Boca's dark eyes softened slightly. "I would like to talk to this major, but I have been unable to find him."

"I suggest you contact Sheriff Hill to arrange a meeting in his office. I came upon your brother only moments after the shooting. I can tell you that the major expressed deep regret at the death of your brother."

"I find the sincerity of the major's sentiments difficult to believe," Boca replied.

"Why is that?"

Sergio Boca twisted his long mustache. "I have reason to suspect my brother had dealings with this man before."

The judge pulled off his spectacles and waved them at the man across the desk. "Mr. Boca, are you saying your brother, Rudy, knew Major Fallon Lansford prior to this shooting?"

"It is my suspicion. But that was not the major's name at the time. It is this idea, this intuition, that has brought me all the way from New Mexico."

"Can you identify the major on sight?"

"That I cannot do. I never met him. But there are some in Pagosa Springs, Colorado, who know very well what he looks like. I live in New Mexico. I heard the story only after Rudy was in prison."

The judge opened a drawer and pulled out a long sheet of paper. "May I jot down a few notes?"

"Certainly."

The judge pulled the stopper out of the bottle of black India ink. "Please start from the beginning."

Sergio Boca held on to the arms of the chair as if someone were about to pull it out from under him. "Rudy worked odd jobs out of Pagosa Springs. Mainly he gambled, chased women, and got in fights. However, about two years ago a man from the East, wearing fancy suits and calling himself Captain Landford Falcon, came to Pagosa Springs with an ambitious proposal to build a soldiers' hospital there."

A cold chill slid down the judge's spine as the metal nib scratched across the page. "He wanted to build a soldiers' hospital?" he repeated.

"For Civil War veterans, he claimed. It would take care of disabled and elderly veterans from both sides of the war."

"Wouldn't that be a government project?" the judge asked.

"According to Rudy, the captain stated that the federal government was not convinced of the need. But if a local community could show the need and potential for such a hospital, the government would buy it from the community for a handsome profit to the local investors."

"That, I suppose, is a possibility. It certainly makes a selling point."

Boca loosened his death grip on the chair arms. "I think he was very convincing. He came with letters of recommendation and a scale model of the hospital."

The judge stopped writing. "What do you mean, a scale model?"

"Little stick buildings, miniature trees, everything . . ." Boca waved his hands wildly. "That's the way Rudy explained it."

"How does your brother come into this?"

"The captain needed someone to stand guard on his property. He was very secretive and afraid others would steal his idea. Rudy began to do other tasks for him. He became a sort of assistant. Rudy was quite proud of the position. He even tried to give up drinking for awhile."

"What happened?" the judge asked. "Did the hospital get built?"

"No, but plenty happened. One of the first people to support the plan was the local mayor, who happened to be the bank president as well. Even more enthusiastic was the bank manager's wife."

The judge circled the word "wife."

"Rudy reported that the captain and the bank manager's wife became . . . eh, lovers. My brother would often sit outside the hotel room to make sure they were not disturbed."

"By her husband, no doubt."

"Meanwhile, the captain built up quite an account. Then, suddenly —"

"Let me guess," the judge interrupted. "The captain disappeared with the money and the wife."

"Not exactly. The banker was discovered dead in the hotel room. The banker's wife claimed Rudy broke into their room, tried to force himself on her, and when the banker defended his wife's honor, Rudy shot him. The community was ready to hang my brother."

"What did Rudy say happened?"

"He said that while the captain and the banker's wife were in the hotel room, he got disgusted with his role of guarding the door and went to the saloon for a drink. He got involved in a monte game, got drunk, lost a lot of money, and didn't get back until three in the morning. When he arrived at the room, the wife threw open the door and screamed that Rudy had shot her husband."

"What about this Captain Falcon?"

"He was asleep at his boardinghouse room when the sheriff went to question him. He denied any involvement with the woman, although everyone in town knew it was true."

"So, what happened to the soldiers' hospital project?"

"It is a very small town, Judge. The scandal was too much. The captain folded up and left."

"And the banker's wife?"

"She moved soon afterward."

"And the hospital account?"

"It was left in the bank, at least part of it. No one except the bank manager and the captain knew what the balance should be, and the bank president was dead."

"And the captain vanished." The judge jotted down a few more notes. "How did your brother escape hanging?"

"The story gets stranger. It took several weeks for the trial and the sentencing. They sent my brother to Denver. While he was there awaiting an appeal, the bank manager's wife returned to Pagosa Springs and confessed."

The judge stared into the small man's dark eyes. "Confessed to what?"

"To having an affair with the captain, skimming the funds, and shooting her husband."

"She shot her own husband?" The judge dipped his pen in the inkwell and wrote.

"She said her husband found her and the captain in the hotel room, pulled a gun on them, and when she tried to wrestle the gun away, it discharged and killed her husband. She claimed it was her idea to skim the funds and run off, but the captain wanted to stay and build the hospital."

"What happened to her?"

"A jury acquitted her. They called it accidental homicide."

The judge pulled out a second piece of clean white paper. "And your brother?"

"They released him. He moved to Arizona, I thought. I didn't know he was in Nevada until I received word of his death."

"Mr. Boca, even if we could prove that the Pagosa Springs captain is the same man as Major Lansford, the truth remains that your brother, in a drunken rage, tried to assault Miss Fidora. He was stopped from that attack by any means possible. That, by itself, does not mean a crime has been committed."

"I will give Major Lansford the first shot, but I will not give him the second. I will not leave Carson City until I talk to him," Boca announced.

"All right," the judge said. "I will explain to the sheriff and arrange a meeting, if you like. In the meantime, I urge you not to prowl the streets or go after Lansford on your own. I cannot stress clearly enough my belief that a man is innocent until proven guilty."

Boca stood up and nodded. "I will wait for your word. I am at the Ormsby House. But I will not wait indefinitely."

"You certainly know how to warm a woman's heart." Judith peeked out from under the buffalo robe as the carriage rolled out Fifth Street past the state orphans' asylum. "Do you always wait for the coldest day of the week for a ride, or does it just seem that way?"

"We need to talk, and our house is as busy as the train station," the judge said. "Besides, you haven't seen Duffy's cabin yet."

"I must admit the story you told me about Captain Falcon in Pagosa Springs is very distressing. But we have no idea if that is our Major Lansford."

"It is circumstantial at this juncture. But at least three things deeply disturb me," the judge said.

"Fidora's payoff?"

"That's one. Do you know what Fidora heard Rudy Boca and the major say?"

"She told me they cursed each other."

"And that there was a pause between shots?"

"That's how she remembers it."

"Then the major bought her off?"

Judith nodded. "He said, 'I'm sure you saw exactly what happened,' then handed her twenty dollars."

The judge slapped the lead lines on the horse's rump. The spirited black horse broke into a trot. "Then there's the remark you overheard about a Tiffany appraisal, the day we went out to Nine-Mile Butte. Does the major have some Tiffanys among his backers?"

"I don't know," Judith said. "Do you think they've found some gold out at Nine-Mile?"

"One doesn't appraise gold. You assay it. Gemstones are appraised."

"And real estate," she added.

"That's true. That is a very good point. Perhaps there's some surveyor named Tiffany." The judge pulled his scarf over his ears. "This is getting confusing and far-fetched. Are we defending the major or making excuses for him?"

"Perhaps it's time to sit down with Major Lansford and lay all these things out," Judith suggested.

"That might be so, but it will certainly sound like we're on a vendetta," the judge said. "Especially if he has a simple answer for all these questions. He may assume we're spying on him."

"We are being prudent to investigate his background and credulity so that government entities and individuals alike might make wise decisions about possible future investments," Judith said.

"You're beginning to sound like Fidora."

Judith laid her gloved hand on his coat sleeve. "She really did OK?"

"She had every line memorized."

"She came back to the house saying, 'I never knew that clothes and speech made such a difference in the way people thought about you.' "

"Someday you might even teach her how to quilt."

"What in heaven's name for?"

"I want you and me to be praying about this," the judge said. "If it seems to be the Lord's leading, I'll tell the sheriff what we know, and the mayor and any others we think of. But first, we'll need to set up a meeting with the major before this goes any further."

Judith sighed. "If he turns out to be a scoundrel, it will crush Marthellen. I don't think either of us could bear it."

"That's possible, but if the major is also Captain Falcon of Pagosa Springs, he's the type of man to use women to achieve his goals."

"But it sounds like the captain truly wanted to complete the soldiers' hospital," Judith said. "It seems he was undone by his private affairs spilling over into his public projects. Perhaps the captain, that is, the major has learned his lesson. If this truly is his past, maybe he's sincere with the sanatorium . . . and with Marthellen."

"There's something else I wanted to discuss with you," the judge said. "Do you notice a haunting similarity between Marthellen and Major Lansford . . . and Roberta and her Mr. Wilton Longbake?"

"I don't believe Mr. Longbake's a rogue. Do you?"

"It was roguish to leave her waiting at the station."

"There could be a completely satisfactory explanation."

"There better be," he huffed.

"I think I should get you off that subject. I'm glad we finally received a letter from David," she said, "and to learn that Patricia was peaceful at the end." Judith tried to fight the tears.

"She's in glory now," the judge said.

Judith nodded, then sighed. "I wish David and the children could make it back home before March."

"The Lord's work doesn't stop because

of the death of a saint."

"I know, but I want my grandchildren. I want them home with me right now." She reached for her handkerchief, the one Patricia had stitched for her.

"We've had the most depressing news lately," the judge said. "Surely we can talk about something lighter."

Judith rubbed her nose with her gloved hand. "Daisie Belle brought over our talking squirrel costumes today."

"Were they as humorous as you expected?"

"Worse. They make us look bucktoothed and goofy."

"Perhaps you could alter them a tad."

"Perhaps I could destroy them completely."

"Turner told me Drake took a turn last night. Did you hear about that?"

"That's what Daisie Belle said. Doctor Jacobs diagnosed it as pneumonia. So much for humorous diversion."

"Has anyone told Duffy yet?"

"They were hoping you would."

The judge took a moment to swallow. "I'm not sure Duffy could handle the news."

"I believe Duffy is stronger than we give him credit for."

Snowflakes began a soft flurry out of the sky.

"Mrs. Kingston, did you ever consider that our life sometimes reads like one of Stuart Brannon's novels that you hide at the bottom of your dresser drawer?"

She slipped her arm into his. "But I haven't figured out which one."

After supper, Judge Kingston carried hot, steaming black coffee into the living room and shoved another log on the fire. Judith joined him, toting a double-dose mug of hot chocolate.

"If I had known we were going to have the evening to ourselves, we wouldn't have gone for a ride in that blizzard today," he announced.

"It wasn't a blizzard then, but it sure is now. I believe this is the first evening we've had to ourselves since your daughter came home."

"My daughter?" he teased. "She's just like her mother."

"Oh, dear, do I get the blame?" Judith rolled the Chesterfield settee closer to the fire and sat down.

"Or the praise." The judge sat down beside her. "Is Roberta spending the night at Peachy's?"

"She said that was the plan, unless they get into a tussle."

The Nevada street door opened. They heard someone enter. "I believe it's Marthellen," Judith said.

"How can you tell?"

"She has such a soft step."

Marthellen Farnsworth appeared at the kitchen doorway with her own cup of rich, deep chocolate. "May I join you?"

Marthellen slumped down in the brown leather chair and stared into the flames.

"I thought you went with the major," Judith said.

"With this snowstorm and all, I decided I needed some rest."

"Where did he go?" the judge asked.

"To Reno. He had some water-testing equipment shipped out and the company only paid to have it delivered to Reno. The Virginia City and Truckee wouldn't freight it down COD because he hadn't established an account."

"So he had to go prepay them to freight it?" the judge asked.

"Yes. He went to the bank to get some money, then took the train up to Reno."

"Then he'll come back on the late train?" Judith asked.

"No, he said he'd wait until morning, since I wasn't going with him. I was just too exhausted."

296

"You've been very busy," Judith said. "You're getting physically run down."

"Oh, that too. But what I'm really tired of trying to figure out is this relationship," Marthellen said. "Fal only seems happy with me when I'm busy running errands for him. He was quite upset when I refused to go with him tonight." Marthellen unfastened her small, round rhinestone earrings.

"He obviously enjoys your company," Judith said.

"No, he obviously enjoys having me do things for him."

"You two have spent a lot of time together. You're bound to rub a little, especially when you've been so intense on this huge project. A relaxing night at home might be just what the relationship needs."

"It's certainly what I need." Marthellen laid the earrings on the table next to the stained-glass lantern. "I told him not to stop by until noon."

"Good for you," Judith said.

"I'll need to talk to him when he returns," the judge mentioned.

"What about?" Marthellen asked.

The judge glanced at Judith. "I visited with Rudy Boca's brother today. He still has some questions about the shooting."

"Fal knows about that. He's carrying two guns."

"Two?" Judith said.

"He has a beautiful pearl-handled sneak gun."

The judge leaned back against the settee and closed his eyes. "Marthellen, has the major ever mentioned living in Pagosa Springs, Colorado?"

"He sure has. We spent a whole evening talking about it."

The judge sat straight up on the edge of the chair and stared at the housekeeper. "I just heard rumors . . ."

"Fal said he tried to sell the idea about a sanatorium to the people there. They have a mineral springs, too."

"A sanatorium in Pagosa Springs?" Judith said. "That's such a tiny spot in the road."

"That sanatorium was on a much smaller scale than the one he's designed for us. But they backed out of the deal after he spent a lot of time and money organizing it."

"Did he say why they backed out?" the judge asked.

"The banker lacked vision."

He rubbed his temples. *He lacks a good deal more than vision, my dear.*

At the sound of a knock at the door, the judge jumped to his feet, but Marthellen moved more quickly and jabbed her finger in his stomach as she passed him. "Sit down, Judge, I'm still the housekeeper here."

She led Turner Bowman into the room after he stamped snow off his boots.

"Judge, I think I did it," Turner said.

"You went to Virginia City and got financing to buy and rebuild the mill?"

"Yep."

"How many investors did you locate?"

"Just two, but they're rich enough."

"And they're putting up both the purchase and the repair money?"

"Well, they want to come down tomorrow and check everything out. After that, they'll set up a separate company. I'll be the superintendent and have a share of the profit."

"That's wonderful, Turner! I knew you could do it."

"It's an answer to prayer, Judge, that's what it is. This means jobs for the crew and work for everyone. 'Course, there are a couple of things to work out."

"Such as?"

"They want someone, you know, older than me to run the business office."

"Do they have a person in mind?"

"Nope. But they were hoping I'd have someone lined up to interview when they came down."

"By tomorrow?"

"Yeah. That's a challenge, isn't it? Say, Judge, you wouldn't want to retire and —"

"No, but thanks for the offer."

"I was just teasing, mainly."

"Who are your backers?" Judith asked.

"Oh, man, I can't believe I didn't tell you that yet. That's why I came straight here. I was visiting outside the stock exchange in Virginia City and who should I bump into? None other than George Hearst and Roberta's fella, Mr. Wilton Longbake."

Judith and the judge stared at each other. Marthellen's cup rattled on her saucer.

"Longbake's in Virginia City? I thought the man was in San Francisco," the judge said. His words came out in a staccato, bullet-like fashion.

"He was in San Francisco, but Hearst wanted to show him the Ophir Mine, so they took the train right back to Virginia City," Turner said.

"But they had to come through Carson City to get to Virginia City," Judith said.

"I reckon they did."

Judith clenched her fists and looked over at the judge. *And he didn't stop to see Roberta?*

"He had important business to take care of," Turner said. "Anyway, I talked to them for hours."

The judge got up and paced the room. "I can't believe this."

"It's true," Turner said, beaming. "They're really going to give me the money. At least, it's almost a sure thing. Is Roberta home? I want to tell her about me swinging this deal to reopen Consolidated."

"She has gone to Peachy's house," Judith told him.

"Great, I can tell them both at once," Turner said.

Judith got up, grabbed Turner by the arm, and led him to the front door. "Please don't tell Peachy and Roberta tonight," she pleaded.

"Why not?"

"Will you promise me? Wait until to-morrow." Judith gave him her most serious face.

"But they will both be so happy for me," Turner said.

"Everyone in town is going to be so proud and happy for you, but not tonight. Trust me."

"All right, Judith, I'll . . . I'll just go tell some of the crew."

"Thank you, Turner."

When he opened the door, a gust of freezing wind blew in. "What's the judge so riled about?" he asked.

"He's not riled," Judith assured him. "He hasn't begun to quote Ecclesiastes yet."

"No one can treat my daughter with such disregard," the judge ranted when Judith returned to the warmth of the living room. "You treat the woman you're going to marry with consideration and respect, not as an afterthought. 'That which is crooked cannot be made straight.' 'There's a time to cast away stones, and a time to gather stones together.'"

It was half an hour before Judith and Marthellen coaxed the judge to have a piece of apple pie. It was an hour later before he unfastened the top button on his shirt and loosened his tie. He had just allowed Judith to tug off his polished black boots when there was a rapid knock at the front door.

"I'll answer it." Marthellen raced to the door.

"If it's Longbake, tell him I'll meet him

tomorrow," the judge called out, "with dueling pistols!"

Colonel Jacobs was covered with snow, out of breath, and more red-faced than usual.

"What's wrong, Colonel?" Judith said.

"I was at Mrs. Emory's. It's Drake Day . . . he can barely breathe . . . my brother's there with him . . . he said, go get Judith and the judge to pray with Drake."

Judith's hand flew to her mouth.

"We'll pull on our coats and be right up," the judge called out. "Is Duffy there?"

"No, he wanted to stay out at his place tonight."

"Could you go out and bring him in?" Judith asked.

The colonel hesitated. "I'm not sure where his place is, especially with the snow."

"I'll go with you," Marthellen offered, then glanced at the judge.

"By all means, go on. But be careful. We don't need any more tragedies."

The judge sat down and grabbed his boots. "Once again, the Lord has corrected my thinking," he said.

Judith tugged on her heavy wool coat, scarf, hat, and gloves. "How's that?"

"I've spent the last couple of hours fuming about a perceived snub of my daughter, while Drake Day has been battling for his life. My word, I can be such a petty man."

She handed him his coat and hat. *Judge Hollis A. Kingston, you have never in your life been a petty man.*

CHAPTER NINE

"He's dead, ain't he, Judge?" Duffy blurted out. A snowy Carson City night swirled around him, but he refused to come inside.

The judge stared up at a thick blanket of clouds above the stark white forms of frost-coated trees in Mrs. Emory's backyard. Not a star in sight. By the light flickering in the window, the judge could see Duffy's scruffy wild hair shooting out from under his hat. He slipped an arm around the man's shoulder. "Yes, he is, Duffy. I'm sorry."

"He fought that sickness, Judge. My brother fought it to the end."

"Yes, he did."

"Why do you suppose this happened, Judge?"

"Because we live in a world full of sickness and death."

"I know that. But why Drake? It don't make sense. He was smart and hardworking. He has a little boy. If the Lord needed someone else up there, he should have taken me. I ain't got nothin'. I ain't nothin'. It should have been me."

The judge was bone cold, but also numb, past caring about the weather. "The heart of God has never missed a beat. He doesn't make any mistakes, Duffy."

"Can we bury Drake out at my place? I'd surely like his marker close by."

"I'm sure that can be arranged."

Duffy's voice was clear and strong. "Do you know the last thing Drake told me?"

"What was that?"

"He said he was going off to see Mama and that I was supposed to look after Douglas."

Judge Kingston blew steam from his mouth. "What was the last thing you told Drake?"

"I told him I'd look after Douglas until my dyin' day . . . and . . ."

"And what?" the judge pressed.

"I asked him to tell Mama that I really missed her."

Lord, have special mercy on Duffy. He's going to need a lot of strength and wisdom and. . . .

"Douglas is going to live with me, Judge." His words were halfway between a question and a statement.

"It will be nice that you'll have a companion, Duffy."

"Do you reckon he'll grow up thinkin' I'm his daddy?"

"That could be."

"Ain't that somethin'? But there's one thing that really troubles me. I ain't got no bed for Douglas. I ain't got no furniture at all. But I'll make me some. I sleep on the ground all the time, but my brother's boy ought to have a bed . . . with a feather pilla and them clean white sheets. Yessir, he deserves the best."

"Don't you worry about those things. As soon as the cabin is finished, we'll throw you a housewarming."

"I done got me a stove, Judge."

"A housewarming is like a party where everyone brings presents for your house. It will give your friends an opportunity to bring you some furnishings. Why, I wouldn't be surprised if a couple of beds show up."

Duffy clutched the judge's arm. "Two? Why do I want two beds?"

"You might want to use one yourself."

"Why would I want to do that?"

"To give Douglas a good example."

Duffy paused. "I reckon you're right about that." He leaned on one foot, then another. "I changed my mind about somethin'. Do you reckon I can go in now and see Drake one last time?"

The judge opened the door and Duffy followed him in.

"You'll catch your death of cold," Marthellen scolded.

Several blankets covered Judith as she stood on the Nevada Street porch staring across in the night at the shadowy form of the Presbyterian Church. Her ears were so numb she could hardly hear Marthellen.

"I felt stuffy inside."

Marthellen stepped out on the porch beside her. "Did we build too big a fire?"

"No, I mean stuffy inside my heart, my lungs. Death has a way of bringing reality into perspective."

Marthellen held up a blue porcelain mug. "Would you like a sip of my tea? It's chamomile."

Judith took several sips. "Here it is, our first real white-out of snow, and I can't enjoy it."

"You know what this reminds me of?" Marthellen said.

"The night Bence died?"

"I do believe the Lord taught me more about living and love on that day than

308

any other in my life."

"Isn't it interesting that often through death, the Lord teaches us about the priorities of life and the depth of love?"

"Why do you think that is?"

"I suppose because he has our undivided attention for a moment. Most of the time we don't really focus on him completely . . . or at all."

A carriage rolled south on the deserted Nevada Street, laying down tracks on the snow floor. When it got even with the church, Marthellen slipped her arm around Judith. "It's Kitzmeyer's hearse," she whispered.

The two women posed in the darkness as silent witnesses.

"I hardly knew Drake," Marthellen finally said. "But after years of Duffy talking about him, I felt like he was part of the community. What was he like?"

"The only real visit I had with him was his last hours."

"Was he like Duffy?"

"He was like Duffy would have been if the mine shaft hadn't collapsed and pinned him in for three days. He seemed alert, thoughtful, caring. But he was scared."

"About dying?"

Judith rubbed her nose with a blanket

edge. "And about what would happen to Douglas."

"What did you tell him?"

"The judge kept reassuring him with Scripture and prayer. I think it helped. He finally just relaxed, closed his eyes, and quit breathing." Judith released her grip on Marthellen's waist. "I don't think I'll ever get used to the finality of death."

"Do you ever wonder how your last hour will be spent?" Marthellen asked.

"I don't know if I've thought much about the last hour. I suppose I'll be selfish and want my husband, children, and grandchildren with me. And my friends," she added with a stiff smile. "But I don't suppose many of us get to set the scene for our last moments on earth."

"I hope I don't have a lot of regrets," Marthellen said.

"About things you did? Or things you didn't do?"

"Mainly things I didn't do. I find God's forgiveness quicker in the mistakes I've made. The opportunities I've missed seem to nag me forever."

Judith tugged on Marthellen's arm. "Do you think someday soon we'll regret standing outside in below-freezing weather until we caught some terrible flu?"

"We ought to go to bed. There's nothing more we can do."

They entered the Kingston house and shuffled toward the living room fireplace. "Are you sleepy?" Judith asked.

"It doesn't seem like a night for sleeping. When will the judge be home?"

"Not until tomorrow."

"He's staying with Duffy and Douglas?"

Judith slumped down on the sofa, pulling her feet up beside her, the blanket to her neck. "No, he and the sheriff took a little trip."

Marthellen stared at Judith. "In the middle of the night?"

"Something came up."

"Where did they go?"

Judith refused to look at Marthellen. "They needed to go to Reno. The last train had already left, so they took off on horseback."

"Reno? There's not much there besides the Lake House Hotel and a railroad station. If the major had known they were going to Reno, he could have waited and . . ." Marthellen's words died off and the ladies sat in tense silence.

The flame silhouettes from the fireplace splashed across the room, but Judith shivered.

"Are they going for the major?" Marthellen said.

Judith's voice was soft, but her heart beat fast. "Yes."

"I knew it was too good to be true."

"Mr. Tjader from the bank needed some answers to some questions."

"They couldn't wait until morning, when he returns?"

Judith's words were barely audible. "They weren't sure he'd be coming back."

"But I'm here, and he said he loves me. He wanted me to go with him tonight. Of course he'll be back."

Judith had never felt so helpless in her life. "I hurt so much for you, I don't even know what to say."

"I'm sure the major has an explanation."

"Perhaps so. I truly hope so."

"It was about Pagosa Springs, wasn't it?" Marthellen said.

Judith laid her head back against the sofa. "That was part of it."

"What do they think happened in Pagosa Springs?"

"I do know that the bank president was killed."

The old melancholy showed on Marthellen's face. She had lost all the light sparked by the past few weeks. "By the major?"

"No." Judith closed her eyes. "By the major's girlfriend."

"Who was that?"

"The bank president's wife."

Marthellen feigned defiance. "You can't trust rumors. Surely you don't believe . . ."

"The judge got a telegram confirmation from Pagosa Springs."

The pine embers popped in the fireplace. The pendulum from the grandfather clock swung back and forth. Judith heard a sob.

"He treated me nice, Judith. He can't be all bad."

"Some people's biggest battles are the wars between good and evil that go on inside themselves. We can't always see that," Judith said. "In the major's case, we don't know yet which side has won."

"Yes, maybe he's changed. Maybe he wants to settle down now and he's sincere about this project. Perhaps he learned his lesson and he sincerely wants to . . ." Marthellen paused, then said, "You know, it doesn't surprise me. Other than you and the judge, I've never had anything nice ever happen to me. I guess I've already had more than my share."

Judith leaned forward and studied Marthellen's eyes. "Do you regret the past few weeks?"

"There were moments I will remember forever. Good moments."

"And the others?"

"I had hints."

"Oh?"

"Right after we started seeing one another, the major had me pick up his mail. He received a package about the size of a cigar box from Tiffany's and . . ."

Judith sat straight up. "Tiffany's of New York?"

"Yes, the jewelry store."

Judith smiled and tried to relax. "I looked in their window once."

"I've only dreamed about it," Marthellen said. "Obviously he bought someone a beautiful piece of jewelry, and I kept waiting for him to give it to me. He never did. I suppose I just didn't live up to his expectations."

"Perhaps he purchased something else," Judith said.

"Be honest, Judith. You never trusted the major, did you?"

"At first, he offended me. Then, I admired his incredible vision and ability to get things done. But he always made me feel . . . uneasy. I really don't know him well enough to say more than that. I did like the way he put such life into you."

Marthellen dropped her head to her

chest. "How that man could kiss. The housekeeper and the rogue major. It sounds like a novel."

"*El Padron's Daughter* had a plot like that," Judith said. "That's book #5 in the 'Stuart Brannon on the Pecos' series. There was a beautiful señorita and a handsome border bandito."

"What happened?"

"The señorita killed the bandito when she found him in the arms of another woman."

"What did Stuart Brannon do?"

"He chased her all the way to Brownsville and brought her back to stand trial. When it was discovered the bandito had a price on his head, she was acquitted and paid a reward."

Marthellen laughed. "I don't think I have to worry about the major having another woman, at least not in Carson City. He was too busy for me, most days."

"That's one thing I can say for him. He's industrious and ambitious."

Marthellen's face crumpled again. "I will become the laughingstock of Carson. Like Audrey Adair, last summer. I feel like a fool, swooping around town like a foolish, desperate old lady."

"That's bunk. Besides, Audrey is enjoying her life in San Francisco and has remarried Mr. McKensie. You and the major make a striking couple. And if this relationship falls through, you're liable to have more suitors after this all settles down."

"Why would you say that?"

"Some of the men of this town saw the real Marthellen Farnsworth for the first time."

"What do you mean, the real Marthellen?"

"The lady of poise, determination, and mature handsomeness."

"Judith Kingston, you are a flatterer."

"I'll tell you what, if between now and Christmas no man asks you out, I'll cook the Christmas dinner, and you can sit in the living room reading a book," Judith challenged.

"I couldn't take that bet. There's no way you could win."

"Then what do you have to lose?"

"Will you cook the pumpkin soup?"

"Certainly, but you and I will be the only ones who eat it."

"OK," Marthellen agreed, "I'll make the wager on one condition."

"What's that?"

"That you let me read *El Padron's Daughter.*"

Snow blew sideways, chilling their bodies and slamming against their faces. The snow floor hadn't yet packed down. The trail was covered, the brush caked — a regal coating that promised desert life some potential. But there had been too much whiteness for too long, making a slow trip for the weary travelers.

It was still dark when they reached the banks of the Truckee River. The judge pulled down the wool muffler covering his mouth. "You got any movement left in your hands?" he asked the sheriff.

"A little. But I think I left my toes back in Washoe City. You think we should have waited for the morning train?"

"Flannel bedding would be wonderful right now," the judge said. "We'd better warm up before we confront the major."

"Let's build a fire. It won't break daylight for another hour, and the eastbound doesn't come through for a couple more hours after that. If he's here, he'll stay here awhile longer."

The judge tugged on his rabbit fur-lined gloves. "You figure he's going east?"

"If not, he'll have longer to wait for the westbound."

Both men dismounted. A sharp pain

shot up the judge's legs, from his knees to his hips. His right shoulder cramped and he couldn't turn his neck to the right.

Sharp branches scratched against their feet and legs as they gathered scraps of sage and willow by the light of a waning moon.

The flames of the campfire brought feeling, mostly pain, back to the judge's hands. "Roberta wanted snow for Christmas," he said.

"Trouble is, this could all be gone by then," the sheriff said. "The other trouble is, Major Lansford might not be going east or west. If he was smart, he'd buy a horse and ride up to Susanville. Or if he didn't want to be followed, he could ride through the Black Rock Desert."

Smoke stung the judge's eyes. "I don't believe he thinks he's being followed tonight."

"But he did know that Boca's brother was in town with revenge on his mind. He must have suspected something in the air."

"But he'd figure no one would be foolish enough to push horses through the dead of night in this weather." The judge stared back at the Sierras. "I know he's not going to San Francisco. Tell me again exactly what he told Sam Tjader at the bank."

The sheriff pulled the collar of his coat up over his ears. "That he needed to transfer the sanatorium funds to the Bank of California in order to secure the San Francisco backing."

The judge balanced a handful of willow sticks on the blaze. "So he withdrew all the money?"

"All but ten dollars."

"That was generous of him."

"That was so he could leave the account open," Sheriff Hill reported. "He told Tjader that as soon as the San Francisco money was in, he would transfer the money back to Carson City."

"And Tjader believed that?"

"For a few hours, anyway."

"The major told Marthellen he was going to Reno to pick up some water-testing equipment," the judge reported. "He even wanted her to come along."

"Why would he drag a nice lady like Marthellen Farnsworth into all of this?"

"Maybe to divert attention. Or maybe because he didn't know exactly what he was going to do. Perhaps he had a change of mind when Marthellen refused to come along. He may have thought she'd heard the Sergio Boca stories and was pulling away from him." The judge's right leg cramped. He stuck it out in front of him.

"Showing an interest in Marthellen made him look like he wanted to settle in the community," the sheriff said. "The two of them going on a train jaunt would be less suspicious. Everyone would expect them to come back."

"But what would he do with Marthellen if he was absconding with funds? Abandon her?" the judge challenged.

"It's possible he really cares for her and wanted her to run away with him," the sheriff said. "I'm surprised she didn't. He's very persuasive. I can't believe he got Eastern backers to cough up that much for a sanatorium in the West. Tjader said the major had been expecting even more money from them. I guess he couldn't wait." The sheriff pulled out his revolver and checked the chambers.

"So the major had $90,000 on him when he left town?" the judge asked.

"Ninety-two thousand, six hundred and fifty."

The judge slapped his gloved hands together, trying to increase circulation. "Why did the bank president wait until nine o'clock at night to tell you this?"

"He thought it would just cause needless

worry or bring unfair accusation against the major."

"It brings accusation, all right. Especially since $30,000 of it comes from city, county, and state funds."

"What if the major is telling the truth?"

"To whom? To Tjader? To Marthellen? To the Eastern backers? To the citizens of Carson City? Just which story is true?"

"If we don't find him here," the sheriff said, "we'll have to telegram around the state. He could even have headed for Mexico."

The judge squinted at the sheriff. "Does the major seem the kind of man to take four weeks to ride through the Mojave and Sonoran Deserts, across Navajo and Apache lands, in order to sneak into the Sierra Madres?"

"You're right, Judge. He'll be at the train station. But he may put up a fight."

"For $90,000? You bet he'll fight," the judge declared.

"Do you think he'll have partners?"

"He didn't seem to have any compadres in Carson City except Marthellen. He may be too greedy to split the pot and too confident to think he needs help."

"We can see across the river now. You warm enough to ride to Lake Hotel?"

"I'm fine. We could try to slip into the hotel before it gets too light."

The night clerk at the Lake Hotel was asleep at the counter, his nose in the crease of the guest register. Sheriff Hill jerked the register out from under the man's head and let his face bump on the wooden counter, but the clerk didn't wake up.

Judge Kingston scanned the register. "There's no Major Lansford, but the last customer of the night was Lieutenant Colonel Landford Falcon."

The sheriff stared down at the register. "He gave himself a promotion?"

"Ninety thousand dollars does elevate a person's position, I suppose."

"It isn't a good sign . . . him usin' an alias. What does the asterisk after his name mean?"

"I have no idea and the night clerk isn't in any shape to tell us."

The sheriff turned the collar of his coat down. "If he wasn't snorin' and snortin', I'd think he was dead."

"Lieutenant Colonel Falcon is in room number nine." The judge tugged off his black leather gloves and shoved them in his coat pocket. "What if he won't welcome us in when we knock? How do we get into the room?"

"That's where we need an old lawman's technique."

"Good," the judge said. "You certainly qualify as an old lawman."

The sheriff walked to the back of the counter and lifted a brass ring of keys from the clerk's pocket. He pulled his hat low in front, and the judge followed him up the stairs, carrying a short-barreled, single-shot shotgun.

Pans were clanging from the hotel kitchen, but there was no movement in the hall except the flicker of a kerosene lantern. Daylight had begun to filter through chenille and lace curtains.

The sheriff unfastened his heavy wool coat and pulled out a Colt .44. Both men stepped lightly down the hall toward the door with a brass number nine. The sheriff flipped through the brass ring of assorted keys, held up one, and slipped it in the keyhole. The judge stepped back and pointed the shotgun toward the door.

The key clanked and clicked but didn't twist. The sheriff tried to force the key. "It ain't workin'," he grumbled.

The judge thought he heard bed springs squeak. He plucked the keys from the sheriff's hands. "That was number six. Look, number nine is underscored, you old lawman."

Feet shuffled inside the room. "Who's out there?" a man's voice called out.

The judge and the sheriff stepped to the side of the door.

"Who's out there?" the voice called again.

The judge heard the unmistakable cock of a gun hammer. "It's Judge Hollis Kingston, Major."

There was a pause. "What are you doing here?"

"It's a long story. Can I come in?"

"I'd rather you didn't. I'm . . . I'm not feeling very well. Could I talk with you later?"

"Just tell me, is Marthellen Farnsworth in the room with you?"

"My word, no. Why would you ask that?"

"She didn't come home last night and Judith is terribly worried." The judge stepped forward to slip the right key in the hole. "She was just sure she had run off with you and eloped."

"She's not here. Let me sleep."

The judge motioned for the sheriff to knock on the door. As he did, the judge twisted the key one full rotation.

"What do you want?" the major called out.

The judge slowly twisted the cold brass handle and threw open the door. Guns drawn, he and the sheriff barged into the room.

Major Lansford clutched a trembling blonde woman, dressed in pink gauze vest and drawers with ribbed bodice, low neck, no sleeves, and a cocked gun to her head.

The judge aimed the shotgun at the major. *Now we know what the asterisk means.*

"He's crazy," the woman shouted. "I ain't done nothin'. I ain't a part of this. Make him let me go."

"Major," the sheriff began, "we came here peaceful like. We just want you to answer a few questions."

"There's nothing peaceful about deception, forced entry, and barging in with guns drawn," the major growled.

"You're quite right about that, Lansford," the judge concurred. "But we are going to take you back to Carson City."

"That Colorado man lunged at me with a knife. It was self-defense. You don't have any reason to haul me back there."

"We have about ninety-two reasons," the judge replied.

"Ninety-two thousand, six hundred and fifty, to be exact," the sheriff said.

"Besides," the judge said, "how did you know he was from Colorado? Everyone in town thought he came up from Silver Peak."

"Let me go. You're hurting me," the woman cried.

"That money belongs to me," Lansford said.

"It belongs to the Humboldt Springs Sanatorium Project," the judge said.

"I am going to open an account with the Bank of California. I explained that all to Tjader. Talk to him. He understands."

"You've got money in that suitcase and you argued with me over a half-eagle?" the woman said. "I should have slit your throat and taken it all."

Lansford ignored her, saying, "This all can be explained . . ."

"I hope you're talking about the money and the sanatorium project," the sheriff said. "Your personal morals ain't of concern to me. Let the woman go."

"I'm going to take the money and the woman. When I look out that window and see you two cross the Truckee River, then I'll turn her loose."

The judge turned as though to retreat

326

out the door. Instead, he stepped to the right and picked up the heavy leather satchel.

"Put that down," the major shouted.

"I'm certainly glad you took it in greenbacks and not gold. I could have broken my back," the judge said.

"Toss that satchel here. That's mine."

The sheriff inched closer to him. "Yours? I believe it belongs to the city of Carson City, county of Ormsby, state of Nevada, and a few suckers from New York City."

"Stay there," the major commanded. "Toss the suitcase over and back out of this room. Now!"

Major Lansford jammed the barrel of the revolver under the cheekbone of the woman.

"Don't let him shoot me," she whimpered.

The judge's glance met the sheriff's. "We don't want this woman hurt. Let's get out of here," he said.

The judge turned his back to face the door.

"Give me that case," the major shouted.

The judge spun around, allowing the case to swing at full pendulum. He slung it high in the air, straight at the woman and the major.

Lansford jerked her to the side, keeping

the gun at her cheek and his eyes on the judge. The woman shrieked.

"No!" Lansford screamed as he dived for the case.

The brass-cornered leather case crashed through the second-story window behind them and tumbled to the ground behind the hotel.

The sheriff grabbed the major's arm, and the judge shoved a shotgun into his ribs.

The woman ran out of the room, grabbing a heavy muslin nightrobe.

"You better go retrieve the money," the sheriff told the judge, "or that soiled dove will be on her way to San Francisco."

Judge Kingston raced down the stairs. The clerk stood at the front door, staring out into the street.

"Did a woman run out this door?" the judge asked.

"Wearing only her night clothes," the man said, his speech slurred. "She'll catch her death . . ."

The sky was clear with a soft pink skim of cloud fingers. The sun reflected yellow off the top of the snow-covered Sierras. The judge jogged through the sage-powdered snow and saw the woman frantically trying to open the locked case.

"He owes me eight more dollars," she yelled.

The judge reached inside his heavy wool topcoat and pulled out a gold coin. "Here, your debt is settled."

She grabbed the coin. "Let me look in there. I ain't never seen that much money before."

"Neither have I. But the case will remain locked until we return to Carson City."

"You ain't goin' to open it?"

"No." The judge pulled off his overcoat and draped it around her shoulders. "Go on back in and get dressed."

The woman flung down his coat and ran off, stockinged feet kicking up snow.

"You got the suitcase?" the sheriff shouted. The judge glanced up to see Sheriff Hill and the major staring out the broken glass. A few other curtains had opened, framing gawking faces.

A sharp pain shot through the judge's shoulder as he picked up the case. "I've got it," he called back. *However, I threw my arm out tossing it across the hotel room.* "By the way, Marthellen says the major carries a pearl-handled sneak gun."

Sheriff Hill spun around out of sight. The judge heard a scuffle.

"Don't matter how many guns he has now," the sheriff called down.

CHAPTER TEN

At daybreak, Tray Weston drove the carriage in which Judith and Marthellen rode, heading south of town. They were protected from the chill air by a huge buffalo robe covering them up to their necks.

"I don't know why the sheriff took off like that in the night and didn't have me come along," Tray complained. "I'm his deputy."

"That's precisely why he left you here," Judith said. "He wanted to leave the city in competent hands."

"Well, if I'm in charge, what am I doin' drivin' two women out to Nine-Mile Butte?"

"You're investigating a possible crime," Judith announced.

Tray rubbed his unshaven chin. "What crime?"

"We can't tell you yet."

"I feel like a hack driver. You could have gotten Chug Conly to do this."

"But we need your expertise with weapons," Marthellen said.

"You expectin' trouble?"

"One never knows," Judith said.

"At Nine-Mile Butte?" Tray turned his head around and looked at the women. "Crosley and that Arizona bunch is out there. You ain't expectin' me to go against all of them, are you?"

Judith wound her wool muffler another time around her neck. "I don't anticipate trouble. We're just taking precautions."

Tray turned back to the road and spoke louder. "Did you ever have one of them dreams where you were falling and falling in the dark, but you didn't know where it was going to end? That's the way I feel now. With all the rumors flying around, I'm in the dark, falling, and I don't know where it's headed."

"That's a very apt metaphor, Mr. Weston," Judith said.

He searched the horizon. "Where?"

Marthellen cleared her throat. " 'Behold, he shall come up as clouds, and his chariots shall be as a whirlwind; his horses are swifter than eagles. Woe unto us! for we are spoiled.' " She turned to Judith. "You didn't think I was learning it, did you?"

"I'm impressed."

"What does that Bible verse have to do with anything?" Tray asked.

"What we're doing out here, Mr. Weston, is chasing a whirlwind," Judith explained. "The major blew into town like a whirlwind a few weeks ago. He caught us off guard and tried to spoil us."

"And now we're trying to catch the whirlwind," Marthellen added.

"If I've got to seize that whole Arizona bunch to do it, we're going to be in a big predicament," Tray said.

"Nonsense. I'm sure Marthellen and I can take care of them ourselves," Judith said.

Marthellen chewed on her lip. "We can?"

The sun was up when they reached the closed gate at the bottom of Nine-Mile Butte. A glaze of snow accentuated the higher Pine Nut range covered by fir.

Ritter Crosley moseyed toward them from a small fire. He tipped his hat. "Awful cold and early to be out for a ride."

"I had very little sleep last night, worrying so about this sanatorium project," Judith said. "I wonder if we might just ride up and take a look around?"

"I had a jerky night of it myself out in that blizzard," Crosley retorted. "It's made me a bit jumpy and grouchy this morning. I ain't inclined to be too sociable."

"Let the ladies go through," Tray said, sitting tall.

"If it were up to me, Deputy, you could have the whole blame mountain. It's too icy, naked, and downright unfriendly. We're going to pull out for Arizona as soon as the major shows up with our pay. But until then, I can't let you . . . or nobody . . . on that mountain. A man has to keep his word."

"You've got no legal claim," Tray insisted.

"And you ain't in no good position to force nothin'," Crosley said. "You push our hand and I guarantee someone will get hurt. And I don't want that to happen."

Judith put her hand on Tray Weston's shoulder, then said, "Mr. Crosley, do you mind if we warm ourselves at your fire, as we did the other day, before we turn home?"

The burly man smiled. "Of course, you're all welcome. I can handle that, meager though my fire is this mornin'." He stepped over to the carriage and raised his hand to help the women down. "You're welcome too, Deputy."

"I'll stay here," Tray said.

Marthellen and Judith hiked to the fire. Señor Nadie was again hunched over the flames, huge red bandannas tied under his hat and around his neck.

"Ain't got nothin' to sit on except that stump or boulder," Crosley said.

"You take the stump, it's flatter," Judith said to Marthellen. Her shoes sunk into mud where the flames had thawed the frozen ground. She tried to position herself on the boulder, then promptly slipped off. "Oh, dear," she cried out as she jammed her hands into the sticky cold gook.

Crosley jumped over and helped pull her to her feet.

Judith's bare hands dripped with mud. "Thank you. I believe I'd better stand." She reached up to brush her bangs back from her eyes and smeared a thick streak across her forehead.

"Judith," Marthellen called, "you're daubing it all over yourself."

Judith slapped her cheek. "Oh, dear," she groaned. "I'm getting this all over me. Do you have any hot water?"

"We got nothin' but coffee," Señor Nadie replied. "And what I have in here." He pulled out a leather-wrapped canteen with cork. "It's not water. In fact," he turned it upside down without spilling any, "I reckon it's froze up."

"That won't do. I'll have to have some hot water right away."

"We ain't got none," Mr. Crosley replied. "Maybe you ought to get right back to town."

"Like this?" Judith gasped. "I can't have anyone see me like this."

"If you hurry, no one will see you."

"You mean you would deny me the opportunity to wash my face?" Judith sniffled. A tear streaked her muddy face. "How about the mineral springs on top of the butte?"

"Mrs. Kingston, you ought to be one of them actresses at the Opera House," Ritter Crosley said, laughing.

"Well, I do have a minor part in Daisie Belle Emory's Christmas pageant."

"If I was her, I'd give you the lead."

"Thank you, Mr. Crosley. Besides, I happen to know that Major Fallon Lansford has been . . . uh . . . detained. Do we get to go up to the mineral springs to clean up?"

"Only one of you is dirty."

"I can fix that." Judith raised her muddy hands and stepped toward Marthellen.

"Wait," Crosley called out. "I reckon a man has to help a woman in need. Open that gate, Nadie. We'll usher these ladies in distress up to the hot springs."

After Judith and Marthellen were seated in the carriage, Tray Weston reined the horses, and the carriage rattled up the butte, following Crosley and Nadie, on horseback.

Marthellen leaned close to Judith. "Mrs. Kingston, you surely are something."

"Nonsense. I merely help people do what they really want to do. Mr. Crosley is a decent man in a gunfighter sort of way."

"What are we going to do when we get to the top? They won't allow us to do any exploring."

"I'm sure something will work out."

The Nine-Mile Butte hot springs bubbled out of a pile of boulders at the height of the hill. Nearby, Judith spied holes dug in the ground, about four feet in diameter and four feet deep.

"What are those?" Marthellen inquired.

Judith pulled off a muddy glove and tossed it over the side of the carriage. "Tray," she called out, "stop the carriage, please. I dropped my glove."

He reined in the horses and Judith climbed down.

"You cain't get down here, Mrs. Kingston," Crosley yelled.

She scrambled after the glove. Then, it went sailing across the mountaintop and disappeared into the bottom of one of the test holes. "Oh, dear, something was slithering and it startled me. I'll have to retrieve my glove."

"Oh, no, you don't. I'll fetch it for you." Crosley jumped off his horse and down into the hole.

Judith looked down into the opening. "Is that a shovel and sieve in the bottom?" she asked.

"All I claim to see is one muddy glove," Ritter Crosley said.

"What do you think they were sieving out of the dirt?" Judith asked.

"Who knows? I know nothing about sanatoriums." Crosley threw the glove to her and began to climb out.

"Mr. Crosley, would a man look for gold with a shovel and a sieve?"

"Nope. There ain't no gold up here anyway."

"Then, why don't you shovel a scoop of that soil and sieve it out," Judith suggested, "as long as you're down there anyway?"

Ritter rubbed his unshaven face. "Mrs. Kingston, you can skin a man quicker than any lady I've ever met . . . and I've met me some."

"Thank you, Mr. Crosley, but you really should call me Judith, like everyone else does."

He climbed out of the hole.

"Aren't you going to dig, Mr. Crosley?" she pressed.

"No, ma'am. I was curious about them holes last week, so I snuck up here and shifted through ever' one."

"You did? What did you find?"

"Rocks. Nothing but worthless, rough little rocks about the size of your fingernail. And they were all found at the three-foot level. I've seen gold, silver, copper, and lead mines, but these are just hard little stones."

"How hard?" Judith pressed.

"I couldn't bust one open using my pistol as a hammer," he said.

"Do you have them on you? Could I see one?" she asked.

He reached into his vest pocket and pulled out a stone. It felt very rough in Judith's ungloved hand.

"I saw something similar once in Washington, D.C.," Judith commented. "It was a diamond, straight from the mines of British South Africa, before it was cut and polished."

"A diamond?" Crosley gasped. "There aren't no diamond mines around here."

"Nor would you find them all at the same level," Señor Nadie asserted. "My

338

grandfather knew about such things."

"You think they were salted?" Tray Weston asked as he plucked the stone out of her hand.

Judith pulled on her muddy glove and rubbed her hands together. "It would be one way to get Eastern backers to invest in your project."

Tray tossed the rock high and caught it. "You think they're worth much?"

"I don't know. I'd like to ask Mr. Levinski to look at them," Judith said.

"You want them all?" Crosley asked.

"Just three."

"What do I do with the rest of them?"

"I believe mining laws give you permission to keep what you dig off public lands. I will return these to you as well," Judith said. "Undoubtedly they have some worth or the major would never have gone to the trouble. On the other hand, they wouldn't be extremely valuable or he'd never have gone north and left them lying out here."

"What do you mean, gone north?" Crosley said.

"Didn't you know he left town?" Marthellen asked.

"He owes us some pay. Maybe we ought to go after him."

"If I were you," Judith said, "I'd sift

through every hole one more time. As soon as people around town hear about this, they'll turn this butte upside down looking for diamonds. Meanwhile, we need to get back."

Crosley pushed his hat back. "Don't you want to wash your face first?"

"Oh, no! What's a little dirt?" Judith tucked three small rocks into Marthellen's hand.

Judith pulled back the draperies a crack and watched a tall, thin man with black silk top hat climb out of Chug Conly's hack.

"Is that him?" she asked.

"Yes," Roberta said. "I'll go back to Marthellen's room."

Judith nodded and swung open the door before the man reached the porch. He grinned broadly and held out his hand. She scooted right past him and toward the hack driver. "Chug," she called out.

Chug Conley reined up on the lead lines and tipped his hat. "Mornin', Judith."

"How is Mrs. Conly doing?"

"Very well, thank you. She's got her appetite back."

"That's wonderful. Do you think she'd like to try a jar of pickled okra? I seem to have more than I can use."

"I don't want to put you to no trouble."

"Nonsense, let me go get you some."

Judith scurried past the man in the top hat and into the house. When she reached the kitchen, Roberta whispered, "Where is he?"

"Still standing on the step, his hand out, and a silly look on his face."

"I wish I could see."

"Are you sure you want to go through with this?" Judith asked.

"I'm sure," Roberta said.

Judith again sped past the man and handed the jar of okra to the waiting hack driver. The carriage eased out onto Musser Street. Then Judith turned and sauntered up to the man. "Sorry to keep you waiting. What did you say your name was?"

"Longbake, I'm . . ."

"Oh, Mr. Longbake, we didn't know you were coming. What a surprise. We've been waiting for your son, Wilton, but he didn't show up and . . ."

"No, no, I'm Wilton Longbake," he said.

Judith studied the man her daughter might marry. At first impression, he didn't seem quite as handsome as the major, but much more charming than Colonel Jacobs. His eyes were friendly, in a controlled kind of way. He had high, pronounced cheeks and an unfurrowed brow. He had more hair on his face than on top of his head, but it was all trimmed smooth, with flecks of gray in the brown. He seemed amused rather than offended with Judith's behavior.

She slipped her arm in his. "Come in, come in. I was afraid business had called you back East."

They strolled into an empty living room.

"I thought Mr. Bowman would tell you of my delay," he said.

"Oh, yes, Turner is very reliable. But you're such a busy man. We didn't know what to expect."

"I hope I haven't come at a bad time," he said as she took his black silk coat and hat.

"Of course not. We've been anxiously waiting for this. Waiting and waiting. Please sit down. I'll hang up your things."

"Is Roberta here?"

"I believe she's tied up. I'll let her know you're here."

Judith scooted back into the kitchen and hung his coat and hat by the back door.

"Shall I check on him now?" Marthellen asked.

"Wait until he gets restless," Roberta

said. "I'll go get Peachy." She slipped into Marthellen's room and out the back door.

Judith poured herself a cup of black tea and slowly sipped it.

"Are you sure this isn't revenge?" Marthellen asked.

"Of course not. We're just helping Wil Longbake to understand the consequences of his actions. I'm sure he'll thank us for it when he comprehends the ramifications."

Marthellen and Judith drank a full cup in giddy silence.

Finally, a voice called out from the living room, "I say, is anyone out there?"

Judith pointed to Marthellen. She ambled out of the kitchen and Judith strained to hear the conversation.

"Hello, Mr. Longbake, I'm Marthellen Farnsworth."

"Yes, you must be the maid."

"That's an interesting thought. I've never been called the maid before."

"What are you called, Mrs. Farnsworth?"

"Just Marthellen. May I bring you some tea or coffee?"

"Coffee would be nice, thank you."

"I'll be back in a moment."

"Uh, is Mrs. Kingston in the kitchen?"

"I believe so."

"Might I have a word with her?"

Marthellen returned to the kitchen and puttered with the coffee while Judith stalled.

"I think he has a passing resemblance to the judge," Marthellen remarked. "The eyes aren't as deep-set and there's more hair, but a casual observer . . ."

"Nonsense," Judith said.

"But that may explain part of the attraction."

Marthellen made a quick exit of the kitchen. "Here's your coffee, Mr. Longbake. Did you want cream or sugar?"

"Did you mention my request to Mrs. Kingston?"

"She said she'd be right out."

"Thank you, Marthellen."

"You're welcome, Wil."

"Most people call me Mr. Longbake."

"What for? That makes you sound so middle-aged. Just because a man is starting to gray is no reason to treat him like an old man, I say. Young people today don't understand us middle-aged people, do they?"

"Well, I never thought . . ."

Marthellen slipped back into the kitchen. "Your turn," she said.

Judith waited a moment, then strolled out. Wilton Longbake jumped to his feet.

"Mrs. Kingston, did you find Roberta?"

"Please call me Judith. Everyone in the state of Nevada calls me Judith."

"And Roberta?"

"She calls me Mother."

"No, I mean, did you find Roberta?"

"She had to step out for a minute. You know how young ladies are. She said she had a surprise for you."

"A surprise?"

There was a knock at the front door and Judith scooted across the room. She opened the door to find Daisie Belle Emory and Colonel Jacobs.

Daisie Belle bounced in, wearing a dress with bright pink satin jacket and lace overlay, juliet sleeves, two-tiered chantilly lace skirt, sequined bow, and feather boa. She dragged the colonel across the room.

"Oh, you must be Roberta's beau," she gushed, then clutched his arm. "I feel like I know everything about you." Daisie Belle plopped down on the settee and patted the cushion for the colonel to join her.

"Roberta has been talking to you?" Wil probed.

"Not really, but I took the most marvelous trip to Europe a few years ago. Mrs. Longbake was in our group. I mean, your former wife. I suppose that was right after the divorce. Poor dear, I know it was a difficult time for her. I imagine many of those things she told me had only a small fraction of truth to them."

Wilton Longbake rose from the sofa and stood in front of the blazing fireplace. He was not smiling.

"Were you in the war, Wilton?" Daisie Belle asked.

"As a matter of fact, I was."

"Were you at Gettysburg?"

"No, I missed that engagement."

"Then, you must hear the colonel's stories. Tell Wil all about it, Colonel Jacobs."

"Eh, yes." The colonel rubbed his chin. "Where should I start?"

"Do begin with that exciting scene when the cannon melted. Wil, you are going to absolutely be enthralled with this story."

Judith waltzed back into the kitchen as the colonel droned on.

"I'm starting to feel sorry for him," Marthellen said.

"But we've just begun."

A knock at the side door sent Judith through the dining room and out to the Nevada Street entrance.

"Am I on time?" Willie Jane asked.

Judith led her into the living room.

"Listen, everyone, we have a real treat. Willie Jane is going to sing in church next Sunday, and she wants to rehearse. Daisie Belle, why don't you accompany her on the piano?" She turned to Longbake. "She has such a pure, though untrained, voice."

Longbake nodded at Willie Jane, then asked again, "Where's Roberta?"

"Still preparing your surprise," Judith replied.

Marthellen slipped out from the kitchen to listen to Willie Jane sing James Montgomery's "In the Hour of Trial." When she finished all the verses, there was banging on the side door.

"I thought Peachy was coming in the front," Marthellen whispered.

"So did I," Judith replied.

Duffy Day, in tattered coveralls and heavy coat, gripped a piece of paper. Douglas was at his side.

"Uncle Duffy said if you offered us chocolate, we would have to come in," the boy said.

"Duffy, would you actually enter my house?" Judith asked.

"Yes, ma'am, I think I'll give it a try."

"I'll fetch the chocolate," Marthellen announced from behind her.

"Douglas," Mrs. Emory called out from

the piano bench, "come sit by your Aunt Daisie Belle."

"I got me a letter," Duffy said, beaming.

"May I read it?" Judith asked.

"Yep. Say . . . who's this fella?" He pointed at Longbake.

"He's Roberta's beau."

"Is he the one that left her standin' at the station like an old wheelbarrow full of barn manure?"

"Now, Duffy, Mr. Longbake was occupied with business." Judith turned around, her eyes apologetic. "Duffy does have a way with words, doesn't he?"

"We weren't busy that day," Duffy continued. "There was a whole bunch of us standin' around with nothin' better to do than look foolish."

"I, eh, apologize for any inconvenience I might have caused," Longbake said.

"Oh, Wil," Judith fussed, "don't think anything about it. A man has to do what is important." She turned back to Duffy. "What kind of letter did you get?"

"Read it aloud," he insisted as he handed it to her.

"Dear Drake . . ." Judith paused.

Duffy turned to Longbake, "My brother went to be with Mama in heaven, so it's all right if I read his mail."

"Dear Drake," Judith continued. "I trust you finally got rid of that cough. I'll be in Carson City on Christmas. Tell Douglas that his mother still loves him. I'll see both of you then. Sincerely, Barbara Susanna Day."

"Douglas' mother?" Willie Jane exclaimed.

"Ain't that going to be fine?" Duffy said. "Is it OK for her to come over here for Christmas dinner, Judith?"

"We'd be, eh . . . delighted," Judith stammered.

"But, do I have to marry her? I read in the Bible once about men who married their brothers' wives."

Judith patted him on the arm. "No, Duffy, you don't have to marry her."

"Good, 'cause I didn't want to have to build another bedroom out at the cabin. We already have two."

Marthellen returned with the hot chocolate just as there was another rap at the front door. Judith found Levi Boyer and Marcy Cipiro, arm in arm. "Is the judge here? He's not in his office," Levi said.

"He's down at the sheriff's office."

"Ain't that somethin' about the major?" Levi said.

Judith looked around for Marthellen,

who had disappeared into the kitchen. "Yes, it's a shock to all of us."

"You want to hear another shocker?" Levi said. "Me and Marcy's getting married."

"We knew that, Levi."

"He means today," Marcy said.

Judith led the couple into the crowded living room. "Levi and Marcy are getting married today," she announced.

"When?" Willie Jane asked.

"As soon as we find the judge," Levi said.

"How marvelous!" Daisie Belle said. "I'll buy you something this afternoon."

"No need for . . ." Levi began. He was diverted by Marcy's elbow in his side. "That would be mighty fine, Mrs. Emory," he finished saying.

"I'll get you some coffee," Judith said and headed for the kitchen.

"Did Roberta plan this thing with Levi and Marcy?" Marthellen asked her.

"I don't think so. I believe they just wandered by."

Peachy Denair, wearing a hat whose brim was loaded with artificial lilacs and buttercups, breezed through the front door. "My, this looks like a party."

"It's practically a wedding," Willie Jane announced.

Peachy's hand went over her wide, full mouth.

"Levi and Marcy," Willie Jane said.

"My heart stopped for a minute." Peachy sauntered over to Wilton Longbake and slipped her arm in his. "I am Roberta's best and closest friend in all the world. She has told me everything about you." She rolled her eyes in prime Peachy style. "And I do mean everything. Personally, I've always dreamed of working in New York. I think it's the perfect size for a town. When you and Roberta get married, you'll need to hire someone else at the factory. Do you think there's any chance I could get her job?"

Shuffling and stamping of feet at the side door prevented Longbake's response. Judge Kingston and Turner Bowman squeezed into the room.

"Good morning, folks," the judge announced. "Don't let me stop the festivities."

Turner walked over to the fireplace where Peachy still cradled the New Yorker's arm.

"Mr. Longbake," he said, "I've just spent an hour going over details with Mr. Hearst. We can go out to the mill anytime you're ready. Stevens left the keys with the bank

351

and Mr. Tjader is going out with us."

The judge slipped over next to Judith and Marthellen. "My word, what are you doing to the poor man?"

"It's your daughter's idea. At least, most of it," Judith whispered.

"Where is she?"

"I have no idea."

"Tell me about the major," Marthellen said.

"He gave me this." He handed Marthellen a note. She slowly opened it, then looked at Judith, her eyes full of questions.

Judith read the careful penmanship on the letterhead of Humboldt Springs Sanatorium: "Marthellen, I wish we had met thirty years earlier. Perhaps we could have spared one another much misery. Thank you for your tender heart."

The note wasn't signed. *Perhaps he didn't know what name to use,* Judith thought.

"He confessed," the judge declared. "It was the diamonds that broke his resolve. All we had was a case of presumption until we faced him with that fraud. When I told him the jeweler identified them as industrial diamonds from South Africa, purchased in Amsterdam for Tiffany's of New York, he admitted he was going to abscond with the money. He claims he was hoping

Marthellen would go with him. We owe a debt to Mr. Levinski at the jewelry store."

Judith bit her lip. "Mr. Levinski is in Elko. I made that part up to test the major, to see what he would do."

"Judith," the judge roared. "I don't appreciate your putting me in such a position."

Judith rubbed her nose. "Fortunately, it worked. It was a plot from Stuart Brannon's *Emerald Smugglers of El Paso.*"

Turner Bowman led Longbake through the crowd. "Judge," Longbake said, "I am so happy to meet you. It's been quite a reception."

"It looks like half the city of Carson City is in my living room," the judge said. "I would apologize, except it often is this way."

"Would this be an awkward time for me to ask you for permission to marry your daughter? Our time together seems very limited."

"That decision will be Roberta's. I don't believe she's convinced of it quite yet."

"She was when she left New York," Longbake said. "What happened to change her mind?"

"I believe you get all the credit for that," the judge said.

"May I speak to her?"

"Of course, but that, too, is her decision."

Longbake glanced at Bowman. "I'm afraid I need to go with Mr. Hearst out to see the Consolidated Mill reduction plant. I was hoping to see Roberta . . ."

Judith patted his arm. "I'm sure she'll be in shortly. Could you wait a few more minutes?"

He pulled out a pocket watch. "A man can play the fool for only so long."

"Some men do it for a lifetime," Judith said.

"Hi, everyone, how do you like it?" A roar of applause and laughter swept through the crowded room as Roberta danced in from the kitchen, wearing pointed furry ears, a round black nose, and long whiskers.

"It's wonderful," Daisie Belle cooed.

Douglas Day, with full chocolate mustache, kept clapping.

"Roberta, what is this all about?" Longbake said.

"This is my outfit for the Christmas pageant, Wil. I thought you'd enjoy it."

"I really must talk to you."

"Do you like my squirrel costume?" she pressed.

"It's interesting. Now, can we go? I —"

"My friends think it's wonderful, but you say it's interesting. I suppose that's the difference between New York and Nevada."

"I don't understand. Can we talk . . . alone?"

"Yes, just a minute." Roberta turned to the assembled throng. "After I make an important announcement." Her whiskers wiggled as she spoke. "I want you to know that all of you have helped me to make two important decisions."

Turner's eyes sparkled. "Are you dropping out of college and moving back to Carson City?"

"OK, three important decisions. Yes, I am moving back to my hometown." She turned to Longbake. "Second, Wil, I'm not going to marry you at this time. I am not convinced you're mature enough quite yet for a deep, sacrificial, loving relationship."

Judith felt the man's intense discomfort. Now she was feeling sorry for him.

"What's the third thing?" Peachy called out.

"The third thing is, I am going to be my father's new law clerk." Roberta's fuzzy pointed ears twitched.

Judith clutched the judge's arm and

pulled his head lower. "I didn't know you asked her to do that."

The judge pulled off his spectacles and pressed his temples with his right hand. He felt the veins in his neck begin to tighten. "Neither did I, dear Judith, neither did I."